MW01600013

The Shaman's Granddaughter

Faye Westlake Newman

The Shaman's Granddaughter

A Modern Native American Story with Roots 4,000 or More Years Old.

With the exception of certain locations in the beautiful State of Oregon, this is a work of fiction. Any resemblance to any person, place, or action, is purely coincidental. It is meant to entertain. Any errors in my depiction of Native American philosophy or religion are mine and mine alone, and again, this is a work of fiction. There is no intent to disrespect or denigrate. If this work does so, I apologize. I have used some Native American mythology in the story and invented more. The story of the migration through White Spirit Bear country is my own imagined tale; the Kermode bear population does exist along the Washington coast and its white members are revered as Spirit Bears by the First Nations Tribes of Washington. They are black bears with a high percentage of the genes which make them white, resulting in an estimated 1 in 10 occurrence, far greater than the general black bear population.

It is my belief that we have done ourselves a great disservice in allowing and perpetrating the destruction of Native American custom and philosophy. I wish I knew much more.

Dedications

I dedicate this effort, for whatever it is worth, to my mother, Alma J. Boggs, who wanted to live long enough to see me publish a book, and always had faith. Sadly, she didn't, but perhaps she knows, anyway; to my brother, Billy, who has always been supportive in all ways; to my grandchildren, who collectively make life worth living; and to those who have helped this process from the beginning, and from whom I learned far more than I thought I didn't know: Betty Wetzell, Angela Lebakken, Phil Hahn, Sandy Kretschmar, Ina Christensen, Caron Backhouse, Sue Martino, and Elaine Smith.

Thank you, all of you, for enriching my life beyond measure.

Chapter 1: Moonlight and Ivy

Death is a very dull, dreary affair
And my advice to you is to
Have nothing whatsoever to do with it.
~W. Somerset Maugham

Chapter 1: Moonlight and Ivy

Feather-like astilbe shimmered and waved in failing light. Bark mulch paths Alexis Bishop and her mother had created together years ago needed a new layer, and the gardenia needed dead heading. No one had been here to tend them. The gardener mowed and trimmed grass. He wasn't into flower care or weeding. Maybe it was time to look for a gardener who gave them their money's worth. Maybe it was time not to give a flying fig about the stupid garden.

A restlessness stirred inside her, one not explained by all the current stresses in her life. Visiting the home she and her mother had shared until her mother's death when she was twelve brought back memories, but years separated her from those. This was a fluttering of wings in her stomach, a racing heartbeat, an urgent need to do something, but what? This feeling of helplessness was a stranger to her.

Maybe it was time to focus on what had brought her home from D.C. in the first place. She drew a deep breath and released it, silently asking her grandfather to send her energy she needed to take her father back to the desert while he still lived.

"It is not my job to give your father false hope," the doctor had said. "He is dying, plain and simple."

"You said that to him?"

"More or less," he had answered. He had continued, but she had stopped listening.

"While there is life, there is hope," she said. "I will not let you destroy it. We won't need your services anymore."

"Your father is my patient," he snapped.

"Do I have to bring my copy of his power of attorney? We no longer need your services." There was no such power of attorney and Alexis hoped she would not have to back up her threat, because she was sure her father wouldn't agree to sign one.

Now, she meandered through the garden, avoiding the square of light that shone from her father's temporary bedroom window. The climbing rose needed feeding, the raspberries hadn't been pruned, and the damnable ivy was creeping back through the fence cracks from their neighbor's yard. Despite neglect, the garden was a favorite place. As she repeated the deep breathing, tranquility seeped into her like water drawn into a sponge. Only her private mini-garden in D. C. gave her this same sense of peace. The one she had not yet shared with Terry.

What lay behind that? Eight months into an intimate relationship and she had not shared her most cherished place in the capitol with him.

The thought of Terry brought his gleaming blue eyes to mind. She brushed off the niggling doubt thoughts of him brought, fished her phone out of her purse, and pressed the single digit that dialed his number.

"Hey, babe," he answered, his deep voice softened by concern. "How's it going?"

Alexis sighed. "God knows. The doctor says Dad's dying, and I know if he stays here, he will."

"How long are *you* going to stay there?" He didn't mean on the coast. He meant in Oregon. He wanted her to come home to D.C.

"As long as I'm needed."

There was silence.

She spoke first. "Bouncing from Redmond to the coast is wearing me out. Wade works like a demon, and it's only a matter of time before his wife rebels at his never being home."

"From what you've told me, Wade is a great lawyer."

"He is, but he's overwhelmed, and I'm splitting my time between Dad and the practice, not doing justice to either."

Terry snorted. "Half your time is worth two good lawyers. We sure as hell miss you here. Maybe I should fly out, if only to see you tired. That's a picture I can't imagine."

"We can't both be gone. Our boss would have you for breakfast," she said, sure he wouldn't come.

"Never mind the DA. He can't fire me now. He's spending too much time campaigning. And whining about you being gone."

"All I can say is I will be there when I get there."

"Gotta go, sweetheart. Love you."

"You, too. Go home and get some sleep," she said.

Alexis glanced at her watch: eleven o'clock Eastern Time, though not yet dark here on the west coast. Still, she had known he was in the office, maybe pulling an all-nighter. One more quandary to add to all the others stacking up in her life: a lover she was no longer sure she loved.

Facing south, direction of earth spirit, power of life and growth, Alexis kicked off her shoes and, crossing her ankles, gracefully sank to the grass. Cherry tree branches hanging over the fence between back yards stood out in stark silhouette against the full moon. She raised her arms high and wide in supplication to the Ancestral Grandfathers and chanted in the language of her Cherokee forebears. Most of the three languages of her more familiar Warm Springs ancestors had been lost to the mists of time and the obliteration of their culture. She didn't know Cherokee well, not because Granddad hadn't tried to teach her. Still, she sang the words she knew, letting her heart speak those she didn't.

"Wani wachiyelo Ate omakiyayo

wani wachiyelo Ate omakiyayo . . ."

Her voice trailed off. The chant was wrong. She had spoken as if her father sang the song: "Father save me, I want to live."

Her earthly grandfather's voice spoke in her head. "Grandfathers know your heart, daughter of my daughter. Your prayer has reached their ears. They will answer."

In what way? They always answered, and seldom acceded to her dictates. She had not accepted Granddad's beliefs that transition was sometimes to be desired or that life continued after death. And yet, part of her did. Everything she knew led to that conclusion. So why was she unwilling to let her father go? He wanted to die, but that was pain talking. When the pain ended, his desire to live would right itself.

Alexis had not stopped missing her mother every single day since she had disappeared. Alexis was Grant and Adoni Bishop's only child, as Adoni had been an only child—there were no aunts, no uncles, not even a true blood cousin. If she lost her father, and, as she eventually would, her grandfather, Alexis would be alone in the world. There were many friends, but friends were not family. She would have no one.

No one except Terry. Some part of her knew that Terry was not whatever it was she sought as family. A fellow attorney she had known since law school, he had shared her own ambition from the beginning, and the two had planned their careers together, to gather the most legal experience possible in the shortest time. Both had joined first the Public Defender's office, and then the District Attorney's, to gain quality court experience. In addition, both had volunteered time to Legal Aid, to broaden their knowledge into the arenas of tax, real estate, and family law.

They had remained friends through two boyfriends for her and an engagement for him. When his girl broke up with him, they had taken the next step in their relationship as easily as they shared a meal. Sometimes Alexis wondered if it really meant any more than that. What did she want from him that she didn't have? Trust? Alexis had no reason *not* to trust him. Then why didn't he even know that she was half Native American? He wouldn't care. Would he? Why hadn't she told him about the secret retreat on the roof of the building that housed the apartment they shared? Why didn't . . . She gave up. This was an argument with herself no one could win. Alexis suppressed the deep, aching fear of being left alone.

She prayed again for the east wind, the breath of new beginnings, and hope for a brighter future. The energy this west wind brought carried nothing but the dark promise of death. Only the life-sucking ivy answered, its raucous motion like silent, derisive laughter.

Her prayer complete, she stood up. Perhaps it was time to let the tall firs go. The ivy was killing them. The thought brought a deep sadness to her, an emptiness that felt as if it would never be filled again. She recognized that response as substitution for fears about her father.

Alexis went in the house to his room and sat with her eyes closed, sometimes praying in silence, and sometimes thinking about her life and the fact that only a father, a grandfather, and a housekeeper filled its empty spaces. When her chair became uncomfortable, she stood and stared out at the trees and the full moon.

Her father coughed, bringing her attention back to him.

"I want to go home," he said, without opening his eyes. His voice, thick with emotion, too much medication, and the cancer eating away at him, shot a spear of agony through her. She knew what he meant; they owned this house together, her mother having left Alexis her share of it. It had only been 'home' for several months, during his treatment at a nearby cancer clinic. His true home was a ranch in Central Oregon, south of Warm Springs Indian Reservation. Home was a desert with blue skies and hot sun, not this relentless overcast, drizzle, and cold wind. She understood. She'd been away from high desert country for eight years; barely back a month before Dad's illness had taken them to the coast and a new oncologist. The last of many doctors.

She swallowed, but the lump in her throat had been there so long it seemed to have grown roots.

"The next time the power company tops those trees, I'll have them cut to the ground and removed," she said. Her voice sounded hoarse. "They're ugly. We can plant fruit trees."

"To hell with the trees! Take me home!" Another paroxysm of coughing racked his body and he clutched his chest until she wondered if this was, after all, the end. But his protest had carried too much strength for that.

Masking an onslaught of terror, Alexis shook her head. "You *are* home."

A swish of cotton announced the arrival of the hospice night nurse with her needle full of morphine.

"No!" Grant barked. "Take that crap away. I'm tired of being dead before I'm dead!"

"Dad, *please*." She could watch him suffer or he could drift in a morphine fog. Rotten choices, but she'd passed the limit of her ability to watch him do battle with pain. The war he waged had taken its toll on her, too. She'd lost two pants sizes and couldn't shake a perpetual headache. The alternative was to let go and let him die. That was what he was asking of her. He wanted to leave doctors and chemotherapy and poking and prodding behind and go home. He wanted to die looking at blue skies and feeling warm again.

"I'm not—"

"No! Alexis, don't even talk to me until I'm on that plane."

Breathing around the ache in her throat, Alexis shook her head at the nurse. He'd made up his mind.

"It's all right, Miss Bishop, you just ring me when he's ready," the woman said, her institutional smile firmly in place. Her eyes said she knew he'd ring the bell.

"Call me," she mouthed silently to Alexis and left the room.

Alexis wouldn't call. When Grant Bishop made up his mind, nothing changed it. Against his stubbornness, the savagery of pain didn't stand a chance.

"I'm going home," he said. "Take me home and get your grandfather."

Her heart leaped. She grinned. "Let's get you dressed."

"About damn time." He struggled to push himself up on his elbow, failed. She snatched clothes from his closet and slammed the door.

The nurse rushed into the room. "What on earth are you doing?"

"Taking him home," Alexis said.

"But . . . doesn't he live here?"

"Only if he wants to die."

"I don't understand."

"Never mind. This isn't home."

"Oh. But you can't take him out at this hour."

"Of course I can. He wants to go home, and he's all grown up. He can go where he pleases."

"I'm calling the doctor. You can't—"

"Call the marines, if you like. But either get out of here or help me get him dressed. And bring the wheelchair, please. Just a minute, Dad. I'll call for a car and get Pete up. Why don't you let her give you that shot, so it won't be such a rough trip?"

"Huh! So you can knock me out and forget about taking me home? No way. Just get me my pants. No, first tell Pete to get the plane ready."

"He's waiting for my call, Dad."

"Pretty damn sure of yourself, aren't you?" He coughed again. She knew he was fully aware she would not take him back to the ranch until he agreed to let her call Granddad. She couldn't. She had no more strength for watching him give up and die there than she had here. The thought of the soothing quality of her grandfather's presence jolted her to faster action.

His nurse tried again. "Miss Bishop . . ."

"He's considered terminal, isn't he? Isn't that why you're here?" Alexis asked.

"Well ... people *have* recovered . . ."

"Sure they have. And he will. But not here. And he has the right to choose."

As Alexis helped her father into a wheelchair, he grabbed the nurse's wrist.

"Thank you," he croaked, and coughed.

Alexis couldn't speak.

Eyes glittering, she managed a smile and a nod. Now he had a chance.

Chapter 2: West Wind

"Home advantage gives you an advantage."
~unknown

To Alexis, anxious as she was, it seemed to take forever to get Dad and his supplies into the car, to the airport, and boarded on their business jet. As they wheeled him across the tarmac and lifted him aboard, her father had shivered despite warmed blankets.

Drugs were wearing off faster, his pain more apparent. Alexis contained her impatience with an effort as a drizzle misted the plane's windows with a vision-blurring film. As soon as he was settled, she covered Dad and patted his face dry. Someone, she thought, needed to tell Punxatawny Phil that six weeks from February did not take them into June, even on the coast. Listening to Dad breathe, she wondered where in the universe God had gone.

Giving her dad time to recover from the effort of moving, she pretended not to notice his discomfort as they flew over the long, graceful sweep of McCullough Bridge and the bay and hills that surrounded it. Then there was no more ground view, only the rain-blurred stars and the full moon.

"We'll make good time," their pilot said into the intercom. "We have a strong tail wind."

"I know," Alexis muttered, "West wind. I was hoping for . . ." She let her voice trail off. If he could hear, Pete would not

16

understand her reference to Native American wind symbolism. Craving a head wind to slow them down and use more fuel would make no sense to him.

Her father emitted a lengthy snore. Alexis sighed and turned from the window. She sat on the edge of her seat and leaned across the aisle, tenting her fingers to peer over them. Grant's gaunt, craggy face bore a striking resemblance to the bark of the trees she had fretted over back at the house, gray and deeply crevassed. His two-hundred-pound frame had shrunk to one hundred forty. The disease ravaged his lungs with the same mindless viciousness as ivy sucked life from the trees. Unshakable. Immovable.

Irrationally, she felt an ache of sadness for the doomed trees. She made a short, snorting sound in the back of her throat, stifling an even more irrational laugh.

Grant Bishop's sunken eyes fluttered and opened. He slept in brief snatches now, especially without medication.

"Are we going home?" he asked.

"Yes, Dad, we're on our way."

"Good. I want to die in my own bed."

"You're not going to die. I won't let you."

"Your . . ." He coughed. "Arrogance knows no bounds."

She sat back and turned away. The urge to argue ran deep. They had always debated the smallest things, but this was no time to spend his energy in pointless argument. Besides, he was right. Arrogance had always been a characteristic ascribed to her, and she had long since abandoned the effort to argue that confidence was not arrogance unless she couldn't back it up. And she could. Always. She would not let him die. She would not.

After they cleared the hills, their plane was tossed around as if thrown by some insane juggler with too many clubs in the air, making her stomach roil almost as much as Dad's. Eyeing him, Alexis vowed she would never again take off into the summer whirlwind that surrounded North Bend Airport.

She clenched the arms of her seat until her fingernails ached. Her father was jostled about on a bed secured to the wall, despite being strapped down from waist to ankles. They'd have tied him completely, but he needed freedom to use the plane's ample supply of vomit bags, and anything snugged around his chest caused pain. As she saw her father suffer, a great ache grew inside Alexis. She almost wished she had denied him the trip to the ranch, after all, except that she knew it was his only chance to survive the ravages of the monster inside him.

The cabin was not cold, but she clutched her jacket around herself anyway, knowing the shivers for what they were: nerves. What if they were too late? What if Dad's stubbornness had taken him too far on the road to death to recover, even with Granddad's help?

Alexis didn't begin to relax until the familiar multiple peaks of Broken Top came into view. The long extinct volcano had been part of her view of life for as long as she could remember, and had always drawn her attention.

Dad muttered between bouts of illness. "Hell of a note, when I have to agree to see a witch doctor, before my own daughter will honor my wishes about where I want to die," Grant said between bouts of nausea.

"Dad, please. Let's save this, at least until we get home."

"Why? Will your attitude be different?"

Even now, patience was not her strongest quality. "Do you think my attitude is the one that needs changing when you call Granddad a witch doctor?" she retorted.

"You don't really believe Chases Bear can do what specialists in three states couldn't, do you?"

"I do, and so do you. You'd rather pet a rattlesnake than admit it." *She* would rather pet a rattlesnake than admit her doubts about her grandfather's ability to help at this late stage. If he'd been called from the start . . .

Something in her tone must have struck a nerve. "You're not planning to go live on the rez with that madman after I'm dead, are you?" he asked.

"Since you're not going to die any time soon, it's a moot point, isn't it?"

"Christ! A million-dollar education, all that experience, and you would throw it away for what? A few square feet of dry sagebrush, weird herbs and a tribal shack?"

"Fancy homes and private planes aren't everything!"

"Oh, spare me!" He coughed until his eyes watered, and turned his back to her.

The sun ignited the eastern horizon as Pete circled twice to be sure the long, paved driveway that served as a landing strip was unoccupied. He finally set the small jet down on the ranch, nine miles northwest of Redmond, touching down smoothly, but their ill passenger felt it and lifted himself to his elbows, retching. The plane's wheels traveling over the surface sent him into another fit of coughing. Alexis cringed. The Cadillac waited at the end of the tarmac, parked safely to the side. Alexis couldn't see him, but she knew Harmon occupied the driver's seat. In fifteen years, their driver had not missed a landing.

As they taxied to a stop, she saw Harmon get out of the car and light a cigarette. He'd have just time for a drag before squeezing the butt out and meeting the plane.

Grant leaned over the side of the bed. Alexis slid a wastebasket into line with his mouth. She ignored the glare he sent her way, reminding her that he would rather have barfed all over the floor than have her notice. Sympathy warred with annoyance. Much worse was the fear that he might not survive the trip to the ranch house, after all.

When he finished, she slid the container under his cot with her toe and held a warm, wet towel to his face. She stood and opened the cabin door. Harmon, slender and fit, despite his age, sprinted across the pavement and up the few steps to the cabin. His nose twitched, but he said nothing about the malodorous atmosphere.

Alexis dropped to the ground, caught the bag Pete tossed down and ran to slide it into the Caddy's open trunk, leaving room for Dad's medical paraphernalia.

Harmon carried an emaciated Grant in his arms as one might carry a child. She held the car door for them, and then waited outside, while Harmon settled and covered Grant. Alexis gazed at the striated red and gold cliffs, carved by wind and rain, over who knew how many millennia. She found herself as grateful to be home as she knew her father would be. Despite the early hour, the rising sun warmed her. She drew deeply of the thin, high desert air, fresh and clean, dry, and natural.

Some movement seen from the corner of her eye caused her to look in that direction. She scanned the cliffs, searching for what had drawn her attention. Nothing. No light, no movement, no reflection. Nevertheless, a chill crept up the back of her neck and nerves came alive in her scalp, feeling like thousands of tiny pins pricking her skin. Whatever was there, at the crest of the hills, or in one of the wind-dug caves, felt sinister, like some frightening *thing* lying in wait—for what? Or for whom?

Pete's eyes registered sympathy as he murmured, "I'm sorry," to Alexis. Her eyes filled.

He made three trips with suitcases, cane, walker, and a blanket before tossing an offhand salute and climbing back in the plane. Sitting in the front beside Harmon, Alexis heard the roar of the aircraft drown the purr of the car's motor.

Catching a distant whiff of Harm's dead cigarette, she opened her window and let the wind lift her hair and dry stress perspiration from her neck.

Mercifully, Grant fell asleep. Nearly as exhausted as he was, she leaned back and rested her eyes, glad to be out of the incessant summer wind on the coast. She had hated June in Coos Bay even when her mother was alive.

"How was the trip?" Harmon asked. She looked over the seat, but her father, apparently at peace for the first time in weeks, snored softly. He was home. He had always loved the open, rugged territory his great-grandparents had settled, well over a century past.

"Rough," she murmured. "The trip was hard on him, and he refused medication, for fear I'd turn the plane around and take him back to the hospital."

"Wouldn't you?"

"Not this time, Harm. There's nothing more they can do. Hospice doesn't take patients unless the doctor says they're terminal. 'Weeks or months left to live.' The doctors gave up on him."

"So he's come home to die?"

"No. He just thinks he has."

Harmon took his eyes off the road long enough to glance at her.

"You'll call your grandfather?" Like Dad, Harmon had expressed his opinion that Granddad was more than a little crazy.

"To get me to bring him home, Dad agreed."

Reluctantly. Alexis stared out at a distant series of striated red mesas that formed the perimeter of the ranch. Where beyond them would she find her mother's father, a transplanted Cherokee medicine man?

Modern medicine had given Grant Bishop no hope of survival and little respite from pain. Only the Spiritual Grandfathers remained to help him. Alexis had no illusions about why her father had agreed she could call his dead wife's father.

There was no guarantee Granddad wouldn't refuse to treat her father. Chases Bear still blamed Grant Bishop for taking his daughter away from her people and leaving her to die alone. After seventeen years, Granddad remained convinced that if either Dad or Alexis' mother had called him when she became ill, she might still be alive. Alexis didn't know the truth, because no one had ever told her—assuming they knew—what illness had taken Adoni Bishop. Alexis had been twelve when her mother brought her to the ranch, left her with Grant's housekeeper, and then disappeared from her life. As a result, Grant Bishop, wealthy rancher and prominent lawyer, had raised Alexis in his stimulating world of global travel and Ivy League schools, always returning to the sun-splashed country of his ancestors and hers, always happiest at home, summer or snow-blanketed winter.

Months after she had left, Granddad had held an Indian death ceremony for his daughter, still without explaining to Alexis what illness had taken Adoni, or where—or if—he had found her body.

Shaking off the past, Alexis got out first and held the door for Harmon to wheel Dad inside the massive ranch house. She and Harm helped him into a hospital bed in the den and gave him medication. When Dad slept, she climbed the curving sweep of staircase to her room off the balcony.

Upstairs, in a hot, scented bath, she soaked the ache out of her body, if not her soul. When the bedside telephone rang, she wrapped herself in a sheet towel and grabbed the phone to avoid waking Grant.

"Omigod! Alex! It *is* you! You're home! I heard you were home! When'd ya get in? How's your dad? How long do you get to stay?" Alexis held the phone several inches from her ear until her oldest friend took a breath. The 'moccasin telegraph,' the native news system, had worked with its usual efficiency. There was probably not a soul on the nearby reservation who didn't know that Grant Bishop and his daughter were home.

"Whoa, Chili! One thing at a time. I'm home. Dad's very sick. I'm here until he's . . . well. And, let's see—oh, yeah— when did we get in? About three hours ago. Long enough to get Dad settled and asleep, and for me to take a soak. I'm hoping Mary's downstairs making breakfast, because my stomach has shrunk to half its size on my own cooking. Come for dinner tonight if you can."

"Ahh, I'd like that, but Bobby's got a bug and I don't think you need the mama of a sickie in your daddy's house right now. Maybe in a couple days."

"Did you send for Granddad?"

"Oh, like I had to," Chili said. Alexis could see in her mind the curl of her friend's lip, indicating she should know better than to ask. "Chases Bear was on my doorstep before I noticed Bobby had a fever."

"Of course he was. Foolish of me to ask." *So why wasn't he here this morning? Why hadn't he gone to Alexis' mother the moment she became ill? What did he know that she didn't?*

"He did his thing—shook rattles over Bobby, and gave him some kind of awful-smelling concoction that Bobby says tastes like dead 'possum and prob'ly is," Chili added. "At least he can breathe, but he's still coughing. Anyways, his cough is loosening up, and his fever's broke, so I guess he'll be all right in a day or two."

"Oh, I'm glad. Do you know where Granddad is now?"

"Yeah, him and Patrick are camping out on Tenino Creek. Pat's testing water quality. Chases Bear's going off over to Bend early tomorrow to take a look at a pregnant girl that's two weeks overdue, if she don't pop loose tonight. Patrick's not s'pose to be back at the cop shop on the Rez until Monday, so he'll still be there. Maybe he can tell you where to find your grandpa better'n I can. Why? You gonna see if he'll break down and do a ceremony for your dad?"

"I think he will. I hope so. I am just not sure whether he will kill him or cure him. Chili, I need to go. I'm standing here nearly naked and I want to be around if Dad wakes. Hugs to the kids, and you, too. I'll see you in a few."

"Great! Can't wait to catch up."

Disconnecting, Alexis smiled, thinking of her best friend with one tawny, spiky-haired kid slung on her hip and another underfoot while she did dishes, made beds and sang to them. Her house was not fancy, but it looked as clean as a white bunny and her children were the most pampered and best behaved on the reservation. Chili made it all look easy. Alexis knew it was no such thing, but there were moments when she envied her friend's simplistic and love-filled life.

Mary Noreen, their housekeeper and Alexis' substitute mother since her real mother's death, was in the kitchen. Alexis, in shorts and a loose white shirt, descended the massive staircase and found her. She sniffed the air.

"Oh, yum, Mary. No one can cook like you. The soup smells great. And do I smell heal-all, with garlic and mint?"

"Of course you do, Missy. Except it's called sicklewort. It'll clean toxins out of the blood. It's what I had on hand when I heard you were coming."

Garlic was Granddad's version of an antiviral and antibacterial, and mint had properties of both plus the ability to make it more palatable. Since her childhood, her family had used the brew at the first sign of a sniffle. Alexis was not confident of its value against lung cancer, but it was harmless and might help him feel better.

Stewed chicken bubbled gently under a glass lid that revealed plump dumplings floating atop meat and broth. A steaming tureen of the soup and a big cup waited for Dad to wake. Delectable as the chicken soup smelled, Alexis hoped for a plate of scrambled eggs, peppers and onions with potatoes for herself.

Alexis hugged Mary. "You'll fix him, won't you?"

"If there's fixin' to do, my girl. It's in the Grandfathers' hands now."

Alexis sighed. "Yeah, I know. Is the stubborn old bull going to let me bring *my* grandfather?"

"Could be. 'Pends how scared he is."

"Of dying? Grant Bishop? When he goes, he'll rule heaven before the day's over."

Mary chuckled. "Or hell."

Chapter 3: Rendezvous

Some people come into our lives and
Leave footprints on our hearts and
We are never ever the same.
~ Flavia Weedn

Cisco slipped among sparse lodge-pole pines, his presence revealed by the occasional snap of a twig. With only a patterned blanket between her jeans and his strong back, Alexis felt herself a part of her familiar paint horse.

Alexis stopped briefly, lifted her chin and sniffed the air. The residual scent of Pat's campfire drifted past. Turning Cisco west, she caught the odor of roast rabbit Pat had eaten for dinner and smiled. It was laced with the scent of whiskey he would have used to tenderize it and then to wash it down. She stopped Cisco with knee and seat pressure and slid off his back, letting the reins drop to the ground.

Pausing again, Alexis considered the sense of betrayal she felt about Terry. It was no different from the way she had felt about Pat, when she and Terry had started dating. Neither was logical, but when had her heart ever behaved logically? Pat had been her first love, the only one before college. Their on again, off again affair, begun when both were teenagers, had always been full of fire and excitement, but without commitment. Terry Wells was different. College buddies, close friends, and later co-workers, the two had settled into a living arrangement almost by accident, when Terry's apartment had been sold and he found himself homeless. The 'temporary' stay, which they concealed at work, had lasted nearly eight months now. Although he had not said so, Alexis thought he loved her and would eventually ask her to marry him. What she didn't know was how she felt about him. Affection, certainly, contentment in his company, definitely. She and Terry were compatible and had much in common. Their personal future, at this point, was a blank page. If she loved him, surely she would not be looking forward to seeing Pat like this.

"No grazing," Alexis whispered to Cisco. "I'll be back." She was wasting her breath. There would be grass stains ground onto the bit when they went home, since she had neglected to bring a halter.

Alexis crouched and slipped through the brush, any sound covered by the gurgle of Tenino Creek rushing over well-worn rocks. The open flap of Pat's two-man tent faced a cold campfire circled by a double layer of stones with two feet of cleared space between fire residue and rock. A battered coffeepot perched on the stones. Knowing his habits, she guessed it held water for drowning embers. His food bag hung from a tree well away from the tent. The faint crackle of a battery-operated police scanner, turned low, sounded from inside. Near the opening, Alexis toed her feet out of moccasins and carried them.

She stepped quickly inside and to the right, to avoid silhouetting herself against evening light. Barefoot, wearing jeans and no shirt, Patrick lay atop a sleeping bag with one hand behind his head on a rolled blanket, watching her entrance. The other hand held a steel blue Smith & Wesson revolver, pointed at her midsection.

"Oh, it's you," he said, feigning boredom. He slid the gun back into its holster. "Heard you were back."

Alexis yelped and tackled him, landing on his middle. Air whooshed out of him and she laughed. He grabbed Alexis and rolled over with her back on the hard, pebbly earth, and then drew her closer as his mouth sought hers. He was laughing too hard to kiss her, but his hands roved over her body, claiming every part of her.

"Yeah—you heard I was back and sent word where I could find you," she said.

"Who? Who told you where to find me?" Mock innocence convinced neither of them.

She bit his chin.

"Animal," he growled.

"Let go, and I'll leave," she teased.

"Mm, hmm. After."

Alexis stilled. Suddenly, she could not do this. Not while she shared a home with someone else back in Washington. "No, Patrick," she murmured.

He lifted himself to his elbows, looking into her eyes.

"No." Alexis said again. "Pat. . . I'm sorry." Now it was herself she betrayed. Desire fully aroused, she wanted him as she always had, with the same overwhelming need. But she couldn't.

He kissed her tenderly and held her. "You sure?" he whispered.

"Yes. I'm . . . I'm seeing someone."

He rolled away from her. "Bound to happen," he said. "You been gone a long time." A wistful note in his voice made her open her eyes, but his face, in deep shadow, offered no more understanding. She sat up.

"How's your dad?" he asked. His rich, deep voice sounded gravelly. He rubbed his temples.

"He'll live," she said, "like it or not."

"Opinion or fact?"

"Both."

Pat chuckled from deep in his throat, and kissed her again, lightly this time, without the fire. She let him, but managed not to respond. She squirmed away from him and scrambled to her feet, knowing that if she stayed one more second, she would be lost. Running from the tent, she found her horse a dozen feet into the woods. She grabbed his mane and leaped aboard.

"Witch!" he called after her. She looked over her shoulder, between the trees. He stood in front of the tent, holding her moccasins. His smile failed to reach his eyes. Alexis urged Cisco to run faster.

Alexis hurried to where she had parked the truck and trailer alongside a narrow rut of a road leading from the Warm Springs Reservation. Though the edge of their property lay only three miles south, it would have been an eight-mile ride, cross-country, to the house. She dragged a pair of running shoes from beneath the pickup seat and put them on. Then she brushed sweat off Cisco, walked him cool, and loaded him into the trailer. She hoped Dad would be asleep when she got home, entailing no explanation of where she had been. Light was fading as the sun dropped behind Mount Jefferson to the west.

Alexis wanted her father to be well, and soon. She wanted to turn around and run back into Patrick Collins' arms where they had spent many hours of their teens in the years before she left home. She was back now, and wanted to be here. Was this where she belonged, and not in the hotbed of power and possibility that was Washington, D.C? Was this country meant to be merely a place for taking breaks from a hectic life in the nation's capital, or was this, in fact, where she was meant to live? A lot depended on the men in her life—all of them, Dad, Granddad, Pat, and Terry, though none of them would make her decision for her. For now, she seemed to be flying a holding pattern.

She reminded herself that a trailer rolled behind the truck, and Cisco would be struggling to keep his feet as she traveled the bumpy road to the highway. From there, twenty minutes brought them to the ranch, where she stopped and unloaded him in front of the barn. At the barn door, Cisco shied and pulled away.

"Whoa!" Alexis ordered, reaching higher up the lead rope, tugging. Nevertheless, Cisco danced backward.

"What's wrong with you?" Alexis asked Cisco. A sound from behind, inside the big, open barn door, made her step close to Cisco, stroking his neck. "Easy," she murmured.

Listening but hearing nothing, she ground tied the gelding. He moved toward the illusory safety of the trailer and sought comfort in a few blades of grass nearby, his eyes wide and still watchful.

Approaching cautiously from beside the barn door, Alexis reached inside to a shelf where her father kept a long Kel-Light, the heavy-duty, weighted flashlights carried by police officers. Switching it on, she held it away from her body, in case someone decided to use it for target practice, and flashed it around the wide, open aisle. Nothing. Starting with the nearest stall on the left, on silent feet, she carefully checked each roomy, open box. Still nothing. Not until she turned into the aisle at the far end of the barn did Alexis notice anything out of the ordinary. There, the narrow back door stood open. Footprints scuffed the soil. On closer examination, a dark spot on the dusty floor appeared to be blood. Fear crept into her. The sense of something evil returned with a vengeance.

"Casey?" she called. A moan sounded from outside the door. "Casey! Casey, where are you?" The young barn manager should have greeted her by now. She flashed the light over the yard, spotting a form lying on the ground. He was trying to get up. Hurrying, she nevertheless took care to check the area for intruders, shining the light throughout the circular corral. Nothing. Casey groaned again as she reached his side. The overwhelming sense of some dark evil chilled her through.

"Casey! Don't get up. I'll bring help. Where are you hurt?"

"All over. My head, my arm, my ribs."

"Who did this?"

"Don't know. Two of 'em. Man, woman. Too dark to see. Guy held me—"

"Okay. Stop talking. I'm calling the sheriff's office."

Alexis dialed 911 on her cell phone, identified herself, and asked for an ambulance and an officer to investigate a barn invasion, with injuries. Back inside, she found a clean horse blanket and returned to cover Casey, praying the nearest deputy was closer than the far end of the county. The kid turn on his side, curling into a fetal position. He wrapped his thin arms around himself and moaned again. Alexis hoped he hadn't suffered internal injuries. She made him as comfortable as possible and searched the area, finding scuffed footprints in the soil all around inside and outside the barn, but no other sign. When she saw tire prints near her own vehicle, she concluded that the culprits had made their escape before her arrival.

Fear gave way to fury. She would find the bastards who had attacked an innocent kid working his way through school. And when she did . . .

Chapter 4: Vision Quest

*Going into the Spirit World is very serious.
The most important thing is being clear in your heart
As to what you are seeking for yourself and the people of the
world. "*
~William Walking Sacred, Lakota Sioux

Alexis burned with fury. Granddad would remind her of
the old saying that holding a grudge is like carrying a hot coal
waiting to throw it at someone. He would also remind her that
she must not approach the sacred grandfathers in prayer with
anger in her heart. She must cleanse herself of it first. For once,
she was grateful her bedridden father couldn't see and argue with
her about what she needed to do.

With Casey laid up, she cleaned Cisco's and Ranger's
stalls, and brushed both horses, reminding herself that Ranger
needed exercise, too. She swept the barn, saddled Ranger, and
rode him to a wooded area along the Deschutes River where the
trees were young, limber, and plentiful. Lodge pole pines, they
had long been called, for the very good reason that they made
suitable lodge poles. She searched until she found several of the
right length and limberness. She cut them, sharpened them on
both ends and pushed them into the ground, crossing poles over
one another to create a structure about four feet high. She cleared
a space outside, located enough large rocks for circle—never a
challenge in the stony desert— and searched the area for fallen

branches, with which she built a good hot fire inside the bones of the sweat lodge. Alexis untied the metal container of an old coffee pot from her saddle, filled it from the clear water of the Deschutes, and set it inside, near the fire. She unrolled a pack from behind the saddle to reveal a motley assortment of mats and aged saddle blankets and used them to cover the sweat lodge. While the fire burned, she sat cross-legged, feeding it, and thinking about the odd sense of evil she'd felt and the feeling's reappearance when she'd found Casey. Odd seemed a good word for the feeling. Made up of part scent, part skin sensation, and part deep-down feeling of dread, awareness brought no enlightenment as to its cause. Its odor, distant but distinct, reminded her of the stench of death or decay, which anyone raised in the high desert wilderness knew well. The skin sensation felt like icy pinpricks, each miniscule by itself, but together, like a cold blanket over her body. The dread—no, not dread—*fear* lived deep down inside her in a place she couldn't reach. Fear of what? Of death? Alexis had been brought up knowing death as a mere transition from this life to some other, of unknown expression. Pure spirit, perhaps, or a lovely place many thought of as heaven. Or was it some different expression of life, something completely unfamiliar, that her limited experience could not even imagine? As a result of certainty that death was transition, not ending, she had never feared mortality.

Yet this awareness of evil was made up essentially of fear that was elemental, of her fabric, body and soul.

Alexis set stones from those she had gathered around and partially in the fire. She stacked a second layer, allowing these to lean a little toward the heat and fed the fire until she thought the stones were hot enough. She slipped out, changed to halter top and cotton shorts, and took the pot of water into the sweat lodge. There, she dribbled water over hot stones until the makeshift lodge filled with hot, deep-soaking steam. She made two more trips for water until she saturated the space with steam. Then she sat facing the hot stones, cleared her mind, and merely *was.*

At one point, Alexis slipped briefly out of her meditation to giggle at the passing thought of what her sophisticated friends and fellow attorneys in DC would think if they could see her, barefoot, ankles crossed, breathing steam in a sweat lodge. Forcing the thought away, she centered her mind to the reason for the sweat: Casey Bolt, an 18 year-old boy from the rez trying to earn money for school. Who would wish him harm? Why? Why had his presence been accompanied by the sense of evil? She'd seen victims of beatings before, both here and in the city. She'd prosecuted their assailants. No such occurrence had been accompanied by this evil sensation.

Alexis closed her eyes, opened herself to receive, and prayed for release of her anger. She asked the Grandfathers to see to justice, and to relieve her of the need for anger. She prayed for peace of mind to focus on her father's good health, and allowed herself to feel the gratitude his recovery would bring. When she felt at peace, she rose, left the lodge and dismantled it, cleaning up after herself. Examining her feelings, all she found was urgency to enter the Sacred Cave.

Alexis hurried back to the barn. It wasn't far enough to give Ranger a good run, so she made time to work her father's horse. Tall and rangy, the gelding, now fifteen, had been able in his youth to chase cattle all day. She wondered if her dad had been riding him before the illness. In long distances, could the bay still outrun Cisco, who was more agile and faster in short distances but couldn't keep up in a mile or more?

In the circular corral behind the barn, Alexis haltered Ranger and attached a longe line, a long, flat, cotton line, to the chin strap and let it out. With a cluck of her tongue and a gesture, she started him trotting in a circle around her, gradually asking him to increase speed until he reached a fast, collected canter around her while she turned in place to watch him. His movements were as fluid as always, his feet well placed. He looked healthy and energetic. Someone, perhaps Casey, had been exercising him. She would tell her father how well the horse looked. It would please him. Finished, she let him cool, brushed him down and put him away before saddling Cisco. She wanted to make her prayers in the cave, and had more than enough of them. Mary had agreed to watch over Grant.

Alexis closed the barn, wishing it could be locked. Ranchers do not lock animals inside barns. Fire is a greater fear than unknown attackers. She mounted the horse she had loved since he was a foal.

Cisco stretched his legs, leaping stones, skirting holes, and finding the trail with the unerring accuracy born of familiarity. Temporarily released from the stifling rooms where she'd spent day after day, week after week, Alexis exulted in the freedom of wind lifting her hair, stinging her eyes, burning her cheeks. In tank top, jeans, and moccasin boots, she scarcely felt the hot afternoon sun beating on her. The wind of motion flowed over skin already well-tanned and burn-resistant. The padded, hornless Australian saddle conformed to her body, fitted to her by many hours in its seat.

Nearly four miles from the ranch, the Paint gelding panted as the trail steepened and they climbed a narrow path diagonally up the side of a flat-topped, red bluff jutting out of the top of a low hill.

On top of the ridge, she turned her horse. They crossed the flat and started down a similar path on the opposite side. On leather-booted hocks, Cisco scooted ten or twelve feet to a ledge overlooking miles of sage-spotted, dry, rocky soil, dotted with clusters of piñon pines and more rugged, vertical rocks standing like sentinels among the dry sage.

Alexis leaped out of the saddle, dropped the reins under Cisco's chin, crouched and placed both hands flat on the rocky earth, bending and straightening her legs to stretch saddle kinks out. Years had passed since she'd ridden enough to keep them supple. Muscles eased, she faced the mouth of a natural cave, wind-worn into the side of the bluff.

Pleasant tingles danced over her bare arms and neck as she stepped into cool, moist shade. From somewhere inside the earth, a gurgle of water sent its soothing welcome. Her nervousness eased as she felt the comforting presence of the Grandfathers. Alexis sensed the presence of other creatures: a scorpion perched on a shadowed outcrop along one wall, a yellow-headed, green, collared lizard waking from a snooze in the shade. Deeper in the cave, she felt the occasional flutter of bats the size of hummingbirds hanging from the ceiling. Only the scorpion was undisturbed by her presence. A bobcat had been here, but was gone, long enough ago that his scent had dissipated, but not the essence of his spirit. In this sacred place, Alexis' every sense felt alive and attuned to her surroundings.

She let her fingers play over cool walls while her eyes adjusted to dim light. After a few minutes, she made out the primitive outlines of the horse and the buffalo carved deep into the surface, both stained red as dried blood. The inky pool of water in front of the wall bearing the petroglyphs was too wide to step over, too deep to wade. The stream curved in a wide half circle around an island of rock at the feet of the two-dimensional animals. She tugged a small glass vial from her pocket, crossed her ankles and sank to the floor. Breathing deeply, she waited until her spirit subsided and her mind emptied.

The plea that had brought her to the cave sifted gently into her consciousness, letters floating in air. Words she had spoken before leaving the house and then sent in silent prayer to the four winds. She ached with fear that they were too late. Dad had spent most of the morning vomiting until there was nothing left in his stomach, and pain wracked his body. If only she'd long ago acquiesced to Granddad's desire that she learn the Healing Way, maybe she could have taken better care of her father. Prayers filled every corner of her mind, leaving no room for any other thought. *Let my father live. Show me where I belong. Guide my every step. I will follow.*

Alexis released the prayer and carefully poured a capful of Granddad's dark liquid into the vial's lid and swallowed it, wincing at its bitter taste. In a moment, the bitterness faded and a sweet, rich flavor like sugared espresso took its place.

"If ever the taste does not change, you must leave the cave without looking back. If you undertake a journey with bitterness in your mouth—or in your heart— you will not return," Granddad had said. "The sweetness of life must bring you back, or you will stay with the Ancestors forever." She closed her eyes, inhaled and exhaled, deeply, several times. She waited.

After an unknown time, she inhaled again, and yet again, her mind empty of all thoughts except the awareness brought by her senses. A tiny, not audible, but perceptible, *pop*! And she felt herself slip free of her body. From above, she looked back to see herself, still seated, ankles crossed, still breathing. She allowed herself to drift, feather-like, to earth, and sat facing herself as if in mirror image, on the island of rock beneath the feet of the horse and the buffalo. She felt herself slipping away and the physical form across the water disappeared from view. A song of happiness filled her and she basked in gratitude for her return to this sacred place. She had so missed it!

Alexis drifted in a crisp, clean, blue field, then walked to the gnarled roots of a tree and stepped beneath them into a dark passage. Daylight, the scent of grass and wildflowers, and a fresh, sweet breeze filled her senses as she found firm footing on the grass. Thundering hoofs beat a rhythm in front of her. The buffalo raced through her and beyond; the horse stopped and snorted. Grabbing his mane, she threw herself onto his back without effort, and sat there, erect, as he followed the buffalo. Her legs, bare like the rest of her, clung to his sides, feeling the undulation of his muscles as he ran. A spear appeared in her hand. They caught up with the buffalo and she leaned down, positioning herself to drive the spear deep in his side, into his heart, as if she had done it many times before.

The buffalo's shaggy hair turned white and he—or she—grew small—a calf.

Alexis sat up straight, squeezing her legs together. The horse stopped. The buffalo faded and disappeared. She spun her horse and returned to the tree, feeling weighted, heavy. When she had slipped through the passage, there was a *ping*! And she was back inside her body, earthbound, seated on the floor, facing the island of stone. Tears blurred her vision and traced a path over her cheeks. She had spoken none of her prayers aloud in the vision, but had no doubt the Grandfathers had heard. She looked up.

The painted buffalo on the wall across the water glowed white in the shadows.

Puzzled by the vision, Alexis stood, wiped tears from her face and felt her way to the cave's entrance. Cisco shied away and she waited until the scent of the spirit world left her. When he would allow her to mount, she trotted him back to the ranch, watching the sun spray crimson light over wispy clouds on the horizon. She still did not know if her father would live and trembled with fear that he might not.

Alexis had even less certainty of her place in the world—with or without Dad— than before the vision quest.

Chapter 5: Chases Bear

When I bestride him, I soar. I am a hawk; he trots the air;
The earth sings when he touches it;
The basest horn of his hoof is more musical
Than the pipe of Hermes.
~ William Shakespeare

Her father slept fitfully through his first night home, as evidenced by mangled bedding, and dozed off and on all next day. He woke to stare out the window to the high desert he loved, occasionally to eat or take medicine, or both, and to visit the bathroom. Once he had stopped taking harsh chemicals, his nausea settled. He said he was acceding to the inevitable. Alexis saw it as clearing poisons out of his system, so a more natural means stood a chance to heal him.

However, she hadn't heard a word from her grandfather and it had been nearly a week. Waiting uneasily, she paced, snapped at Mary, and apologized. She finger combed her hair until it looked a mess. She made her supplications to the Spirits of the Grandfathers, and it was time to speak with the one still living. If he could not come to her, she would go to him.

Chili answered the phone on the first ring.

"Lexie! How's it going? How is your daddy?"

"He's still here. That's why I'm calling. Do you know where Granddad is?"

"He went over to Redmond, and I heard that girl that was overdue had a rough birth. She had a big baby and lost too much blood. He took care of her for a couple days, and then he went over to the old folks' home by the casino to check on Granny Bamer. She had a stroke, but she come out of it okay, I heard."

"Chili!"

"Oh, God, I'm sorry, Lexie, but I don't know exactly where he is now. I'll check around and see if I can find out and give you a call back, hon."

"Call my cell, Chili. I'll be on my way to the rez by then."

"Will do. Be careful. I heard there was a wreck out on Highway 105. Big rig and a pickup, I heard."

"Maybe that's where he's been," Alex answered.

"No, I don't think so. One driver was a fatal and the trucker went to the hospital in Redmond. That part was on the TV news."

"Okay, thanks, Chili. I'll be there in a while. I'll bring Cisco in case I have to search for him."

"Yeah. I'll do my best. See you soon."

Alexis took care entering the barn, having no desire to repeat Casey's experience with whomever had beaten him. The horses greeted her with gentle whickers, telling her clearly no one was there to bother her. By the time she fed them, cleaned their stalls, and turned Ranger into the round pen for a little exercise, the sun had cleared the horizon. She hooked the trailer to the ranch pickup and opened the back doors. Cisco walked in of his own accord.

"Going somewhere?"

Alexis jumped and looked up from her task. "Harm! Do you have to walk like a cat?"

He grinned. "Sorry."

"I'll be back in a few hours."

"Going after your grandpa, aren't you?"

"Yes. And I don't want to hear any objections. I'll get enough from Dad."

"I got none, missy. I s'pose anything's worth a try. Nothing else has worked."

"Well, I'm glad to have your unbridled enthusiasm, Harm." She'd heard heaviness in his voice, and examined his brown, weathered face, regretting her sarcasm. Harm worked for her father, but the two had been friends as long as she could remember.

"Call my cell if Dad needs me, Harm. I'll be back as soon as possible."

The old man nodded, turned, and walked away. The slump of his shoulders told her he, too, was grieving. Alexis wiped her eyes, gave Cisco a pat on the rump, and locked him in. It was an hour's drive to Warm Springs pulling the trailer.

Chili Wenway's home was a neat, small, frame structure much like others on a gravel street not far from Warm Springs' only shopping center, a strip mall near the reservation entrance. Like its neighbors, the house had no garage. Unlike its neighbors, it boasted a covered porch, a fresh coat of paint, and a well-kept front yard. For all intents and purposes, Chili was a female head of household. Chili's husband, Benjamin, was currently on his third tour in Afghanistan. Alexis fervently hoped it would end soon, and not just for Chili's sake. But Ben's hazard pay allowed Chili to raise their three children without working and to spend the money it took to keep up their home.

As Alexis pulled the horse trailer up in front of the house, her heart leaped. Something—or someone—was lying on the porch like a pile of rags.

That someone appeared to be a woman, slumped in a heap at the door. Alexis threw the gears into park, jolting the trailer, turned off the engine, and jumped out of the cab.

"Chiiilllii!" she screamed, running toward the figure. Reaching the woman, she dropped to her knees, seeing immediately that it wasn't her friend. The front door sprang open.

"What?" Chili cried. "Oh, my Lord! Lila!"

"Thank God," Alexis said. "I thought it might be you. Here, help me."

The girl on the floor looked to be fourteen or fifteen. Her hair was tangled, full of thistles and leaves, skin blazing to the touch, face bruised and scratched, shirt torn, baring one shoulder, and her breath came in shallow gasps. Between them, Chili and Alexis lifted and carried her into the house, where they laid her on a sofa. Some of the wounds seeped blood. Alexis lifted her feet to the sofa and bent to listen to her heart.

"Is this your missing cousin?" Alexis asked.

Chili nodded. She ran to another room and returned with a bowl of water and several washcloths. Alexis could hear children playing in another room.

"Did you find out where Granddad went?"

Chili nodded again, her mouth set in a grim line. "Yes. Out Shitike Creek. He said someone needed him."

"Do you think it was Lila?"

"He wouldn't say. He wouldn't let Gale go with him." *If it was Lila he went for, he wouldn't want this girl's mother with him when he found her. But where was he?* Alexis scowled. She dipped a cloth in the water and let a few drops seep into Lila's mouth. The girl's eyes fluttered and opened.

"Ch-chases Bear," she muttered, her voice husky. "Help him."

"Where?" Alexis asked. There was a familiar scent on the girl's sticky, dust-covered hands.

"Sh-Shitike creek. In the rocks south . . . of the old boarding school. I hid him in the rocks." She looked pale. She seemed to be fighting to keep her eyes open. Chili gently dabbed blood away from Lila's cheek and one eye. Both looked as if they might need stitches.

"You hid him? How badly is he hurt?"

"I think his leg is broken. And he was unconscious, at first. But he started to wake up. I told him I was going for help."

"There are people you could ask for help between here and Shitike Creek."

Lila ignored her. "Be careful, Miss Bishop. Those guys will do anything to hide . . ."

"Hide what?"

Lila clamped her lips shut and said no more.

"Chili, call Patrick, if he's back from Tenino Creek. And get her mother to decide if this girl is going to the hospital," Alexis said.

"Lexie, you can't go alone. Wait for Pat."

"No! Don't call the police. Please!" the girl begged. Then she passed out again.

From the door, Alexis took her cell out of her pocket and showed it to Chili. "I will," she mouthed silently, and left.

Unloading and saddling Cisco took under five minutes. She turned northeast out of Chili's driveway and clucked him to a trot until they were off of paved roads, heading cross-country toward the 200-year-old school building. She brought him to a canter, fear for her grandfather's well-being stronger than her fear for her safety and that of the horse on the rocky, uneven ground. When they reached the edge of town and turned up into the hills, she let him set his own pace. Shitike Creek was reachable by road to the southwest, but the old boarding school, on its northeast end, was closer this way. She fumbled her cell out and tapped the single digit that called Pat's phone.

"Alexis! What's happenin'?"

"Thank God I got you. Lila, the girl who's been missing, showed up on Chili's doorstep, all beat up. She probably needs a doctor. She's semi-conscious, but I think somebody beat her."

"You on a horse?"

"How can you tell? Granddad's up by the old school building off Shitike Creek. Lila says he's hurt, and she hid him in the rocks out there. I'm on my way to find him."

"Right behind you, babe."

"No, take care of Lila first and see she's in a safe place. I don't know who did this. She clammed up when I asked."

"Don't worry about Lila. I'll make sure she's okay. I'll meet you at the school."

Pat would be driving. He'd come around by the road, and the way he drove, would likely beat her to the school. For a moment, she felt silly for bringing a horse, but only for a moment. After he reached the school, Pat would be afoot. No one knew better than he that there were many places on the rez where a car, even his four-wheel-drive, couldn't go. She hadn't asked if Granddad had his mule. Of course he did. Someone needed him and walking would take too long.

Alexis knew the way. She'd be unlikely ever to forget. As kids, she, Chili, Pat and their friends had used every square mile of the rez as their playground. On horseback, on foot, in their cars as they grew older, they'd explored everywhere, without fear. Apparently, if Lila's face was any indication, the reservation had changed. What hadn't changed was the rough, rocky ground she was covering, and she worried about Cisco's legs, but he was as surefooted a horse as she'd ever ridden. He leaped over stones and sagebrush as if he hadn't aged a day. The pungent scents of sage and dust drifted to Alexis' nose on a stiff breeze and made her sneeze. She rode with long, loose reins, giving Cisco little direction. He would choose his footing more accurately than she could.

The school ahead of them was some two hundred years old. As children, they had snuck in windows and explored every inch, ignoring rodent droppings and dust. They must have developed immunity to every disease known to man. As, in all likelihood, had her grandfather, traveling the rez year after year, treating all sorts of illnesses and injuries. For the first time, it occurred to her that her grandfather could be seriously injured. What if he died? What if she lost him? Then she'd lose them both, Dad and Granddad. Heart pounding, she leaned forward in the saddle and urged Cisco faster. He kicked up his heels, happy to oblige, and broke into a fast gallop.

Leaping over sage, Cisco avoided dangers as if he were a mountain goat. There was nothing new about this place to him, either. "Don't let him step in a gopher hole," she prayed.

Well before the sun reached its apex, they looked down at the school from the crest of a knoll. Gray, faded boards had most likely never seen a hint of paint. No intact panes remained of the cross-sectioned windows, and a hitch rail adorned the low porch. There were two rooms, long since emptied of any contents. Dusty fields of weeds surrounded the building. Pat hadn't arrived yet. It must have taken him awhile to see to Lila's safety. A battered Jeep C10, the old WWII style, was parked on the far side, but no one seemed to be near it. Alexis surveyed the area where she was and determined which way was south. Then she recalled the rocks Lila had meant, and turned that direction just as she caught a glimpse of movement near the Jeep. At the same moment, she heard the low growl of an approaching vehicle. That would be Pat's patrol car. Backing up to reduce the likelihood of being seen by those who had arrived in the Jeep, she called Pat from her cell and warned him he'd have company.

Alexis turned her attention to finding Granddad. Air roared in and out of Cisco's lungs and she rocked as he panted. Breathing as hard as her horse, she wiped perspiration from around her eyes and left them surrounded by grimy dust she could feel. She wound her way among and around the deep red stones, aware Granddad would be in shade. Equally aware that the only poisonous snake found in Oregon could be seeking shade here as well, she slackened the reins and let Cisco find his own way. His nose and ears were far more useful than her eyes and ears. They didn't search long. Cisco whickered and pointed his ears forward, then picked up his pace. She saw the mule before she saw Granddad, lying near the mule's feet in the shade of a rock that was thirty feet high and probably twice that around. She grabbed her canteen and dismounted, anxiously searching his face. A moment later, on her knees at his side, she sighed her relief: he was breathing, though too warm by half. Lifting one eyelid, then the other, she saw that they both dilated, but not at the same speed. What had he said that meant in the distant reaches of her history? Concussion? Maybe. She couldn't dredge up the memory. Starting at his neck and shoulders, she ran her hands swiftly over his head and neck, and down over his ribs, and each leg. His left side gave her a shock. Blood seeped from beneath a rough poultice. Bending to smell it—and not very close—she knew he'd been conscious when Lila left him here. How else would she have known what to do for him? The poultice was made of crushed, soft, end-of-the-branch, sage leaves. A sticky substance made up of honey, cider, and minced garlic. Her grandfather had used the poultice on a hundred wounds she's suffered or seen in her youth. The combination was concocted of ingredients selected to protect from infection: honey and apple cider for acid-alkali balance; sage to purify; garlic to kill bacteria and viruses, none of which had been known by the ancestors who had passed down the formula. All they knew was that, backed by eons of trial and error, the treatment worked. She didn't need to look to know that all the ingredients except sage were packed on the mule's back. They always were. Alexis smiled. He would survive. Lifting the edges of the mess to look at his wound, she sat back on her heels, fingers shaking. Nothing but a bullet could have made that groove. She pressed the mat back down and called Pat. Someone had shot her grandfather.

Before he answered, shots rang out from below the knoll. Keeping low, Alexis crept over far enough to see below. Pat crouched behind the open door of his patrol car, firing toward the building. Someone fired back from the shadows.

"Where's my woman?" someone shouted. "You got her?"

"What woman?" Pat called out.

"You know what woman. And don't worry, we know where yours is. When we done with you, we head up in those rocks up there—" A shot raised dust twenty feet below where Alexis lay. "And get both her and her grandpa. Then maybe I'll make a trade with Lila's mama. Bishop money should help her make up her mind."

"Best thing you can do is toss your guns out here and walk out with your hands behind your heads."

"Best thing *you* can do is scoot on outta here and leave a man to take care of his own."

"I don't see a man—only a child molester and a baby raper."

Whoever was in the building wasn't listening any more. Alexis watched as three men ran out the back way, piled into the Jeep, and sped away. Pat remained where he was. Alexis guessed that he wasn't sure they hadn't left some behind to set a trap for him. She texted a message to him: "3 left in Jeep."

Pat stood up. So he knew there were three. He waved his gun, telling her he'd seen the message. He paced, shoulders tight, a deep scowl creasing his forehead when he looked up in her direction. He turned on his heel, as if making up his mind, and ran into the school, taking the short stair in one leap, and disappeared inside. Alexis doubted he could have seen her. She squirmed her way back to Granddad. He stirred, holding his torn shirt to his side.

"It's okay, Granddad. I'm here. You did a good job on the poultice."

"Lila Boden did," he muttered, his voice hoarse. She tipped her canteen to his lips and helped him raise his head and shoulders to drink. She allowed him only a few sips. He didn't argue for more.

"Gosh-awful headache," he croaked.

"I'll bet. Does it mean concussion if your eyes dilate, but not at the same rate?"

"Maybe. What else . . . you remember . . . I taught you?"

"Not to play with snakes," she said, laughing, and gave him another sip.

"Don't make me laugh."

"Does it hurt?"

"Not as bad. Sage helps pain. Another . . . thing to remember."

"Well, stop teaching for now and tell me if you are strong enough to ride that choppy old mule, or shall I get you on a real horse? One who knows how to move, even with the likes of you on his back?" People teased him—and her—about the slouchy way her grandfather sat a saddle and bounced in it. She guessed she'd bounce almost as much in the effort to ride Jack, Chases Bear's mule. But smooth or not, if she had to, she'd ride him.

"He's not riding anywhere," Pat said, coming over the rise.

Alexis grinned. "Could you skulk a little louder?" she asked. "You scared me to death after all that ruckus down there." She stood to meet him and both stepped deeper into the shade, out of the noontime sun.

"You should be scared. I wouldn't put it past Harley John Braithwaite to do just what he says he'll do: come after you."

"Braithwaite? How do I know that name?"

"Your father probably told you he defended Braithwaite last year for kidnapping and rape."

"Dad must have loved that. How do you know him?"

"He wasn't very happy about it. Grant was court appointed, no choice. But he didn't have to work hard. The woman disappeared—Sarah McCord—before she was set to testify and hasn't been seen since."

"*That* my father wouldn't like one bit. So if Granddad isn't riding a horse or a mule, how's he getting out of here?"

"An ambulance is meeting us at the schoolhouse."

"Okay. That takes care of Granddad and you'll be driving your patrol car—"

"Not likely. My patrol car has a bullet hole in the radiator and two flat tires. You and your granddad take the ambulance back to Warm Springs, and I'll bring your animals."

"No." Granddad broke in. "Jack won't let you take him. Knows his way home." He winced.

Alexis hurried back to his side. "What else do you have for pain, Granddad?"

"More sage, wet," he answered with effort. "Softer."

Alexis complied, wondering how long it would take to wash off the overwhelming scent of sage. She crushed it thoroughly, until the mass was wet from the leaf sap. She lifted the old poultice, laid the new one on his side with the old on top, and applied light pressure. The bleeding had stopped. The crease was a flesh wound that might have cracked a rib, not serious. She was more worried about his head. He had a lump on his forehead and he'd been unconscious for who knew how long.

"Does crushed sage help a contusion on your hard head?" she asked.

"No. White . . . bark." He passed out, and Alexis worried. She found the bark in Jack's pack, in the same place he'd always kept it, in various forms, including liquid in a small vial, clearly marked. It would be bitter as walnut shells, but it would work, and he couldn't drink, so drops under the tongue would have to do. She had started to place the drops when Pat interrupted her with a hand over hers.

"Don't," he said.

"But Granddad said . . ."

"I know. I heard. He's not himself."

"I wouldn't be, either, after what he's been through. But he knows medicine."

Pat shook his head. "That bump on his head could be a concussion. He could also have a hematoma. White willow bark is a blood thinner. It's like aspirin."

"He'd know that. He's the medicine man."

He grinned. "For now, you are. Let the medics find out what he has before you give him anything."

"You sound like a cop." She matched his grin.

"Imagine that."

Getting her grandfather off the hill proved to be the least of their difficulties. The ambulance announced its pending arrival within minutes, so they waited. When it came, two young, strong men raced up the hill with a stretcher, lifted him aboard, and spirited him off, still unconscious. Alexis watched, worried.

"He'll be all right," Pat said, coming to stand beside her. "He's tough as an old vulture."

"I know. I'm part of a family of three. Two thirds of us are not well. Pat—how did you come across John Braithwaite?"

"Which time? I've hauled him to the drunk tank a dozen times, and charged him with assault once or twice. Right now I'm looking at him for a handful of forged artifacts that have been showing up in shops around the area."

"How can you tell? People are still making artifacts. Some of them are using the old ways as much as they can."

"The ones they make today, no matter how accurately reproduced, don't look like they've been buried for a couple of centuries and pulled out of a dig somewhere."

"And you think he's involved?"

"I don't know. I don't like him much."

"Now there's a reason you can take to court if ever there was one." She shook her head. "But what had Lila said about someone doing anything to hide— hide what? Forgery?"

Pat grinned and changed the subject. "How's Grant doing?"

"About the same. I came to find Granddad to help. How are you getting back to Warm Springs?"

"I guess I'll test your grandpa's faith in his mule."

Chapter 6: Detour

***No trumpets sound when the important decisions
of our lives are made.
Destiny is made known silently.
~Agnes DeMille***

"If you see this Braithwaite guy," Pat said. "Steer clear of him. He's seriously bad news."

"I would do that," Alexis said, "Except I wouldn't know him from a lamppost."

"You won't mistake him for a lamppost." Pat's voice grated. "He's built like a fire plug. Short, stocky, big shoulders. Weightlifter. He's worked out a lot. Nothing else to do in prison."

"Sounds like a charmer. Why was he in prison?"

"Assault. He put his mother in the hospital."

"Oh, really. Why?"

"He never said. Investigators surmised it had a lot to do with the ear-to-throat scar he has where his father tried to take his head off with a meat cleaver."

"Good Lord. I could almost feel sorry for the guy. Almost."

"Yeah. Abused child becomes an abuser. Surprise, surprise."

"How old was he when all this happened?"

"He was seven when his old man whipped his ass and shoved him outside to spend the night in a cold, dark shed with no food or water, and it snowing. In the morning, he stole food and clothes and took off."

"Someone should . . ."

"Yes. Someone should . . . something. I've been tempted more than once to tie his old man to a fire ant hill."

"His father probably has a similar story of his own childhood."

"No excuse." Pat reached for Jack's lead rope, gazing speculatively at the two packs on his back. "We should be turning our attention to getting these two animals home."

She nodded agreement. "Jack would find his way home alone," she said. "Unfortunately, we can't be so sure about the contents of his packs. Not with your disreputable friends around."

Looking at the ground, Pat kicked a rock and toed another one. "I'll lead him on foot," he said.

"That'll take us into next week."

He grinned. "You got a better idea?"

"Yes." Alexis mounted, sidled her horse up next to Pat, and reached out her hand. She kicked her foot out of the stirrup. He slid a toe into it and mounted behind the saddle. Cisco grunted with the added weight. They wouldn't be running any races, but the two equines would walk faster than a man afoot.

Besides, she'd feel far too guilty riding while Pat walked. "Just don't flank my horse, please. I prefer voluntary dismounts."

In fact, she didn't know whether or not Cisco would buck if kicked in his flanks. She hadn't ridden double with anyone since school days. Better safe than sorry.

"What was next for our poor little bad boy?" Alexis asked.

"That was the first of a dozen times his parents were reported to police before Children's Services took him away from both of them. That was the first time Harley ran away."

"He was seven? Where did he go?" Alexis asked.

"He didn't get far. Back to CSD, for a while. Eventually, either he got better at hiding, or the police quit trying to catch him."

"Where does a little kid go when he runs away?" Alexis asked. She could feel sorry for the child whose family had neglected and abused him, but not for the man who had shot and beaten her grandfather.

"Friends, if he has any. Harley didn't. The streets, dumpsters, trash cans, abandoned buildings, doorways, bad experiences. Luckily for him, he escaped any serious encounters that we know of. When he was twelve, some enterprising rookie cop hauled him home and told him to stay there. The cop was the first of many do-gooders, before the kid landed in juvie. He got three squares and no one whacked on him. Not one to fit in, eventually he ran off again, this time back home, 'cause he figured he was tough enough by then to handle his father."

"Hence the cleaver scar?"

"Yes." His voice sounded grim in her ear. "How is Casey?" he asked.

"He'll be okay. A few bruises, a knot on his head, and a fractured rib. Why do you ask?" *While we were talking about Braithwaite.*

"No reason. Just wondered."

To Alexis, Pat sounded far too casual for 'no reason' to be completely forthcoming. Casey's beating was still under investigation. Alexis let it go, accustomed to cops who withheld information during an investigation, especially from lawyers.

She loosened the reins and let Cisco set his own pace and pick his footing. Pat rested his hands on her hips. In the past, he'd have wrapped his arms around her waist. The Aussie saddle, a cross between western and English, leaning toward English, had a sleek, smooth, cantle, not much support for his hands. He worked to hang on when Cisco stepped up to a trot. She had no doubt Pat could ride the lively gait from his unstable perch behind her saddle, though it couldn't be comfortable. Jack kept up, laden as he was, without difficulty, but she'd have hated to be on *his* back. That bounce would rattle the teeth of a jackrabbit. Tomorrow, she'd be looking for a good horse for Granddad. If he survived. That thought chilled her to the toes. He had to survive. He had to be well.

Granddad, despite feeble protests when he wakened enough to make them, had been taken to the hospital in Redmond. Fortified by Chili's dependable promise to care for the animals, Alexis left Cisco and Jack in Granddad's lean-to. She bade Pat good-bye, and followed as fast as she dared to the hospital, where she meant to see both her grandfather and Lila Boden.

A doctor met her in the surgical waiting room, needing a next-of-kin signature in order to proceed. There wouldn't be time the next day or the next, for horse hunting.

"We've been waiting for you," the doctor said. "He's just had an MRI and we found a subdural hematoma, a bleeding between the meningeal and dura matter, which adheres to the skull."

"I know what a subdural hematoma is, doctor. If it continues to bleed and applies pressure to the brain, it is life-threatening. He will strangle me, but I will sign for the surgery."

"Why will he strangle you? Does he have a DNR, a Do Not Resuscitate, in place?

"No, of course not. He's a Native American medicine man, and he'd handle it his own way."

The woman gave Alexis a condescending smile. Alexis called the front desk from her cell phone to find out Lila Boden's room number, to learn Lila had checked herself out against medical advice and was gone. Alexis called home to advise Mary what was happening and made herself comfortable in the family waiting room.

It was there that John Stockton caught up with her at last, plopping himself down in the chair next to hers as if he'd been invited. With an effort, Alexis kept the chagrin out of her voice. "Hello, John." His long, denim-clad legs stretched out in front of him. He slid down in the chair until his dark eyes were level with hers.

"You are a hard lady to find, Alex." John was one of few people who ever called her Alex. She occasionally wondered whether he wished she were a man or whether he was simply lazy in his speech. In either case, he had never failed to treat her with the respect due an equal, so it didn't bother her much. Just now, Alexis had enough on her mind and needed no more of John's wheedling her to take on his enormous legal business. A year ago, six months ago, she'd have snapped at the opportunity. At the time, she'd known a half-dozen young attorneys, including Terry Wells, who would have joined the firm with herself, her father, and Wade Corey as senior partners. They'd have gotten the job done. They'd have built up their firm and expanded into other industrial business to insure against the down-sizing that would follow if John someday took his legal work elsewhere. Today, though she had the right to do it, she did not have her father's guidance in matters regarding the law firm he'd built from nothing, and she wouldn't make decisions as weighty as this in his absence. She waited for John to speak.

"What happened? Your father have a relapse?"

While she heard nothing in his tone to indicate it, Alexis sensed that he thought a relapse was to be expected. She kept her manner soft, her voice giving away no more than his. "No. Dad's home, feeling better without the chemo."

He frowned, looking puzzled. "What brings you here, then?" A lifetime of hard work showed in his deeply crevassed face, sun-bronzed color, and rough, calloused hands. No one would have taken him for the multi-billionaire he was.

"My grandfather had an accident today," she answered. "He's in surgery. And a young girl from the res was assaulted. I was hoping to see her, but she checked out against medical advice. She's gone."

"You sound worried."

"I have an idea who might have assaulted her, and I am worried."

"I'm sorry. I know your grandpa means a lot to you. I don't mean to pester you when you've got so much going on, but things are happening and I need you."

"John, I told you . . ."

He held up a hand to stop her. "I know you need to be with your father. But that isn't forever, and I think I have a solution I want to put out there for you."

She eyed him with suspicion. "What kind of solution?"

"You'll see. I want you to meet with me in Portland later this week or next, after your grandpa's better. Me and some other people I want you to know. Now, please tell me you'll think about it before you say no. I'll make an appointment for whenever you think you can spare a few hours, and I'll send my own helicopter to get you to Portland, so you don't have to waste a lot of time. Just say you'll think about it."

"John, there are any number of legal firms suitable for your needs. Why me? Why are you so set on having me take on the work?"

"You know why. I watched you work on my son's case, and then later, you saved me a fortune after all was said and done, a lot more than you charged me. And that was a pretty penny, I want you to know. Worth every cent, but your services don't come cheap. Except at that penny-ante job you have in Washington."

"That job, as I've told you before, is part of my education, John. Think of it as an internship, preparing me for my future. And by the way, I'll pass on the chopper. I hate those noisy machines."

Frowning, Stockman took a toothpick from his breast pocket and chewed it. "If you say no this time, Alex, I'll never bother you again. I'll have to hire someone else, but I'll stop pushing. Just give it a few days' serious thought before you answer. Please."

"It's a deal," she said. "I'll think it over seriously if you will accept my decision."

"Done. Now I'll leave you to your troubles. You have my number."

Chapter 7: Healing Way

May the warm winds of heaven blow gently on your house,
And may the Great Spirit bless all who enter.
May your moccasins make happy tracks in many snows,
And may the rainbow always touch your shoulder.
~ Native American Prayer, Unknown Origin

"Get *all* that trash out of here! The smell of it turns my stomach!" her father growled when Alexis came downstairs the next morning. Shadows under his eyes told her he had not slept. His face remained pasty and his hair so thin she could count the freckles on his scalp.

She hadn't slept, either, for different reasons. "You need to eat," she said.

"When I'm damned good and ready. Get me some coffee and water and get the hell out of my sight." The effort to speak ignited a coughing fit. She waited to speak until he caught his breath.

"Granddad's in the hospital. I'll be in touch with him later."

"I don't give a—in the hospital? What army dragged him to a hospital? Why?"

"It took two of us, and then he had to be unconscious."

"What happened?"

"We aren't sure yet. Apparently, he had a run-in with a man named Braithwaite and came out on the short end of the scrap."

Her father seemed suddenly more alert than he had appeared to be in weeks. "Braithwaite?" He cleared his throat. "Is that low-life out of jail?"

"You ought to know. I heard you defended him."

"Not voluntarily . . . The defenders' office had conflicts because of his history . . . Judge caught me in his sights when he was looking for somebody." He pulled himself up on his pillows and leaned back. "You're not telling me something. How bad is he?"

"Doctor said he has a subdural hematoma." There was no need to explain the bleeding in the brain to a fellow lawyer. "He drifts in and out. They said the next twenty-four hours would determine if he's going to make it, but not how much damage he'll have. That will take a few weeks."

"He hit on the head?"

"He had a goose egg on his forehead, maybe more. And a bullet grazed his ribs."

"A bullet! How did you find out it was Braithwaite? Where did it happen?" He stopped for breath. "Who found him? Is that all you know? What are the police doing?"

"One at a time, Dad. I'm pleased that you care."

He caught his breath, coughed and wiped his face with a tissue. "He's your grandfather. I care about you."

"Lila, Gale Boden's daughter, has been missing. She turned up on Chili's doorstep and told us where to find

Granddad. Lila had been beaten, too. I found Granddad where she had hidden him out in the rocks near the old school on the rez. Pat came and exchanged a few shots with what looked like three people. He recognized Braithwaite."

He leaned back and was silent for a few minutes. "Watch your back, honey. That guy is . . ."

Alexis nodded. "Seriously bad news, according to Pat."

"What are you doing here? Why aren't you with Chases Bear?"

She wiped a tear from her cheek. "I have two of you, Dad. I've only been home a couple of hours, and if you'll be okay, I'm going back. First, I want to ask the tribe's Elders to speak to the Grandfathers for both of you."

He waved a hand. "How is Chases Bear?"

"Surgery was successful. Bleeding stopped. They can't even guess at any brain damage. He's out of recovery, and they expect him to survive."

"Good. Go. Nothing to do here. I'll be around when you get back."

"Promise?"

"Get!"

"I'm gone." She kissed his cheek and left him.

Alexis stopped in the kitchen to tell Mary to offer him food again later. "But steer clear otherwise. He was in a vile mood," she added. *Until she told him her grandfather's life was at risk.* She decided not to follow that thought.

"He's not going to die today if he has the energy to be vile," Mary answered. "I'll call you if you're needed." She wrapped a breakfast sandwich, filled a thermos for Alexis, and hugged her.

Alexis phoned Chili to ask her to contact the Elders and request prayers.

"Already done," Chili said. "For you, for Mr. Bishop, for Chases Bear, and for Lila. The drummers are coming and there'll be a ceremony tonight. Everybody's been told. You don't worry about being here. There will be plenty of people to dance and pray."

"You're a treasure, Chili."

"Your granddaddy has helped a lot of folks, out here and all over. We'll do right by him. He'll be okay."

Alexis thanked her again and said good-bye to her friend.

"There are evil spirits around today, honey," Mary said. "You be careful of your own self."

"I promise to do that." She would be careful. Evil spirits or evil people, they were giving her a distinct chill. Gratefully, she took the food and drink Mary offered and started to leave, deep in thought.

Paradoxically, Dad's foul mood encouraged Alexis. Mary was right. That horrible cough of his made her cringe. Still, if he was energetic enough to order her out, he wouldn't die today. If only Granddad's health looked equally promising.

"Mary," she said suddenly, remembering a few of Granddad's words from the old days. "Do you know where to find any sarsaparilla?" The vining shrub with red berries was common in Oregon, but she knew it preferred moist woodlands in temperate zones for its home. Places such as the one they'd just left.

"Now, you quit worrying about your daddy, Alexis. I've got sarsaparilla root drying on the back porch, and some already ground up. I'll work on his cough today."

"Thank you, Mary. I remember Granddad said once that there are only a couple of drugs not to mix it with. He's not taking either."

"I asked your grandpa what to do about that cough a long time ago, Missy. And how much to use. I sent away for some from the coast tribes when you came home. I knew you'd find a way to get him here." As did Alexis' grandfather, Mary had contacts everywhere.

Alexis hugged her and left for the hospital, eating a breakfast burrito heavy with sausage, peppers, onions, and tomatoes as she drove. Good food, Mary's cooking she had she had not been able to get in D.C.

Evil spirits were about, according to her foster mother. Much more than a housekeeper, Mary Noreen had taken care of

Alexis, guided her, dried her tears and shared her fears and triumphs throughout her teens, and given her an education in ways of women everywhere. Mary derived her spiritual values from her tribal family, including Chases Bear. Alexis loved her. Alexis did not share all of their beliefs, but neither did she reject them. To do that would have been to dishonor both her mother and her grandfather. There had been enough of that in Indian history. Her only question was whether the evil Mary spoke of was limited to Braithwaite and his cohorts, or was there more to worry about? More than cancer and brain injuries and battered teenagers and shots fired at authority? More than decisions about her life that she had begun to see looming like dark clouds hanging over her future? Wasn't that enough?

Her grandfather, awake and alert, sat up in the hospital bed, looking odd with his head swathed in bandages and tufts of unruly dark hair sticking out above them. She kissed his cheek, squeezing his hand.

"You're looking good, Granddad." She pulled up a chair. "Has your doctor seen you today?" She paused and waited for him to compose an answer. The native tradition had served her well in her profession. People, especially nervous or guilty people, often felt a need to fill silences with words rather than take time to think.

"I am good," he said. "Now get me out of here. There is work to do."

"Oh, stop! Granddad, you sound just like my dad. 'Take me home. Take me home.' "

"Why did you bring me here in the first place? These places are no good for people."

"Many would agree with you, I suspect. But there are few better places for safely drilling holes in your head."

"Who decided I needed another hole in my head? I did not agree to such a thing."

"You were in no shape to agree to anything. As your only kin, I did. You were bleeding inside your head, and the doctor determined that she needed to relieve the pressure, or you would die."

"Humph. I am not ready to die. Spirit is not ready for me to die. I have much work to do."

"Yes, well, it's been my experience that Spirit's notions of readiness often clash with ours." She fell silent, again allowing him to think before she spoke, as was proper. Good conversations take time. When he did not say anything, she looked closely at him. His eyes were open. He stared straight ahead. She passed her hand in front of him, frightened at the fixed look on his face. He did not flinch.

A voice startled her. "It's a mini seizure. He's been having them since he came out of surgery." A nurse in a purple top and pants adjusted settings, increasing his oxygen.

Still automatically practicing Granddad's preferred means of communication, she almost missed catching the nurse's attention. The woman was at the door before Alexis stopped her.

"What does it mean?"

The nurse turned around. "Maybe nothing, maybe everything. It depends how much of his brain has been deprived of oxygen by the swelling and bleeding. You need to discuss it with his doctor."

Alexis nodded. She was Granddad's next of kin—his only kin—and the doctor would speak with her. She drew a chair close and sat down, taking his hand, murmuring the few Cherokee prayers she recalled having learned at his feet. Minutes later, his taut body relaxed, his eyes closed, and he fell into a natural sleep, snoring lightly.

Alexis relaxed. Perhaps her prayers had been heard. Feeling overwhelmed and a little dazed, she stood and walked to the wide window that looked down one story on an enclosed courtyard situated on the roof of the first floor. In the center of the court stood a concrete bench of the type made for gardens, a concrete trashcan holder, and a pair of large boulders that could be used as seats. She saw a narrow door set between two groups of windows. Someone had entered it, and not long ago. A dozen or more large black birds foraged in the leaves and dust on the concrete floor or pecked at chunks of bread on the minimalist furnishings.

Were they ravens or crows? Her grandfather had told her there was too little difference to matter. Members of the same family, they differed in size, and the crow had a more slender body, a smaller beak. She decided these were ravens and shivered, drawing her jacket close around her, though the room was warm. Harbingers of change and transformation, ravens suggested something in her life was about to change, drastically. Had it not already? She did not see the glossy, ebony-feathered creatures as omens of death, as others did, but the changes that hung over and threatened her included the real possibility of not one, but two deaths in her small family. She cracked the window open to hear the caws from the birds. Not that it would tell her anything. "Will my father live?" she murmured toward the ravens, who gave no clue.

"Ask the eagle," her grandfather said. She looked, but he seemed asleep, eyes closed, breathing evenly.

Change. Only five weeks ago, Alexis Bishop had been a busy, overworked Assistant District Attorney, helping the staff keep the office humming while their boss, DA Will Harrison, spent his time campaigning and fundraising to keep his job. With cases ranging from minor assaults and driving violations to murder and rape, Alexis had gotten exactly what she had wanted from the legal arena in Washington: an opportunity to compress a lot of courtroom experience into a short period of time. Wherever she landed in private practice, she wanted to arrive armed with more than adequate litigation experience. Wherever she landed, she meant to be the best. Five weeks. Five weeks ago, she had labored into many nights beside equally hard-working young lawyers with similar ambitions. She'd lived in a roomy and expensive apartment not far from City Hall, raised herbs and vegetables on her roof, and walked to work and up and down stairs for exercise, often racing over them against her roommate, ADA Terry Wells. She and Terry were comfortable together, like long-time friends. Their home was full of other friends and laughter on the rare occasions when they had a day off together. Was she happy there? She'd have said yes until the summer heat of the high desert had ignited emotional flames she'd thought long extinguished by time and distance. The heat wasn't only for Patrick, teenaged lover, but for old yearnings she didn't understand. There was restlessness about her life now, an edgy feeling. A certainty that something, something she had long sensed was coming, was about to erupt like a volcano through her life and turn it inside out, before, like Mt. St. Helens, it greened again and came to life with a great newness.

Where would she land when the lava stopped flowing?

"Divine discontent," her grandfather said. She turned to see him smile at her. His eyes gleamed, arousing Alexis' suspicion. Did he think she was ready to sacrifice everything she had worked for to follow the Medicine Way, as he'd asked more than once?

Chapter 8: Forged Culture

***Restlessness is discontent and
Discontent is the first necessity of progress . . .
~Thomas A. Edison***

At three in the morning, having finally left her grandfather sleeping soundly in the hospital, Alexis sat cross-legged on a chair facing a wide-open window. Fresh from a bath, she let a cool nighttime breeze lift and dry her hair while she thought about Granddad's many rambling words spoken over the past hours.

Broken by not less than a dozen of his brief seizures, their conversation had nonetheless been as interesting as any she remembered. Full of their combined ancestral history and the myths of his Cherokee traditions as well as her Northwestern tribal culture, the talk delighted Alexis. She was reminded of the similarities between the distant tribes' customs and tales. She wasn't sure when she had realized that he was passing the stories of the tribes from his safekeeping into her own; as if he feared he would never have the opportunity again. Was it when he woke from one seizure during which he had seemed to be speaking to a third party in the room? When he woke alert and clear-headed and reminded her of medicines and when he had used them, on whom? Or was it when he spoke the prayer of healing for her father, asking the spirit people of his acquaintance to be there for Grant Bishop, that his daughter might not be alone in the world?

These were not, however, the thoughts that kept her staring out at the desert hills overlooking their home at this hour of the morning. She had understood what was meant last night by 'divine discontent.' Emerson had called it "an opportunity to discern your calling." The term seemed too self-explanatory for questions. Besides, it so clearly defined and explained her feelings that she had not questioned its truth. So, okay, she had admitted at last that she was discontented, knowing it for a long-standing condition. About what? And to what end?

Why? Her life in the city had been active, challenging, fun, and often exciting, though equally often mundane. How many Driving Under the Influence cases can one find exciting? How many pages of paperwork, created in triplicate, can hold one's interest? Yet she found every case new and different, and learned from each one, even if only whom she could trust within her own offices. Armed with the firm belief that what she did benefited people, Alexis had given rare thought to the life she'd left behind in the desert. She sought instead to prepare herself for the time when she decided where she would practice law, when at last she felt as ready as she'd ever be.

Terry had teased her about that. "You're like a painter," he had said, "or a writer who is never satisfied with her work and just keeps doing it over and over until she's repeating herself, not improving, just re-doing."

"You don't think I'm improving?" she had asked him.

"In our business, you'll either keep improving throughout your career, or you'll lose interest in it. But you don't have to do all this learning in an educational arena. With your schooling and experience, you could take your pick of positions today in any good firm east of the Mississippi, and learn the rest on the job."

"What about you? You've been in the DA's office as long as I have, Terry."

"Almost. Lacking a month or so. I don't have your quick mind, your ability to tell when a witness is lying, and your almost eidetic memory for details others miss. You're the best at what you do, and you're passionate about it. Will I catch up with you? Maybe I'll come close. Maybe I'll settle for middle of the road, while you soar to the heights of our profession."

"Don't say things like that, Terry. You're good. You know the law and you have a sense about when to broker a deal and when to go for the jugular. That's worth all the details in the world, and I don't have that sense. I'd get half my clients off with a slap on the wrist, even if I knew they belonged in prison for life. The other half, I would fry, just to win. I work the law. You work the people. In that sense you are years ahead of me." She sipped wine from the glass he handed her.

"What else makes us such a good team, babe? We are perfect together, the people person and the legal whiz. What could be better?"

Terry had drawn her into his arms then, entangling her legs with his on the sofa and holding her close. Something had bothered her about their exchange, something she still had not understood. Did she really mean what she'd said about frying half the defendants just to win? She knew she worked harder on some cases than others because winning mattered. What did that say about her?

Behind the hill, a lone car went by on the distant highway, spraying light into the night sky, moving toward the reservation. Who was coming home from town at this late hour? Henry Beck on another bender? Someone who worked a night shift? Braithwaite on the prowl for his underage girl?

Alexis stretched to touch the floor without leaving her squatting position on the chair, relishing the delicious stretch of muscles stiff from sitting too long beside her grandfather's bed. Nevertheless, she was glad she'd stayed. With the exception of a few instances in which he had lost his train of thought, or forgotten a detail of a story, he'd been pretty much himself. He would heal.

""Thank you, Great One," Alexis murmured, allowing gratitude to flood through her entire being, to fill her with the warmth and joy of success and thankfulness. He had taught her long ago that gratitude came before the gifts of the spirits, not after. The idea had seemed foreign at first, until she had seen its work. Then she made it a natural part of herself and her prayers to feel the gratitude and the knowing first and experience the wonder of miracles after they occurred.

She dressed quickly, automatically, with minimal care for her selections, and then pulled her thick hair into first a pony tail and then a knot on the back of her head, ignoring stray curls. Carelessness with her appearance was unlike her, but unimportant at the moment. Dashing downstairs on silent feet, she looked in on her father from the door. He slept, breathing evenly, better, she thought. So she left for his office, to catch up on piles of unfinished work. He would skin her if he knew how much she'd let it go. Or how much she'd left for Wade to do.

Arriving before dawn, she slipped in the side door from the courtyard and went directly to her father's office, stroking the sleek, shining surface of the cherry wood desk he had used throughout his career. Stacks of files teetered on two corners, with more in front of them, momentarily distracting her from the white pasteboard box centered on the open space. The letters USPS were emblazoned across the container, but it held no postage. Frowning, she carefully lifted a corner and peeked in. Seeing nothing dangerous in the contents, she threw it open. Wired to white cardboard cut to fit the box were a number of Native American artifacts: arrowheads, bone needles, bone fish hooks, other small tools. A scrimshaw flute, carved in the shape of a raven, made her stop and draw breath. Carefully, Alexis lifted the surface display to look beneath it. A beaded bag, fringed with bear fur, lay at the bottom. Resting on that lay an exquisite, though primitive, clay bowl of mixed faded colors, as if clay from different locations had been used. Parts of it were chipped away to show a rough surface, while parts of the inside retained a burnish, perhaps rubbed for hours by a piece of hide . . . or was it? She picked up the bowl, held it to the light, and peered closely. No, it was not burnished by hand for many long hours. Angry, she set it down and examined the other articles more closely. Arrowheads chipped by rocks, as in the old days; scrimshaw, legal only if made from the ivory of an extinct animal such as a mammoth; bone fish hooks made from sharpened antlers; these would be harder to identify as forgeries, unless they bore microscopic metal tool marks.

Alexis glanced up from the collection when the door to the courtyard opened and Pat came in.

"I might have known," she said.

He grinned. "What do you think of them?"

"That depends. Does the matter involve anyone who is or could be one of our clients?"

Pat shook his head. "Not to my knowledge. And I won't put you on the witness list for voicing your opinion, anyway."

"Fair enough. What makes you think I know any more than you do?"

"Maybe you don't. I respect your opinion, though."

"All right. In my no-more-expert-than yours-opinion, the bowl, which, if real, could be valued at $30,000 or more, is a forgery. In the time-honored birds of a feather tradition, my guess is that the other pieces are, as well. Where did you get it?" She picked up the object and held it to the light, where she could examine the underside, and pointed to a tiny scratch.

"An art dealer brought my attention to it. He asked that I try to be discreet, as his professional reputation may be at risk, though he hadn't offered the collection for sale yet."

"Honoring that request will keep him on your side, in the event that he spots any more like this."

"My thoughts, exactly. He bought it from an estate. Not much help there—the lady who owned the collection is dead, and there was no record of her original purchase. My guess is she was a collector who wasn't all that finicky about legality. Her nephew said she paid a measly eighteen thousand for it."

"Sans provenance, it wasn't much of a bargain."

"Lillian told her nephew she was bringing the Nation's treasures back to the rez, and nobody cared about proof but white people, anyhow."

"Oh. Lillian Red Sky."

"Yes."

"Paul didn't know where she got it?"

He shook his head, grinning. Like him, she knew everyone who was or ever had been on the rez. She certainly knew which one had become an art dealer. "He said his aunt didn't tell him a lot of things."

Alexis chuckled. "I'll bet not."

Chapter 9: Ice Cave

There is the world of the flesh and there is the Spirit world.
When the flesh is gone the spirit remains.
Those voices speak to those who know how to listen.
Wisdom is born in the heart and then spoken.
~ Wolf Clan Song

Pat left before her father's partner, Wade Corey, arrived in the office. The dawn's first rays competed with fluorescent lamps to gleam on very little visible area of the glossy red wood of her father's desk. Marked with red, blue and black ink depicting the priorities of various appointments, his desk calendar, stood propped on a chair. Alexis had left everything exactly like this except the size of the stacks of file folders obscuring the desktop.

"Good morning," Wade said, his square face wearing a cheerful smile. "Was that Pat Collins I saw heading north?"

"Likely. He was here. He wanted my opinion about some so-called artifacts that he thinks—and I agree—are stolen or forged or both."

"He's been working on that for a while now. Said he had a tip from a local dealer who declined to buy some fishy-looking pieces from a young girl."

"Oh? Did he say who the girl was?"

"No. But he seemed to have an idea about that."

"Thank you, Wade. Keep me informed if you hear more, please? Judging by these piles of folders, I'll be here for the day, if not the night."

Alexis buried herself in the work, barely noticing when Wade left for an hour at noon. Sue interrupted with lunch, which she ate at her desk, but otherwise, she didn't look up before the lights came on that evening. The office still hummed with activity.

Later, when she switched off the desk lamp, achy from hours hunched over the work, everyone had gone. Pale wisps of moonlight gleamed on the clean surface of the desk; her father's calendar was back in its accustomed place, with items crossed off and others added. Tired though she was, she felt deep satisfaction for a job well done. The sentiment was accompanied by a vaguely wistful feeling that she couldn't pin down. She stepped out into the courtyard, a grassy square surrounded by wide sidewalks. In the center was a circle of decorative flagstone that served as a floor for a swing seat, a small table, and a large pot of fragrant geraniums. The day's heat still blanketed this serene space, and coming from the air-conditioned office, she found it comforting.

Alexis chose a spot in the grass, curled forward to touch her toes, to each side, and then backward as far as she could reach. Her muscles rewarded her with the pleasurable sensation of each stretch. She sat on the cool, green grass and with feet spread wide, stretched again. Feeling better, she crossed her ankles, closed her eyes, pushed all thought out of her mind, and opened her hands and heart to receive the blessings of Spirit.

The air chilled and she welcomed it at first, but as seconds passed or hours, she couldn't tell which, she shivered. Opening her eyes, Alexis found only darkness with a cold, pale blue gleam here and there, like the color of ice on blue water. It seemed to take no time and forever for her eyes to adjust. She became aware, first of a great, icy cavern, then a cold wind whistling through the space, creating eerie music as it passed through stalactites and stalagmites. She tasted fear, rising, chilling her further, and causing her to tremble. A huge shadow approached in front of her, moving very fast, and enshrouded her body. The shadow clarified in her vision and became a great white hide, covered with white fur, thrown over her by a man who stood behind it. He was very tall, very large, and white bearded. His crevassed face bore a deep scowl, firm set mouth, and narrowed blue eyes. He, too, wore a fur, but it was darker, brown or black in the gloom, shining, glossy, as if he brushed it often, and it bared one huge, muscular shoulder.

The fur warmed her instantly, through and through. Her teeth stopped chattering. As her eyes met his, she felt a rush of unlimited love and wasn't sure whether it came from her or from him to her, or both. All she knew was that it was the warmest, most beautiful, serene feeling she had ever known.

Who are you? No words came from her mouth.

Neither did he speak. *You will know who I am when there is need.* His voice rang in her mind, deep, gentle, strong. She felt no further need to ask. He took her hand and they walked out of the cave, into a world of deep, virgin white snow. Trees and earth, rocks and streams glistened white in bright moonlight. Stars filled the night sky, shedding light that competed with radiance from the moon. He stood tall, over her head. His hand enveloped hers, warm and powerful. They walked together. She lost all sense of time.

She wore light moccasins with leather soles on the icy surface, so he picked her up as easily as she might pick up an infant. He carried her to a green, grassy place and set her down. She felt again that vast, gentle burst of unlimited love, and he vanished.

She looked at herself, expecting wet feet and white fur. Instead, she wore casual business attire, the same shirt and pants she'd worn to work, sitting in the grass where she had so recently stretched her muscles and meditated. For a moment, she felt bereft, as if she had lost someone who mattered more than anyone in the world. The fleeting sense of loss disappeared as quickly as it came. He would always be with her, whoever he was. She did not even stop to wonder how she knew that. She was still until she knew it was time to move.

Alexis called home to check on her father, left the courtyard and drove to the hospital. She hurried past nurses and attendants as if she belonged there at this late hour, and made her way to her grandfather's bedside. He opened his eyes, smiled at her, and stroked her arm.

"Granddad . . ."

He held up his hand. "We do not speak of union with spirits, my child, for doing so may cause us to doubt. We may speak of messages received in dreams."

"Why dreams?"

"We do not doubt dreams. They simply are."

"In my dream I was dressed in white buffalo fur in a cold, icy land."

He nodded. "You are very cold, still. How is your father?"

"Your guess is as good as mine and you haven't even seen him."

"Get me out of this charnel house, and we will see him. Until then, go home and tell him to get up and get back to work."

"I'll do that, first thing. Charnel house? No wonder nurses whisper about you and don't answer your bell. Neither would I, if you describe my place of work as a place of death and destruction."

He chuckled. "I haven't said it before. Do I look a fool?"

"Do I? I would have to be to go home and tell Dad to get up and go back to work. As for you, you probably scare the staff witless when you hold conversations with people who aren't here."

He peered at her, apparently decided she was not serious, and laughed. "Sometimes one is one's own best company." She laughed with him, knowing full well he had not been talking to himself when she'd heard his side of a conversation. They spoke a while longer. He was falling asleep again when she left for home.

There, she went to the barn instead of the house and saddled Cisco. They both needed the exercise. He was excited, as he'd always been when she rode at night, and danced a bit before she gave him his head and let him choose his gait. He trotted briefly, up the hill overlooking the house, and then broke into a canter, tossing his head and whinnying.

"I know, kiddo," she murmured, petting his neck. "I like the desert at night, too." At the hill crest, she stopped and turned to look down at the house. Lights shone from her father's den and she could see him clearly, in a chair, looking out the window. Could he see her? Probably not, in the light of a half moon. She turned Cisco away and let him run along the ridge. When the land began to slope down, she turned him and ran the other direction, past the house and on for a quarter mile or so, then stopped to let Cisco catch his breath. She felt exhilarated, full of life, and relaxed. Here was another joy she would not find in the city. Did it offset all her years of education, her father's expectations, and her satisfaction with her work? She realized as she formed the thought that she was expressing her feelings in exactly the order of their importance. What did that say about her? Her stomach growled, reminding her that she hadn't eaten since lunch, twelve hours before. She reached inside a bag always kept on her saddle and withdrew a stick of her grandfather's venison jerky. Rock hard, it challenged her jaws, and did little to assuage her hunger.

Shaking her head, she turned Cisco toward the ranch and rode him diagonally down the slope at a cooling walk, mulling the startling and not so startling events of the evening.

Granddad had known the moment she entered his room that something momentous had happened to her. How? Had her expression given it away? Or was he as prescient as she had always believed he was? Would he fully recover from his illness? Would he be able to help her father? Did he need to be well to do that? Was her experience this evening an indication that she was, in fact, as talented as Granddad thought she was? Could Alexis do what she wanted her grandfather to do?

Would she have no other choice in the end? She needed to know a lot more before the answer to that came, if it did.

In the barn, Alexis unsaddled Cisco. She rubbed him down and cleaned his feet. There wasn't much to it. Casey had groomed him earlier in the day, but she enjoyed brushing her horse. The work allowed her time to compose herself and to voice aloud some of the questions that plagued her.

"What should I do, Cisco?" she murmured. "Can I ask Granddad to heal my father while I refuse him the only thing he's ever asked of me?

"Of course I can. Healing my father's illness isn't about me—or at least it's not only about me. Dad's a young man. Too young to stop living. He touches so many lives. There's his work. And he's always helping those who need a hand. He has too much to offer. He'll never admit it, but he needs Granddad. Doctors gave up. They said there was nothing more they could do. Granddad's medicine is all that's left." She paused her vigorous grooming, used a curry comb to cleaned matted hair from the brush, and thumped the brush on a rail to shake out the dust. Cisco's fine hair was completely dry.

What if Granddad's medicine didn't work, either? It didn't always. He said it did. He said saving a life wasn't necessarily healing. Healing was a thing apart from life. Alexis only vaguely understood that. The modern part of her wondered how a person could die and yet be said to be healed. And his conviction didn't apply in all cases. Granddad's bitterness toward her father was evidence enough that he hadn't thought Alexis' mother had been healed when she left her only child and walked into the desert to die. Did Granddad know what had finally happened to Adoni? Alexis wasn't even sure he knew what illness she'd suffered from that led Adoni to believe it was her time, as the message she left Dad had said. All she knew was that one day Adoni had taken Alexis to the ranch, told Mary it was her time, and walked into the desert. Frantic, Mary had tried to reach Grant at work. She'd taken Alexis and tried to follow Adoni. When they failed to find her, she returned to the ranch and found Chases Bear waiting.

Alexis paused her one-sided conversation and pictured her mother in her mind. Not as tall as Alexis was at twelve, Adoni's slenderness had given an impression of height. Her delicate, heart-shaped face, light brown and free of blemishes, had a smooth, curved jaw and high cheekbones typical of her ancestry. Her mass of brown hair had been almost black, much darker than Alexis' hair. Her eyes, too, had been darker, nearly black, while Alexis had an elusive gleam of gold in the brown.

Granddad had listened gravely while Mary explained. Too young, confused and afraid, Alexis had asked him why he had not come sooner.

"She did not whisper to the wind," he'd said. Then he went into the desert to find his daughter.

He had spoken of Adoni in Alexis' presence only once after that. At her insistence, Grant had taken her to visit her grandfather. She'd wanted to ask him what happened to her mother, but the pain in his eyes stopped her. As they prepared to leave, Dad, angry and hurting, had shouted, "Why didn't you and your damned native medicine save her?"

Granddad answered in a soft voice, full of pain. "She ran from us both, but you were the one who wanted to make her an ordinary woman. She died because you couldn't see her for who she was. Neither of us would let Adoni be Adoni."

Alexis had wanted desperately to ask, "What did *I* do? Why did she leave *me*?" But the opportunity was lost in their argument.

"You're an old fool, and you won't get a chance to turn my daughter against me," her father barked.

The right time to talk with either of them never occurred again. Alexis shied away from the subject, for fear she would be told what evil she had done to make her mother prefer death to being with Alexis. And to avoid seeing the pain in their faces again.

"Why didn't you talk to me, Mama?" Alexis murmured to the empty barn. "Why didn't you let me and Granddad help you? Were you so unhappy that you preferred to leave us?" Tears, long unshed, streamed down her face.

"Now my father is ready to leave me, too," she murmured to Cisco. She gave the horse an extra scoop of grain to make up for the exercise and put him away. Swiping at her eyes, she hoped they weren't noticeably red and swollen. Breathing deeply, she squared her shoulders and strode to the house.

Dad was groggy, but awake and seemed not in pain. She checked Mary's notes and saw that he'd taken his last medication over three hours ago.

"You okay, Dad? You can have another pill if you want it."

"No. Hell, I'm only half here as it is, girl. Where've you been? I thought you came in two hours ago."

"I did. I exercised Cisco." She held her breath, waiting for his outburst.

"In the middle of the night?"

She ignored that.

"What did your grandfather have to say?" Now he was awake.

"He said tell you to get out of bed and get back to work."

"Huh! He knows *his* stuff, doesn't he?" He chortled.

"Let me know when you're ready to get up. I'll find something for you to wear other than that ugly nightshirt." She smoothed the covers around him.

He looked at her sharply. "Don't be an idiot. Get out of here and let me die in peace."

"Want something to eat first? Or should I start on your burial ceremony?"

"Yeah, get me some of that jerky I smell on your breath. Unless it's your grandfather's. That stuff would poison a rattlesnake."

"You'd better not have any, then. I thought it was good."

"Humph. You got any?"

"Yes, and I'll get you some if you eat soup, too."

"Yours or Mary's?"

"Mary's, of course. I'll be back with it after I take a quick shower." She started out the door. He stopped her with a yelp.

"Hey! What did you say? Burial ceremony?"

"Oh, you *are* awake. Slow on the uptake, though."

"Watch your mouth. And don't you dare give me any Indian burial ceremony! In fact, don't do anything at all. I don't want a bunch of wailers sitting around dissecting my carcass after I'm gone."

"Funerals, I'm told, are for the living, not the dead. I'll pretty much do whatever I want after you're gone. And if you don't like it, you'd better get out of that bed and go back to work."

"You—you ungrateful . . . you . . ." He looked around, found a spoon on his tray, and flipped it at her. He missed, probably intentionally, and it bounced off the wall beside the door. She looked over her shoulder, giggling, as he laid back on his pillows, breathing hard, his eyes full of mischief despite his words. Alexis skipped a little as she ran up the stairs. Whether prayer or medication had given him respite from his pain, she was grateful, and relieved to see humor return to his eyes. Maybe he was just that glad to be home.

Showered and dressed in jeans, tee shirt, and the moccasins Pat had returned, she was reminded of him and warmed all over at the thought. The image of Terry faded in her mind like an old daguerreotype.

It was unwise to love Pat. He drove too fast, drank too much, and loved too often and too many, to be a good risk. He'd been with a dozen girls and women in the decade and a half Alexis had known him, including a wife. He'd been married less than a year. Alexis had an idea his wife had caught him fooling around, though no one had ever said so. She could hardly complain about him. Though she wandered back to him like a tethered horse, she'd dated, too—enough to fear no one would compare favorably with him.

Pat was the best cop she knew—smart, fair, hard-working and dependable. Officers were happy to call him for backup. He was strong and quick on his feet. He was personable and intelligent. Everyone she knew liked him, even Dad, who had spent too much time defending people to like most cops very much. Despite his womanizing, Pat had a boyish air that fooled no one, but endeared him to people anyway. Loving him was a mistake, no question about it. She was glad he was part of her life, but couldn't think about a future with him. When she had told him so, he'd laughed and called her the smartest woman he'd ever known. If she returned to the desert to stay, it would not be for a future with Pat. Still, the moccasins brought her pleasurable memories of many clandestine meetings over the years since they were teenagers.

And Terry? Steady, intelligent, capable, with skills similar to her own, he should fit well into her life as she had known it this past five years. Her heart did not flutter at the thought of him, as it did for Pat. Did she love him? She lived with him. She looked forward to seeing him at the end of the day, enjoyed working with him on the occasions when they did. She would have described him as her second best friend, next to Chili, whom she hadn't seen for months and even years on end. Was that love?

"Spirit," she whispered, "a clue would be nice, here."

Alexis hurried to the kitchen, prepared fresh green salads and big bowls of soup, surrounded with crackers, and took the tray to the study where they had set up her father's bed.

He ate slowly, but he ate, which encouraged her. She hoped he wouldn't lose his meal again. He'd stopped the chemotherapy when they left the coast. His local doctor had told Alexis the cancer would kill him, but he wouldn't have to spend his last weeks nauseated and miserable from the chemo. His system, the doctor said, would clear out the drugs and he might even get up for a few hours some days. He might feel better for a time before the disease took him down again. He'd weaken, and pain would worsen, until he'd be grateful for the oblivion he now resented and accept morphine without complaint.

Alexis questioned that. Her father was the most bull-headed person alive, save for herself. He would never like being deprived of his senses. But tonight he was alert and eating. Alexis was grateful.

He spoke after a long silence. "Well, are you going to get around to telling me what about the state of my office? Or do I have to find out from the gardener?"

Alexis chuckled. Their driver had once done double duty as a gardener, until Dad decreed he was too old for the task and reduced his duties. Apparently, it was irrelevant that Harm could still take a bear in a fair fight, and lift half his weight in young beef at calving time. His job had been limited to driving and car care for the past decade, and from time to time, Dad still referred to him as the gardener. The idea that he might be in touch with the office and know anything about what happened there came as no surprise. Those who surrounded her father were a tight-knit family, banding together in his support. She would bet nothing that had happened anywhere in his world during this illness had escaped his notice. She made herself comfortable. Telling him all that was going on in the office would take time.

"I caught up on a lot of reports and letters, set the Manning divorce for a hearing in July, finalized the Whitmore adoption, and appealed to the parole board for Johnny Dwight. Want more?"

"Is there more?"

"Oh, yes. Much more. We could do this for what's left of the night. Why don't we just enjoy this food and try for an hour or two of sleep?"

He chuckled. "You always could do more with a day than most people do with a week. I'm . . ." He coughed. "I'm glad you're taking good care of your inheritance."

"I don't want an inheritance," she snapped, more harshly than she intended. "I never thought of you as a quitter, damn it! I had one parent who did that." The stricken look on his face told her she had gone too far, and she regretted it.

"I'm sorry, Dad. I didn't mean that."

"Of course you meant it. I'll stop talking about dying. But I fear you will have to accept, eventually." She took their dishes to the kitchen, fighting the return of tears, and spent extra moments regaining control. Quarreling with him wouldn't help the situation.

When she returned, his eyes were closed and she thought he was asleep, so she switched off the corner lamp.

"What else?" he asked, startling her.

"What? Oh, I thought you were asleep." Leaving the light off so he couldn't see her face, she sat down and told him about her encounter with Pat.

"Stay out of the issue of forged artifacts," he said, his voice firm and insistent. "And stay away from that Braithwaite bastard."

"Dad, do you know something about this? Do you think Braithwaite is involved?"

"I think it's possible."

"Tell me," she insisted. "What are you worried about?"

"I defended him when his girlfriend disappeared. I think he helped her disappear."

"How does that . . ."

"She made Indian pottery. She was good at it. Look in the shelf. Over there, by the window." Alexis turned the light on and went where he'd indicated. He had several very nice pieces of Native American pots in a glass case. Alexis recognized immediately that two of them didn't fit. Most were clean and colorful, with primitive-looking designs—a wolf or a raven, a buffalo, a horse. She knew enough to recognize that the dyes were authentic, red, purple, and green, against lighter earth tones, but recently created. Only two seemed meant to fool anyone. The two she'd noticed looked old, not symmetrical, and slightly imperfect in shape. They had not been turned on a wheel, but formed by hand. The colors were pale and worn versions of the colors of newer pieces, and there were vestiges of burnished places left on them. They looked as if they'd been rubbed for hours, or even days, with leather or some other material that gave them a sleek surface. They could easily have been used, judging by the stains on and inside them; and perhaps then buried, not thrown away as trash. That they were intact was almost

107

unbelievable. One almost never found intact pieces such as this in local dig sites. She refrained from picking them up to examine the colors. If antique, they would be delicate. From here, they looked better than the example Pat had shown her that —no, yesterday—morning. If real, they would sell for seven figures. With solid provenance as to dig site and tribal identity, more.

"Are they forged?"

He knew which ones she meant. "You'd know that better than I would. You spent half your youth on that reservation."

She nodded. "Did you get them from Braithwaite?"

"No. A client—a different one—thought she was giving me something very valuable as thanks, over and above her fee. She paid $62,000 for both."

"Did she say where she got them?"

"No, and if she did, I'd be bound by privilege. You weren't my partner then. But I showed them to your erstwhile boyfriend, Sgt. Collins."

So that's why he was looking for a forger. He'd seen the evidence in her father's study.

Chapter 10: The Medicine Way

If a man is to do something more than human,
he must have more than human powers.
~ Unknown Native American

The following morning, Alexis rose early to pick up her grandfather and take him home from the hospital before going to the law office. As she parked in the hospital lot, her phone rang: John Stockman, with a text message. Again, he wanted to meet her at the office of a well-known attorney in Portland, and would next Friday work for her? She pressed ignore and dropped the phone in her bag.

Alexis' grandfather lived in a clapboard home, miles inside the border of Warm Springs Reservation. His dusty road wound between sage-covered, steep hills littered with porous red rock and sometimes boulders and pillars that looked like the results of a rock-throwing fight between giants. You could see the towering columns of Trout Creek from here, which natives often called Indian Creek, its original name. Granddad's small house was old, but clean and in good shape.

She expected to leave him settled on the sofa or in his bed to rest, but instead left him serenely weeding his herb and vegetable garden, adding more loose straw to preserve the limited water from his well. Despite his absence, the plants looked healthy and green. Perhaps someone watered them for him while he'd been gone.

"Be careful, Granddad," she said over her shoulder as she left him.

"Don't worry, child. The grandfathers are not done with me yet. I have much work to do. Thank you for taking me out of my prison."

Alexis laughed, knowing better than to argue.

"Wait," he said. He led her back inside the house to his vast array of medicines on narrow shelves in the dining area. There, he chose a clear vial of liquid with the appearance of concentrated liquid coffee. When she reached to take it from him, she saw that he had slipped into another seizure. His eyes looked steadily above and beyond her. She waited, afraid, now, to leave him. The episode passed within seconds, and he handed her the vial as if nothing had happened.

"Granddad . . ."

"Do not worry. I am in good hands," he said. "Three drops in a full glass of water, three times a day, if he is awake. He will not like it."

"What if he is not awake?"

"The medicine is strong. If he sleeps through doses, it is doing its job. Do not let him sleep through two in a row."

Alexis removed the cap and held it to her nose. No, he would not like it. She wasn't sure she'd take it herself, regardless of circumstances.

It was pointless to disagree with Granddad about being in good hands. Alexis kissed him on the cheek and left.

She drove the half-hour journey to the ranch, her head buzzing with all the questions and puzzles in her life. What caused Granddad's seizures? Were they, in fact, seizures, or something altogether different? He seemed unconcerned, though she thought he was aware when they occurred. Would he be able to perform a healing ceremony?

Her cell phone rang again, dragging her attention back to the present. John Stockman, CEO and almost sole stockholder of Stockman Construction, a commercial construction company that operated nationwide and was valued in the billions of dollars.

How long would she have to continue hitting 'ignore' on John's calls before he would leave her alone? Why did he want to meet her at a lawyer's office in Portland, fifty miles away?

Most importantly, would her father survive his illness? If he did, where did her future lie? In Salem or Portland, where she could do well in the legal profession she had chosen? Or on the reservation with her grandfather, where he wanted her to learn the Indian Healing Way? Did she have the strength and courage required to follow that sacred path? Alexis Bishop had been raised in comfort and privilege. She had not known a moment of lack in her entire life. Had she not possessed a considerable amount of her own money, as Grant Bishop's sole heir, she and any descendants could be comfortable indefinitely. Could she give up everything to live the life of sacrifice the Medicine Way required?

What did she want to do about Terry Wells? She would miss him if they broke up. They'd been friends long before they had become lovers.

There was no denying that she was drawn to the path Granddad walked. Sacrifice or no, there was a sense of fulfillment here that she found nowhere else, not even in the courtroom, where she had aspired to be since she was old enough to understand the legal system. Well trained for the work, she had added a great deal of experience to her education and did her job very well. With memory skills that were almost eidetic, she had an ability to learn anything she read once. As a result, she often put together pieces of a puzzle before many of her peers recognized there was a puzzle to solve.

The drive home ended while she was still ruminating about her future. As she stepped inside the comfortable coolness of the ranch house, a scene came to mind, as clearly as if she were standing in the midst of it. The image took her breath away. Words came with it: "We must prepare." No sound accompanied the words, a fact from which she surmised the message came from the miraculous mind of her grandfather. His ability to communicate in silence was legendary among his adopted people.

In her mind, she stood atop a sheer, vertically scarred, red rock, peering across a deep, wooded canyon. She recognized Indian Creek, or Trout Creek, as it was now known. The creek bed started north of the town of Madras and continued inside the border of the reservation. The rugged mountain was popular with skilled "crack" rock climbers: those who liked to climb vertical crevices in sheer mountainsides. Also a nesting place for endangered golden eagles, much of it was banned to climbers by the Bureau of Land Management from May to September every year, to protect the nests of this species of great raptors, of which only 4,000 to 5,000 were believed to exist world-wide. The part of the creek that extended onto the reservation was off limits to the public for climbing.

From where she stood, she saw a pair of eagles exchange places in a nest large enough to hold a small car. She wanted to turn and leave, to avoid disturbing the breeding pair, but felt rooted to the spot, unable to walk away. The eagles, sensitive to any presence of intruders anywhere near the nest, appeared not to notice her.

Wind blew over her face. She pushed her hair away, closed her eyes and was still.

"Prepare," the voice whispered in her mind again. Prepare for what?

"As the sun rises," the silent murmur said.

"Alexis?" Mary's querulous voice broke her focus on the rugged canyon. *Sunrise? In Indian Creek?* Sleep was in order tonight—early.

"Hi, Mary." Mary's mouth, set in a grim line, and the muscle strain around her eyes and mouth told Alexis something was wrong.

Her heart skipped a beat. "What? What is it?"

"He has a fever."

Alexis braced herself. Mary wouldn't be reporting a fever unless it was bad. "Thank you," Alexis whispered, and hurried toward the den. Mary was right. Her father's face flushed deep red, and beads of perspiration rose on his forehead and lip. He shivered as if freezing cold. She started to remove the pile of blankets covering him, thought better of it, and brought them close to his chin, unsure why until she felt her grandfather's presence in the room as if he were there in person.

"Fever is nature's tool for curing illness," he had told her once, long ago. "We are too much in a hurry to bring it down, instead of letting it do its work."

"Where do we draw the line?" she murmured now.

"We don't," Mary answered from behind her. "We let Spirit decide."

"You'll have to help me with that," Alexis answered.

"There is nothing wrong with your own judgment. You need only open yourself and believe. But I will be here." The two sat with him for hours, until his fever broke and he opened his eyes. Mary washed his face, hands, and neck. Alexis gave him the water containing drops of Granddad's medicine. He groused, but took it, made a sour face, and soon fell asleep, feverish again. His temperature seemed considerably lower than before, though. Alexis felt encouraged. She left him and, from her own room, called Wade to check in on events at the office. Assured that he and the staff had handled everything of importance, she returned to her father's room and fussed around him a bit while he slept. She'd eaten nothing since dinner yesterday, so she followed her nose to the kitchen for food.

The house seemed steeped in gloom. She had intended to go to bed early. The idea of leaving Dad made her nervous, but there was no choice. If Granddad wanted her at Trout Creek tomorrow at sunup, she would be there. This was no time to listen to doubts.

Helping Mary with the dishes and cleaning her father's room took less than an hour. She puttered in her own bedroom, hanging clothes and collecting soiled ones. Her jaws ached from clenching her teeth.

Finally, she called Terry's cell. A woman answered. Alexis recognized one of the young ADAs who had joined the office after Georgetown's graduation last spring. She sounded confidant until she heard Terry demand his phone. The woman giggled. Alexis drew a deep breath and decided whatever it was, she wasn't in the mood to deal and hung up. Terry Wells was very low on her priority list right now. Tomorrow, maybe.

The phone rang and she reached for the connect button, preferring to speak to John Stockman rather than to be available if Terry called.

"How are you?" John asked, his tone gentle.

"As well as I can expect," she answered.

"Your father?"

"He's holding on. He spent today with a fever, while Mary and I sat with him."

"Ah, hon. I'm sorry you have to go through this. I know it's rough."

"You could say that," she said.

"Look, I don't want to pester you, but I could use a little encouragement that you are thinking about my offer, at least a little."

"John, I am deeply honored that you want our firm to handle your business, but until Dad is better I cannot seriously consider it. I've told you that."

"I know. And I hate to bother you, but I have an issue that needs attention, soon. I managed to put off a meeting in Portland until next Friday. Is there any chance I can talk you into joining me then? You can be home by noon."

"What sort of issue, John?"

"My daughter got in a little trouble with the law. I don't want to go over it on the phone, if you don't mind."

Knowing how he felt about his children, this was the one thing Alexis couldn't deny him. Two years ago, in Camp Pendleton, California, his only son had been charged with raping and killing a young woman he'd been dating. The young man's older sister, a former classmate, had asked Alexis to defend him. Her success in that case was the reason John wanted Alexis to manage his legal business now.

"All right," she said. "I'll look at the case and either take care of it or recommend someone highly capable. I'm sorry, John. I guess I'm not the only one having a rough time."

He loosed a great sigh. "Thank God. I'll text you the location." He said good-bye and clicked off.

Alexis went to bed and slept fitfully, wondering why she had taken on yet one more responsibility. Wondering if she cared that Terry Wells was busy cavorting with another lawyer in their office. Wondering if he was. She had never considered the idea of infidelity on his part. It seemed completely out of character for him. Was it? Maybe she didn't know him as well as she thought.

Chapter 11: Golden Eagle

***I don't believe you have to be better than anyone else;
I believe you have to be better than you thought you could be.***
~Ken Venturi

An hour before sunup, Alexis approached Trout Creek from north of the town of Madras, not far off the reservation. With climbing banned from May until September, the camp was almost deserted. A few families camped there, but no one stirred at this hour. She parked her car in climbers' parking, as close as she could to the trailhead. A long hike faced her before she even approached the crowning, vertical, basalt walls that appeared to grow sixty feet out of the top of the mountain like a coronet on an oversized head. She guessed that the sheer, vertically cracked walls of the topmost bluff were what remained after millennia of weather had broken off the outer edges, causing them to fall and form the much smoother hills that surrounded them. Curious, she had once looked up the reason the basalt, usually gray or black volcanic rock, was red, and learned it was due to oxidation of its high content of iron. Simple rust had given the mountaintop its vivid color.

She wore leather, calf-high, moccasins with thickened soles. Snug leather gloves were thin enough to allow maximum feeling in her fingertips, thick enough to protect her fingers. The rock was porous and sharp-edged. Cuts and abrasions were to be expected.

With a slim flashlight from her belt lighting the trail, she took a deep breath, marshalling her resources, and started her hike to the daunting formation ahead, grateful for good health and conditioning. Though she had not made this climb in years, she'd done it, and thought she could again. She wasn't sure why Granddad had chosen this place for her to prepare—for what? A healing ceremony? And why her? Because he was in no condition to do it? Alexis doubted he would admit that. If he needed to climb this mountain, he would, seizures or no. He had told her to be here.

She heard his voice in her head, repeating what he had told her a thousand times, "We are all, always, in the exact right place at the exact right time. We may never know the reasons, or we may. Perhaps the plane or train we missed will crash. Perhaps we will touch the life of another, however briefly or apparently inconsequentially, and ripples of change will follow. We are all connected, each to the other, to Mother Earth, and to the breath of Spirit. Nothing that happens is inconsequential or coincidental."

She sighed, knowing this task was hers to do, regardless of reasons. She'd climbed many rocks in her past, for no other reason than that they were there. Most often such hijinks had been undertaken in the company of Patrick Collins or Chili Wenway, or both, and with other friends as well. Not since the very earliest attempts had she felt trepidation, as she did now.

Something in the path ahead gave her goose bumps, causing her to wonder if this was, indeed, the best place to prepare for a healing way—assuming that was what she was preparing for.

With or without fear, she was meant to climb that rock. She strode along the rugged path, grateful for having been here before. A sign marked the point at which she entered Indian land and was no longer in violation of BLM rules. The golden eagles would be here, too, but she'd been told in her vision that she would not disturb them. She need only believe that to be true.

Littered with rocks, the path was treacherous. A turned ankle in this wild country could be life threatening. Where she was unsure of her footing, she adopted a shuffle that located loose stones and let her kick them out of her way before she stepped on them in the dark. By the end of this hike, Alexis would be looking for a new pair of moccasins. At steeper points on the trail, she bent to use her hands for better support. Applying one such maneuver, she felt an icy cold shiver travel up her back, and swung around to see who or what was watching her. It had felt eerily as if her back were a target. Seeing nothing and no one, she returned her attention to the uphill trek, picking up her pace as much as she dared. Sweat poured off her face and down her torso before the sky lightened and her path became clear without the flashlight. A timber rattler slithered away and she was grateful she had not met the snake in the dark. She wondered where the cold-blooded creature had found enough warmth on the mountainside during the night. A den near the path, perhaps? In any case, now he was headed upward, seeking the reflected heat of red rocks to warm him as day broke. Light sliding over the top of the cliffs above caused her to reach into a cargo pocket for sunglasses. Barely dawn, and the desert already felt uncomfortably warm, especially after her exertion. Approaching the sheer, vertically scarred and cracked wall, she scanned the area for snakes or their hiding places. Seeing none, she turned her attention to searching for footholds and finger ledges visible from the base of the wall. They were there to be found.

"Thank You, Spirit, for good eyesight," she murmured, planning the initial leg of her journey to the top. She unhooked a bottle from her belt and took a long draft of still-cool water. The top of the wall was out of view, but she judged it to be not less than eighty feet high at this point.

She braced herself. "I can't stand here looking at it." The base of the rock was still in shade. She found her first handhold and stepped to the first foothold. One step at a time. Do not hurry. Impatience was her enemy. Look ahead, plan the next steps, rest in the cracks where she could lean her back against one side, her feet against another. Virgin clean, the wall had no pitons or bolt rings. She climbed as her grandfather had taught her, without support, without artificial assistance. She heard his voice in her head.

"Faith," he said. "Have faith in your skill, faith in God. Accept fear. Be at peace with it. Let it guide your steps until you no longer need it. Then release it to the spirit of the mountain."

Or the spirit of the eagle. With a wingspan measuring eight feet from tip to tip, the golden eagle soared past her, its shadow on the wall drawing her attention. A moment of near terror jolted her as she turned to see if the raptor presented danger. It would protect its nest from any intrusion. Or worse, it might decide the danger she represented was too much and abandon its nesting eggs.

She could not tell if it was male or female; the two look much alike. Its widespread wings resembled fingers at the tips. A small animal was clutched in its blue-black beak. It soared on the canyon breezes and paid no attention to her. She might not have been there at all. She was sure those sharp, hooded eyes could have seen her. It either dismissed her as non-threatening and not food, or it chose not to see her at all.

It was no wonder almost a half-dozen nations had adopted this magnificent bird as their national symbol. The gold part of its wings looked translucent in the sun. She hoped nothing she did would disturb the glorious eagle or its mate, who seemed to be nowhere near at the moment.

Alexis had passed the halfway mark when she felt a sense of something or someone watching. The feeling manifested as a pressure against her spine, an inch below her shoulder blades, almost in line with her heart. She stopped moving. The intensity of feeling remained, neither diminishing nor increasing. She maneuvered herself into a position that allowed her to look backward, across the stream at the foot of the mountains. Nothing. She looked down. Nothing there but the long slope of hillside beneath the bluff. No creature, no person, no threat of any kind, except the one she created for herself by allowing her focus to be broken.

At the upper edge of the bluff, with her fingers inches from the end of her climb, she heard her grandfather's voice. A mixture of fear and anger assaulted her. Why had he undertaken this extreme challenge in his condition? She abandoned caution and scrambled over the edge on her abdomen, clinging to the root of a tree protruding out of the mountainside. Her grandfather stopped chanting and grinned at her. He sat with his ankles crossed in traditional Indian fashion on one end of a prayer rug, as old and worn as he was.

"What are you doing here?" Alexis demanded. "What possessed you to climb this bluff when you are still having seizures? You could have fallen!"

"Have I not told you that Spirit has much work for me?"

Alexis shook her head. She might as well accept his position. Nothing she could say would shake his confidence. He wouldn't even argue. He would smile and wait for her to see the light.

"Well, Grandfather, I think Spirit has made a small miscalculation in choosing our location for whatever task is planned for us today. I cannot think this is a suitable place for prayer."

The old man nodded, his brow furrowed, his mouth firm. "Is this what the eagle told you, child of my child? I saw him pass by."

"The eagle said nothing. He did not acknowledge my presence. It was the arrowhead aimed between my shoulder blades that told me there is evil present in Indian Creek today."

"Ah. And this arrowhead—was it wielded by the hands of man or spirit?"

"I was unable to discern if it was either. I saw nothing but the flight of the eagle as I climbed. And why is it that I have sensed this evil, and you have not?"

"Perhaps its message was for you and not me."

Both of them jumped as the crack of a rifle shot echoed against the canyon walls. Alexis threw herself flat on her abdomen and stretched to look over the distant horizon. Chases Bear sat still, his head cocked sideways as if listening to some faraway voice. Alexis' first thought was for the magnificent eagle that had passed her with food for its young.

Chapter 12: Miscreants

Where there is mystery,
It must generally be suspected
There is also evil.
~Lord Byron

Alexis felt the weight of sadness inside as she recalled the splendid bird with sun gleaming through its golden wings, and feared for its safety. When only 5,000 remained in the entire world, what callous soul could shoot, or shoot at, a creature so wonderful?

She faced her grandfather. From beneath the blanket he wore over his shoulders, he withdrew a small telescope, held it out to her, and pointed toward the western sky. Alexis stepped closer to the edge of the bluff for a better view. She searched until she saw a distant brown speck soaring far higher than it had when it passed her. She focused the glass on the speck, seeing that it was, indeed, an eagle whose golden wings and white tail spot caught the sun. Much relieved, she lowered the spyglass. It was amazingly powerful for being no more than eight inches long. She made a mental note to find one for herself.

As she did, something on the ground further upstream caught her eye: a structure, partially camouflaged. Shaped like a sweat lodge, it seemed from here to be constructed in much the same way, with curved saplings covered by rugs and blankets. Branches atop the rugs concealed its shape to some degree, whether by design or accident, she couldn't tell. Someone who was too far away for her to see clearly sat hunched in front of the only opening, which faced the stream traversing the floor of the rugged canyon. Two other individuals sat more or less opposite the first person. A third sat on a boulder apart from the others. She thought two of the people were men and one a woman, but couldn't swear to it. Of greater interest was a smooth clay construction some thirty feet away from the camouflaged lodge. That, she recognized. It was a kiln for baking pottery.

Another shot rang out, and before she dropped to the ground, she saw a rifle in the hands of the person in front of the shelter. If he was aiming at the eagle, his judgment was off by a mile. Nevertheless, the eagle made a soaring turn and flew higher, faster, and farther away from the threat on the ground. Alexis wondered where its nest was located and if the raptor would return to it. If it didn't, more lovely golden eagles would be lost to the world. Her sadness returned, and with it, the suffocating sense of the presence of evil.

Granddad remained where he was, undisturbed by the incident or the presence of the eagle. "You are right," he said. "This is not where we must prepare for a Healing Way. We will seek another place close to God."

"So you made that hazardous climb for no good reason," Alexis said.

"Nothing is without reason. We are always exactly where we need to be at any given time."

"So we are supposed to see what is here on this day, at this time."

"We are, daughter of my daughter. The reason may become clear to us, or it may never be revealed on this side of the curtain of death. It is the way of Spirit to reveal what we need to know, if we listen closely. The reason may be for the eagle, or for you or for me. Or it may involve the five miscreants in the chasm. We will listen to the wind."

"Five? I saw four."

"Five souls occupy the space below. One is insubstantial."

"What does that mean?" she asked.

"I don't know. I can only feel her presence. I cannot see her."

"How do you know they are miscreants?"

"You have felt the presence of evil, as have I. Had we been above them, or at any other angle than this, perhaps we would not have seen. I think that is their intent."

"Did you see the others?"

"Yes. When next young Casey appears for work, you should ask him why he was here."

"You're just full of surprises today, aren't you? How are we getting down from this place? I am hungry." He reached under his blanket and brought out two sticks of his homemade jerky. It would sustain, but would not fill the belly.

"Gee, thanks."

Going down proved far easier, though longer than going up and made her thoroughly annoyed with her grandfather. He had approached the bluff from the back side, through a series of narrow passages among a litter of boulders, many as large as a house. A few paths meandered under the bluff, through dark, claustrophobic tunnels worn in the basalt.

"How did you find this trail?" Alexis asked.

"Long ago, as a boy, I walked and rode this mountain many times. The trace has not changed since then and perhaps not since animals no longer known to us traveled this way."

"And do you have a thought as to how I will find my way back to my car?"

He chuckled. "I have every confidence in your ability to meet all challenges."

"Uh, huh. And how are *you* getting home? Perhaps I will borrow your mode of transportation and let you walk."

"Given a choice, Jack will almost certainly choose him who fills the manger over a young woman, however beautiful."

"Beauty is rarely beyond the notice of an ass, Granddad."

His laugh eased her tension. "True only of the two-legged variety. Our furred friends are wiser," he said. Alexis checked her cell phone, even knowing there would be no reception from this place. By the third time she looked, she concluded that she had a long walk ahead of her. Her grandfather knew she would not allow him to walk while she rode his mule. She stopped to check the condition of her moccasins and fell behind a little. When she looked up, a four-wheel-drive patrol car was parked at the foot of the trail.

"You tricky old coyote," she muttered under her breath, glaring at her grandfather's receding back. By the time she caught up, the old man was leaning into the car window, talking with Pat Collins. "Were they there?" Pat was asking.

She poked her grandfather's arm. He grinned at her.

"Did you think I would leave you to walk so far alone?"

"I would put nothing past you. It would depend upon your reasons for doing it."

He nodded at that. "With cause, there is little I would not do for your benefit," he said.

"Benefit! You think it is to my benefit to drag me out here to climb the wall—for what? Your entertainment?"

A conspiratorial grin covered Pat's boyish face.

"Did you know about this?" Alexis demanded.

"I didn't even know you were here, Al. Chases Bear just asked me to meet him. He thought he knew the whereabouts of some people I've been looking for."

"And did he?"

"I don't know. You started beating him up before he answered me."

She shook her head. His boyish grin bested her in an argument every time. She looked to her grandfather. "So you expected our discovery in the valley."

"They have been there long enough to dig many holes for waste burial."

"It's nice to know they have that much conscience."

"Maybe," he said. "Maybe conscience does not guide their actions."

"Why else would they dig—" *One of the souls in the valley is insubstantial. Dead? Buried in a hole dug for waste, which no one would dig up?*

"What are the ways you might age pottery to make it look antique?" Pat asked, startling her with this apparent change of subject. She thought about it.

"Maybe something like bury them in soggy waste for a few weeks? Do you think these are your artifact forgers, Pat?" Alexis asked.

He shrugged. "Maybe. I'm a long way from having enough evidence to do anything about it."

"It's Braithwaite, isn't it?"

"Why do you say that?" Pat asked.

"If ever there was an evil man, that Braithwaite is," she said. "Granddad, you know what he's willing to do to you. Why are you out here looking for him?"

"He is not aware of my presence," Chases Bear said. "And Jack and I are going home now. I am sorry, Granddaughter. I underestimated the degree of evil residing in the valley. I did not think their nearness would affect our prayers."

"Not knowing a thing isn't like you."

"It is not," he said. "And will not be again."

Alexis kept her doubts about that statement to herself. While her granddad climbed aboard his mule, she circled the car and got in.

Chapter 13: Four Legs and Spirit

A horse is the projection of peoples' dreams
About themselves - strong, powerful, beautiful –
And it has the capability of giving us escape
From our mundane existence.
~Pam Brown

The distance back to Alexis' car through the reservation Gateway, to the highway, and past Madras, seemed several times farther than she had climbed and descended over the mountain. Alexis could think of nothing to say, uncomfortable in Pat's company after their interrupted rendezvous at Tenino Creek.

He broke the silence. "How's your father?"

"About the same. He sleeps a lot, and had a high fever for a while, but he's not suffering from the effects of chemo."

"Chases Bear said you were here to prepare. For a healing ceremony? For Grant?"

"I assume so. You know Granddad. His messages tend to be long distance or cryptic, or both. In this case, both."

Pat chuckled. "He sent you a mental message?"

"Yes. How do you know about that?"

"He's sent them to me since I was a little kid, running loose on the rez with no one to look out for me."

"I remember. You never told me he spoke to you the way he did to me."

"My parents said I was crazy. I didn't want you to know I was crazy. Besides, you never told me, either."

Alexis made an impatient noise in her throat. "Your parents were rarely in possession of all their faculties, as I recall."

"No one can deny that," he said, his tone rueful. "My parents were the kind of Indians who gave us the reputation for what firewater does to us. I doubt if I ever saw either one completely sober. Chases Bear looked after me more than anyone."

"Apparently, he did well. You went from bad boy, to college, to cop."

"I suspect I owe him my life. Without him, I might have been Harley Braithwaite—or dead. Chases Bear is a good man, Alexis. I was not crazy. He spoke to me wherever I was."

"Yes. And by now, few of our people I know would be surprised to hear it."

"Maybe more than a few, but people have come to recognize his gifts, if they don't understand. He has a way of just appearing where he is needed. That only happens so many times before people figure out he has something special. It scares some."

"Some people have things to hide, I imagine."

"And you have a gift for understatement."

"Our friend Braithwaite must be among those who have things to hide."

"So does Casey Johnson, and the third man. I haven't learned his name yet. We don't see him around much."

"Granddad said Casey was with them in the canyon. I am surprised that he is involved in anything shady. He's always been a good kid, according to Dad."

Pat glanced at her as he turned into the entrance at Trout Creek Campground. "Casey's record's clean, so far. So is Lila's. Her only transgression is being a runaway, as far as I know. Sarah Nunez was clean, too."

"Is she the girl who disappeared? Braithwaite's prior girlfriend?"

"Yes. But she went from missing person, in my opinion, to possible homicide victim."

"Oh, my God. Was she just a kid, too?"

"No. She was twenty-six. A potter. She made pottery for sale. Lila learned from her. That's how she met Braithwaite."

"How old is he?"

"Thirty-one."

"He needs to be arrested for statutory rape."

A moment of awkward silence followed. Alexis opened her mouth to speak.

Pat spoke at the same time. "Who is the guy? Another lawyer?"

"Who?"

"You said you were seeing someone."

"Oh. My mind is still in the canyon. You mean Terry."

"Is that his name?"

"Terry Wells. Yes, he's a lawyer. We've been together several months."

"Several months? Is it serious?"

"I thought so, before I came home. Now, I don't know. This is a different world, like a different life."

"Absence makes . . ."

"Distance," she broke in. "Absence makes distance."

"Which translates to . . .?"

Alexis was spared the need to answer by their arrival at her car.

"Thank you, Pat," she said softly, and stepped out of his vehicle.

At home, Alexis found her dad much as she'd left him; sound asleep, under the influence of Granddad's medicine. Checking with Mary, she was pleased to hear that he had managed to gag down the second dose just after noon. His temperature seemed high, but not drastically so, and he'd stopped shivering.

It was too late for Alexis to go to the office and get much done. She settled for calling to see if she was urgently needed, and wasn't.

Instead, she decided to check the status of the ranch, and called Jerry, their foreman, at his cell number.

"This is Jerry," he answered. He had a voice like the growl of a bear. There was no mistaking who he was.

"Jerry, it's Alexis Bishop. I have a little time this afternoon, and thought it might be good for us to catch up. Are you clear for an hour or two?"

"Uh . . . not really, Mizz Bishop. I've got me a heifer fixing to drop her first, and she don't like it much. I can't seem to get her settled down any, and I'm afraid we gonna have one go bad here if I don't stick it out. How about tomorrow?"

Tomorrow was Friday, and Alexis had promised John she'd see him in Portland. On the other hand, he'd promised to have her back by noon.

"Tomorrow afternoon will be fine, Jerry. Are you in the calving barn?"

"Yes, ma'am. We're in the north end stall. If you catch sight of that Johnson kid, tell him to get his tailfeathers out here, will you? I could use the help."

"Casey's not here today. I'll be out as soon as I can get there. See you soon."

She hung up, swapped her battered moccasins for mucking boots, and sprinted out past the horse barn toward the six-stall covered shelter reserved for the care of sick, injured, and calving cattle. Sheltered from weather beneath a stand of umbrella-shaped myrtle trees, the shelter was little more than a roof over 8 railed pens with a storage shed at one end. The stall Jerry referred to was located at the end of the center aisle, next to the shed, which contained veterinary tools and medicines as well as enough feed for the animals recuperating here. None of the stalls were enclosed. Bishops believed in the health qualities of free-flowing air for sick or suffering animals. The more oxygen, the better, Grant Bishop often said. Hired hands cursed him when they had to work here in winter months, occasionally at below zero temperatures. But Grant Bishop hated to lose a single animal, and to Alexis' knowledge, there hadn't been many deaths. She passed the stall where Jerry worked to calm the heifer, too young and birthing her calf late in the year. If the baby didn't mature well before fall, they'd be keeping both of them in the horse barn close to home, creating extra work for someone. In the old days, Alexis had gleefully taken on that task, loving the calves as she would pets.

Alexis applied cream to her hands to facilitate the donning of elbow- high rubber gloves, and joined Jerry. He'd worked up a sweat trying to corner the young cow and calm her enough to find out if she was as close to giving birth as she seemed.

"Does she know your dog, Jerry?"

"Yeah, but she doesn't seem to want him around right now."

Alexis opened the gate. "Jake!" she called. The blue heeler turned to her, whined, and exited the stall, sitting on his haunches at the fence to watch.

Jerry shook his head. "You're the only other person 'sides me who can order that dog around, an' he'll mind you," he said.

"I raised him from a puppy, Jerry. The first time I came home from college, he was so excited to see me, he peed all over my shoes."

"I'd a shot him on the spot," Jerry said, but his grin told her he wouldn't part with the stocky little heeler in exchange for three of him. Cattle dogs like him were hard to come by, but loyal for life. Alexis decided she wanted one of his next pups. She approached the heifer from slightly off center, so the heifer could see an escape and wouldn't feel trapped. Moving slowly, Alexis scratched the young cow's nose. The animal lifted her head, clearly enjoying the touch.

"When are you breeding Jake again, Jerry?" She carefully made her voice soft and soothing for the sake of the cow. Their patient might not understand the words, but she'd understand the tone. Jerry had brought a bucket of wet COB. Alexis reached into it for a handful of the sticky corn, oats, and barley and held it to the heifer's nose. She wrapped her long, sloppy tongue over the molasses-soaked grain and nibbled. A third figure appeared in the stall wearing long gloves. Alexis glanced up to see Casey rubbing the cow's sides, palpating her swollen belly. Alexis had a lot to say to him, but decided now was not the time. Dropping to his knees, he reached under the heifer.

Casey's head and neck were badly bruised and he had a knot on the side of his head. Perhaps he'd learned that the group in the canyon were bad news.

"Have you seen a doctor?" she murmured. The heifer, calmer now, licked the last of the grain from Alexis' hand and looked for more.

"Your grandpa," Casey answered.

"Did he tell you to come here?"

"No, Miss Bishop, but he gave me permission to come if I wanted to."

"Good," she answered. That meant he was well enough to work, or Casey would be home in bed. This was his second beating in a week, and Alexis vowed silently to get to the bottom of it.

Casey bent his head and pushed—hard—on the heifer's rear flank. The little cow mooed.

"She's breech," Casey said. "And it's not a small calf. We'll have to turn it if we want to save her or the baby. Swap places with me, Jerry. My arms are smaller'n yours."

Smaller, but just as strong, Alexis thought. Jerry moved to take Casey's place, and attempted to manipulate the calf's position from outside, while Casey took off his shirt and rolled the gloves on all the way to his shoulders. A moment later, both arms were up to the glove ends in the cow's birth canal. Alexis dropped to her knees beside her, opposite Jerry, and began palpating the belly, gently shifting, trying to discern the calf's position. The three of them worked for better than an hour, until Casey yelped.

"I got a foot!" He cried. "And another!"

Alexis could tell. The baby's form had lengthened, the bulge reduced in circumference. Now if Casey could just cradle the calf's nose between its front legs, they'd have a baby.

"Do you have a pulse, Casey?"

"Oohh, yeah! Good strong one. This little guy—wait!"

"What?" Alexis asked, alarmed.

"Got a cord around his neck. Jerry, soon as you see his feet, pull. I'm gonna hold the cord off his neck. Miss Bishop, soon as it's out far enough, tie it off and cut the cord. We ain't losing this little one."

"How do I know which side to cut? Oh, duh. Make two ties and cut in the middle."

"That's just right, Missy. We can always cut it shorter when the calf's on the ground." Jerry handed her shears and two cut lengths of twine. His gloved hands were bloody. Casey moaned and huffed with the strain of holding the calf's head, but his arms were no longer as deep inside her body.

"I see a foot!" Alexis cried. One narrow, pointed hoof poked out several inches, and then another. Pulling wasn't much work from there. As soon as the calf's nose left the birth canal, the rest followed almost too quickly. Alexis tied quick double knots around the cord and snipped between them seconds before the calf landed, too slippery for anyone to hold.

"It's a girl," Casey said. "Pretty little thing."

"Not so little," Jerry answered. "Hundred pounds if she's an ounce."

Not little, but definitely pretty, with her dark red hair, white face, and big eyes. Her mother cleaned and nudged her, urging her to her feet. Within minutes, she was perched on long, wide-spread legs, searching under her mama's belly for a nipple.

The three midwives looked at each other, grinning like goofy clowns. There is something about a successful birth, especially a tough one, that lifts the heart and draws people close.

"Let's talk in a while, Casey," Alexis said.

"Miss Bishop, I'm sorry I'm late. I got hung up. . ."

"It's not about being late. We'll save it for later. Get cleaned up. I think Jerry has more work for you. Good job with that calf, Casey. It would have been a lot tougher without you."

"Yeah," Jerry said and clapped Casey on the shoulder.

Alexis peeled off her messy gloves and threw them in the trash, noting that she could use a shower and a change of clothes, herself. She grinned at Jerry.

"Call if you need me. I might as well do something useful around here."

"Will do, boss."

Boss. He only ever called Dad boss. She wanted to rebuke him, to tell him her father wasn't dead yet, but knew better. No point in taking out her frustrations on the help. She was likely to need him for some time.

Back in the house, she saw that her father was still asleep and there was no evidence that he had moved a finger. She slipped in and checked his pulse. He snored. Upstairs, she called Wade again and was assured all was running smoothly. With nothing left to do, she showered and decided a nap sounded nice after getting up before dawn. She closed her eyes and the world around her disappeared. An hour later, she made her way sleepily downstairs when the delectable scent of dinner woke her. She ate scantily, checked on her sleeping father, and stumbled back to bed, asleep within seconds.

Alexis rose as the sun's rays shot their first faint glimmer into the open window in her room. She dressed quickly and tiptoed through the kitchen to the barn. There, she saddled Cisco, mounted, and trotted him to the flat top of a rise overlooking the ranch. At the crest, she looked back and sat staring at the house for several minutes. Sunk in shadow, the structure looked smaller than in daylight. Its two stories spread over 3,000 square feet in the center of a manicured green garden, irrigated by the same pipeline from the Deschutes River that watered pastures and hayfields. The sprinkler reflected stray light from windows and a yard lamp, shimmering here and there like ethereal ghosts, sifting among poplars, encircled by beds of irises.

Lovely as it was, Alexis knew she couldn't occupy their home without her father. If he died, the place would be too full of ghosts from their past. Every shared chess game, debate over legal issues, every hour under his often impatient tutelage, would haunt her. Loss settled over her like dust, suffocating and grave. She spun the horse and tapped him into a canter, running effortlessly across the high meadow, a mile, two, and then three, before the day lightened enough to risk a full-out gallop. Then she leaned into Cisco's neck, tangling her fingers in his mane, burying her face in his coarse hair, and let him fly, escaping her fears.

The unleashed power of his muscles beneath her undulated forward and back, side to side, and up and down, and her body moved with his, the two as if one. Every cell of her being came alive, stretching, contracting, and twisting. One with his motion. The breath of Spirit swept her face, stung her eyes and filled her lungs.

An arroyo gaped ahead, and she felt Cisco's muscles bunch under her saddle. His back lifted, his shoulders rose, and he soared over the chasm, landing on his front legs and lifting off as his hind legs touched the earth.

Miles flew past. At the far end of the meadow, the land sloped down, and she drew Cisco to a stop, both of them gasping for breath. She walked along the edge of the crest, cooling her mount and watching the panoramic view below. A deer family, doe and two fawns, stepped out of a copse and stopped to stare at her as if she'd shone a light in their eyes, still as statues for the space of two breaths. Then they turned and disappeared as one into the woods. Energized and spiritually uplifted, Alexis turned Cisco toward home. The sun glinted off wispy clouds and a faint, white moon touched the mountains. Shadows evaporated, and night-feeding creatures ducked into nests. The scream of an eagle drew her attention to the sky. She stopped to sense him and felt nothing except a gentle breeze in her face before he disappeared in the distance. She returned her horse to the barn, unsaddled him, ran her hands over his hot body, and having found no injuries or blemishes handed him off to Casey to groom and feed.

In the house, her father was awake, sipping coffee. The scent of bacon and waffles wafted from the kitchen. She kissed his cheek.

"Christ! You smell like a sweaty horse. What did you do? Run his legs off?"

"Close enough. Don't eat all the waffles. I'll be right down."

She poured coffee and took it with her to sip while she showered the aches out of her muscles in the bathtub with hot water and Epsom salts. She kept it brief, mouthwatering for breakfast, but the treatment worked. "There's magic in magnesium," she murmured. Toweling her hair, she found a sleeveless cotton shift with a matching jacket and heeled sandals. Simple, cool, professional.

Dad was finished eating. Mary brought her a plate of waffles, fruit and bacon. Alexis took it gratefully and blew her a kiss.

"What's on your agenda today?" her father asked.

"A quick trip to Portland, to see what John Stockman wants. A couple of interviews with aspiring associates. An afternoon with Casey and Jerry, to review ranch work and to try and find out who beat up Casey again."

He stopped to look up, a bite halfway to his mouth. "Casey? When? Where?"

"Not here, Dad. I think he was on the rez, and had a falling out with his companions. Pat's looking into the crew out there."

"Watch your back, young lady. Don't get yourself in danger."

"Working on that, Dad. Not much interested in trouble. I have enough going on."

"Did you say you're hiring?"

"Unless you object."

"Of course not. Just be careful about it. If you hire a lemon, you could be stuck with him for years."

"You're right. And with all my experience, I haven't hired staff. Any advice?"

"I thought you'd never ask. Don't worry about appearance, as long as they're clean. Instruct your existing staff to clue them in on dress codes. Look for balance—not too nervous, not cocky. Check references. See how many jobs they have had. Don't hire anyone with too many short-term jobs."

"If nobody else wants him, why should we?"

"Conversely, if they don't like anyone else, why would they like us?"

"I'm pretty likeable."

"Huh. You have your moments. Go. I'm tired." Indeed, he looked about to fall asleep again.

Chapter 14: Ancient Medicine

Temptation is the devil looking through the keyhole.
Yielding is opening the door and inviting him in.
~Billy Sunday

"Let me know if you need a break," Alexis said to Melanie, her dad's nurse, Mary's daughter.

"I'm fine. I'm not sure your help is good for him," Melanie said.

"What do you mean?"

"Mom told me about the so-called medicine your grandfather sent. Since you gave it to him, Grant has been in the bathroom whenever he's awake."

Alexis returned to her father's temporary quarters and located the vial of medicine. Removing the cap, she smelled it and took time to discern those of its contents she recognized.

"Cascara Sagrada," she murmured. "Of course he has intestinal issues."

"What on earth is Cascara Sagrada?" Melanie asked.

"Sacred Cascara. Bark of the Cascara tree. It's being used as a cleanse, combined with fasting and clear liquids."

"He's certainly fasting, sleeping through most mealtimes." Melanie's voice had sharpened and to Alexis, sounded irritated. Alexis eyed her. The two had lived much of their lives in the same house without becoming friends. Was Melanie the right person to care for her father? Doctors had given up, and though more native blood flowed in Melanie's veins than in Alexis', she was a product of American medical training. Would her attitude affect Dad's acceptance of Granddad's medicine?

As if reading her thoughts, Melanie snapped, "I can care for my patient. I'll discuss this with his physician."

"As long as you do not make decisions about his medication, discuss it with whomever you choose. Better yet, let me do the discussing. You follow instructions."

"Goes with the territory," Melanie answered in a matter-of-fact tone that said she was used to following unpalatable instructions. Alexis detected a smug note that she guessed meant Melanie was certain the doctor would reverse Chases Bear's instructions.

Alexis pocketed the vial. She'd take responsibility for giving her father the prescribed dose herself. She glanced at her watch. John had promised he'd have her back by noon. He'd better have wings if he meant to keep that promise. She could be home by two if the meeting was short. She guessed their conference would be anything but short.

Her stop at Dad's legal offices was necessarily brief. She told Wade where she'd be and that she had agreed to look at the case John had mentioned. She glanced through the mail, noting nothing urgent.

"How's your dad?" Wade asked.

"Sleeping, when he isn't sick."

"Sick? I thought that ended with chemo?"

"It did. I gave him Granddad's medicine."

"Bad reaction?"

"Only what Granddad intended. Intestinal issues."

"Not the first time. If a person won't fast, he makes sure."

"Who's less likely to fast than Dad? Unless you count me."

Wade laughed, nodding. Both Bishops were known to have healthy appetites. "Trust Chases Bear. He knows what he's doing."

"I do trust him—most of the time."

"Why? Is he still having seizures?"

"Yes. Our prayer meeting was aborted yesterday, but not before he climbed a mountain in Indian Creek."

"Aborted?"

"Long story."

"We'll talk later. Drive carefully, Alexis." He gave her an offhand wave and returned to his own office.

Alexis was on the road five minutes later. Melanie's attitude bothered her. The nurse's upbringing had been divided between the rez and the Bishop household. She was one of many kids Grant Bishop had sent to college, and in her case, nurse's training, too. She knew about Native American medicine as well as she knew conventional care. Would she disregard Granddad's instructions? Was that why Granddad had given the vial to Alexis, and not Melanie? Wade's comment about what her grandfather might do to see that his instructions were followed reminded Alexis that Wade came from the rez, too.

Traffic thickened as she entered downtown Portland, forcing her to focus on driving. Alexis knew the location of the building she sought. What lawyer in Oregon wouldn't know where to find the Reinhardt Building?

The thirty-story building with walls that seemed made of glass was named for the founder of the prestigious legal firm that occupied most of its floors, Paul G. Reinhardt. His grandson, William Reinhardt, owned the building and was managing partner of the firm, several times the size it had been in its founder's era.

Alexis parked in an underground garage and took the elevator to the marble-walled enclave of attorneys. Jackson, Paulson, Reinhardt in giant gold-leaf letters graced the otherwise blank wall facing the elevator doors. She recognized Mr. Reinhardt greeting John Stockman with a handshake. John's hair concealed part of a letter on the wall; a foot of space separated Reinhardt's from them. Yet the slender lawyer made the more imposing figure than the big man who had worked a lifetime with his hands.

Alexis hesitated a moment, watching the interchange. It seemed odd, as if staged for her benefit. They looked at her together, as if on cue.

She stepped out of the elevator. A curved counter occupied space in front of a floor-to-ceiling view of the city. A well-groomed woman with salt and pepper hair sat behind the counter beside two empty chairs. A younger woman did something with file folders with her back to the hall. To left and right, wide glass doors opened to unseen places the length of a long hallway. Hunter green carpet covered the center area of the floor, bordered by more marble. The effect was an appearance of wealth, a scene to inspire clients' confidence in the attorneys who worked here. Clearly, they were successful in their work. As John took her arm and guided her over the lush carpet behind Mr. Reinhardt, she wondered if their surroundings had played a part in John's decision to meet with her here, rather than in her own office. He led past a series of double glass doors before entering a pair that opened on a huge interior space made of too much glass. Alexis knew this newer style was in vogue, but felt uncomfortable, a fish in a bowl, where everyone could see every action, every visitor, and every nuance of body language. To her, it seemed contrary to the confidentiality requirements of the profession. By noon, every person in the building would know that a celebrated CEO of one of the nation's largest commercial construction companies had consulted with the managing partner and a young attorney from Central Oregon. Though not as well-known as John, she had defended John's son. Her likeness had graced news magazine covers several times during the trial, and she was not a forgettable person. The environment meant that every attorney in Portland would soon be speculating about the meeting. Legal circles were like small towns: gossip reigned.

The appearance of wealth continued in Reinhardt's office, too: multi-colored, matching vases as tall as she, desks and tables of polished hardwood and glass, shelves lined with leather bound tomes with which she was familiar. There were mementos from world travel, such as the photo of Reinhardt in hunting regalia, holding the huge horn of an African water buffalo, from which she guessed one was meant to assume he had killed it. Its head alone was as tall as Reinhardt's hips. Since she doubted he had eaten it, her estimation of him plummeted. As did her people, she disapproved of killing except for food.

The three of them sat in silence for a few minutes. John, accustomed to her ways, averted his eyes and was still, following her example. Reinhardt tugged at his collar and patted his forehead with a handkerchief before he broke the silence.

"Miss Bishop, I understand you are due home in . . ." he glanced at his watch. "Three hours. Perhaps we should . . ." He fell silent.

John smiled and spoke, "Alexis Bishop, this is Will Reinhardt. Will, Alexis Bishop, brilliant and capable daughter of Attorney Grant Bishop of Redmond."

Reinhardt nodded. Alexis reached across the desk to shake his hand. Reinhardt stood to reach her.

"John? What are we doing here today?" she asked.

"As I told you, my daughter has got into a spot of difficulty with the law. I need the best defense attorney I can find, and we both know that's you."

"What has Paulette done?"

"Oh, no. Not Paulette. Kerrie. The one you went to school with."

Alexis raised her eyebrows. Kerrie was not one she would expect to be in trouble. A stay-at-home mother of two, she was active in volunteerism and social doings, well educated, quiet, and decorative. Her greatest sin was likely social climbing. She had married a fellow grad, Matt Brandman, who became quite successful in banking, and they lived here in Portland. Alexis had not seen her in several years.

"Why isn't she here?"

"Because she wants her involvement kept secret from her husband."

Alexis gave him a sideways look. "How does she plan to do that? Is she entering a nunnery?" Secrets involving wealthy families and crimes were rarely kept from the public, never mind from those closest to the family.

John laughed. "No nunnery, but a cranky divorce is looking pretty likely. We'll need help with that, too, of course."

John made an attempt to smile. "She's not the one who did the crime. She is the one telling it to the FBI."

"Over the same spot of trouble?" she asked.

John nodded agreement. His mirth disappeared and his face hardened. His eyebrows met in the middle. When he didn't answer, she reminded him.

"Feds?"

"FBI, FDIC, hell, prob'ly even the SEC."

"It has to do with banking, then."

John handed her a thick manila envelope. "This will tell you everything you need to know. I'll have Kerrie at your office in Redmond as soon as you call and tell me when. She has a deposition a week from Monday. I'd appreciate it if you would get back to me as soon as you've checked out those papers."

"I can do that. Bring her next Tuesday afternoon, after two p.m."

John's face relaxed into an immense look of relief. "You'll take it then? Without knowing the details?"

Alexis glanced around the open view offices. "I know enough. Kerrie was my roommate, once, and my friend."

"Trust me. She still is." They both became quiet. Adjusting his tie, Reinhardt looked from one to the other as if watching a tennis game.

"John," Alexis said finally, "Why am I really here?"

"You've always been too clever."

Reinhardt looked expectantly at John Stockman, who took a breath before continuing. "As you know, Alex, I want you to handle my business. I want you to have the last word on everything."

She waited.

"I've talked with Mr. Reinhardt, here, and he's agreed to take my business on my terms. I'll bring everything here if you can be my personal and corporate counsel of record, and all important decisions go through you."

"That's an unheard-of arrangement, John, as I'm sure Mr. Reinhardt told you."

"Oh, yeah. We argued a good little bit until we got together on it. He says an outside lawyer can't be in a supervisory position over his associates or partners."

"Well, then."

"So he's willing to take you on as a partner. We agreed, looking at your education, your record in D. C. and your partnership in your father's firm, you're qualified."

Reinhardt broke in. "In terms of education and work history, you are qualified; Further, we know you can afford the fee. We have reservations . . ."

"He thinks you're too young," John interrupted. "And you haven't got enough experience. You'd be the youngest partner ever to work here. But he says that's not a deal breaker, as long as you will confer with him on the work you do for at least the first year—more if needed."

Alexis smiled. "I haven't been second guessed since law school, John."

"And you won't now. I said confer, not defer."

"And I take it you need a fast decision on this, as well?"

"No. You're like me, Alex. Your family comes first. You have problems. I can afford to hold off awhile. Summers and Beebe have sixty days' notice to get their act together and be ready to transfer my records where I tell them."

Alexis didn't know what to say. She'd expected an approach. She hadn't expected this, and wasn't sure she shouldn't get up and walk out. What must Reinhardt think? Did he assume John was buying a prestigious position for a young mistress? What sort of working environment would this be if she pushed her way in under suspicious circumstances ahead of who-knew-how-many associates slaving their way toward a partnership?

"Mr. Reinhardt, I have not heard from you," she said.

"Ah . . . John and I have reached an agreement, Miss Bishop."

"Well, your gain is clear. John estimates not less than sixty million dollars a year in legal fees. As a partner, I would share equally in the proceeds—and production. Are you clear about what John wants from this agreement, if I accept?"

"Umm. Perhaps that's a question best addressed to John."

"Perhaps. I already know his answer. Do you?"

"I'm not sure I need to know."

"What 'n hell are you getting at, Alex?"

"John, when powerful men clear paths for young women, eyebrows dance. You are not so naïve you don't know that."

"I reckon I am, young lady. I am a married man, faithful to my wife, and if I hear any tongues wagging, I'll put a stop to it on the spot."

"Tongues rarely wag within earshot of the subject."

"Is that true, Will? Is this young lady's reputation going to be smeared by joining your firm?" Will colored faintly.

"Not on my level, it won't. You've made the reasons for your confidence in her clear. I am quite impressed with her record."

"Thank you. Relax, gentlemen. If I cannot handle a little innuendo and rumor, I'll collect knitting needles and live on my trust fund. It won't be the first time, or the last, that I've encountered small minds."

"Perhaps we can help with that," Reinhardt said.

Alexis waited.

"How?" John asked.

Reinhardt directed his response to Alexis. "We could disseminate the information that convinced me. Your impressive history of wins in D. C., your high standing in your graduating class, your defense of John's son in California. You've done well, Miss Bishop, and that's an understatement."

"You gonna put it on the front page of the Oregonian?" John asked.

"That part, you can leave to me. I didn't get my job by looking pretty, either."

"Fair enough," John answered.

"John, as you pointed out," Alexis said, "I need to be at the ranch with my father. Thank you for your time, and I will not unnecessarily delay my answer." Alexis rose, dropping the file in her briefcase, and shook hands with them both. John beamed. Will Reinhardt rubbed a spot behind his ear, his brow furrowed. She left them, finding her own way out. The chill décor of the glass rooms made her shiver. She decided if she acquired an office here, there would be some strategic lighting and furniture placement.

Alexis paused at one of the windows with a view of the city, including Kelly Point Park and the confluence of the Columbia and Willamette Rivers, considered a sacred place by her people. She stepped into the enclosure of the elevator, exiting at street level instead of into the garage. Outside, she crossed the street and gazed up at the edifice into which she had been invited.

At her age the prestige of being the youngest partner in Jackson, Paulson, Reinhardt's office alone would give her chosen career a boost unlikely to be offered again in her lifetime. The money, while nice, hardly mattered. One of the reasons John said he wanted her was because she knew how to invest and increase money. It was nothing she'd ever need worry about, even without her future inheritance. In addition, he had said her sharp eye for detail and her ability to recognize when someone was lying had impressed him. She had saved his son from a trumped up murder charge, saved John a great deal of money and advised ways to make more. She had settled contract disputes, created new business avenues, and sorted tax questions. She would have these lawyers believing in her ability before the current year was out. The thought was tempting. Who doesn't want to rise to the top of her profession?

Alexis found the outside entrance to the garage and her car. Portland traffic had thinned somewhat and she was outside the city proper within minutes. She elected to avoid the mass of freeways and exit through the bedroom city of Gresham, taking secondary roads to the northwest corner of the rez. From there, she drove diagonally across to the gateway near Madras.

Focusing on the road and the rich wilderness of her surroundings, Alexis at last found that she could quiet her mind. She sat back in the seat, breathed deeply, and mentally sought her grandfather.

He was waiting.

Chapter 15: Steps

A silly idea is current that good people
Do not know what temptation means.
This is an obvious lie.
Only those who try to resist
Temptation know how strong it is.
~C.S. Lewis

"If he meant to tempt me, he did it well," Alexis whispered to the East Wind, knowing her words would reach her grandfather's awareness. He had always told her that when she wanted to be heard, she must speak to the Four Winds. This message was for the East Wind, the Wind of new beginnings, of reaffirmation of life, especially after trauma.

She *was* tempted. For a woman to reach the height of her professional aspirations, especially a woman as young as she, was an incomparable inducement. From the offices of Jackson, Paulson, Reinhardt, there was no ceiling, glass or otherwise, for her ambition. It was for this very goal that she had planned, worked and practiced in every arena of her profession where she had found opportunity. It was for this that she had sat, hour after hour, listening to her father speak of the law and how it applied to the people he represented.

"The law," he said, "is not an abstract idea framed by legislators, though some of them act as if it were. It is a living, breathing, changing system of protection for all those who live within its parameters. It is the fence around the playground, protecting children. It is the framework of families, the strength of a nation, and the guide toward peace. The law is not an enemy. Those who misinterpret, flout, and disobey, see it as an unattainable ideal, and are in fact, the enemy."

Grant Bishop was an orator, and his words had stayed with her. He was the sort of lawyer she wanted to be. Only now was she seeing that she wanted to do it at his side. Which was stronger, her ambition to reach the zenith of her profession, or her desire to be her father's daughter? Worse yet, where did these awesome ambitions fit with her desire for the sacred spiritual depth and fulfillment of the life her grandfather represented?

Many women think they can "have it all." How many of them faced the "all" that she wanted, needed, yearned to have?

Patience, Granddaughter. Spirit works in Spirit time. When you are ready, the Grandfathers will have work for your hands. You are always where you belong.

"Then what am I doing here, while my father lies sick in his bed, perhaps dying?"

The golden eagle will carry our prayers to the Four Winds at the crest of the second bluff from the south on Trout Creek tomorrow before the sun begins its journey of the day.

"Trout Creek is closed to climbers until September."

Indian Creek is despoiled by evil doers this day. Trout Creek and Indian Creek were two names for the same canyon. She knew her grandfather considered the part that extended onto reservation land to be Indian Creek, the chasm's original name, and the rest, to him, was Trout Creek. To many, all of Indian Creek had been renamed Trout Creek, for what reason, she did not know.

"Granddad!" He was gone. She could do nothing but trust him—and be there.

She was home, and eager to see her father. Someone had thoroughly cleaned the den, leaving a scent of lemon on all the shining surfaces. Glass sparkled. The hospital bed sported fresh linens and neat tucks. Her father woke soon after she entered.

"I didn't mean to disturb you," she said.

"You didn't. I like the scent of your perfume."

"That's nice, except I don't wear any. You must smell my shampoo."

"It reminds me of your mother."

"It should. She taught me how to make it."

The scent of lunch wafted through the house, so Alexis poured fresh water and added three drops from the vial in her pocket, glad Melanie was not here to make an issue of the medicine. He drank it. She poured a glass of clear water and he drank that, too. All of it.

He fell asleep before he finished lunch, mouth open, snoring softly. He had eaten next to nothing. At least there would be little for him to regurgitate. She held the vial to the light. One more day, maybe two, and the vial would be as empty as her father's stomach. Alexis adjusted his bedding, kissed his forehead, took the dishes to the kitchen, and started upstairs. She thought better of it and returned to the kitchen to wash their dishes. It was late. She set up the coffeepot for morning and went upstairs.

From her laptop, she responded to e-mail, typed instructions for Bonnie, and sent a message thanking her. She was busy, at Alexis' request, screening candidates for the positions of paralegal and associate attorney. Alexis would interview those who passed muster with Bonnie. Alexis accessed the Bishop Law office's secure website, scanned a log of the day's events, and added notes about her meeting in Portland. She turned her attention to the envelope containing a file folder full of information about Kerrie. Alexis was not long in discovering the core of the problem Kerrie faced. This was worse than divorce, worse than drunk driving, either of which Alexis might have expected. Kerrie was in an extremely serious position. These crimes could result in lengthy prison sentences for both Kerrie and her husband.

From their actions, she saw that the FBI had gathered information about virtually every deposit and withdrawal from the bank for which Kerrie's husband was responsible.

The FBI was looking for money laundering. The federal audit Alexis read gave every indication that husband and wife were both guilty. Worse, Kerrie had worked there with him off and on, and had signed suspect papers. It would be difficult to prove she had been in the dark about their purpose. Alexis did not question that she was innocent. The Kerrie she knew was a brilliant organizer, a talented decorator, an excellent host for whatever—she would have made a great party planner. She had always expressed little or no interest in business matters, as long as the money was there to provide for her needs and desires. When it wasn't, she paid a visit to her father, who, to Alexis' knowledge, had never hesitated to open his wallet for her. She had no need to earn money illegally.

Concerned, she called John's cell and left him a voice mail accepting the case. How soon she would work on it was anybody's guess. She called it a day—or night—and slept three hours.

Her grandfather's subtle voice in her head nudged her awake. With coffee and yogurt to wake her and provide energy, Alexis was on her way with the light of a full moon as a guide. Sinking behind the mountains and red bluffs, the moon would hide its face soon.

Granddad awaited her at the trailhead, having tied Jack on a long line to a gnarled elm. Granddad carried a pack strapped to his back.

"Let me carry that," she said.

"I am not ready to hand off my duties to you, yet. Let us waste no more time. He adjusted the folded pack and set off at a mile-eating stride up the slope that led to the bluff above. No vehicles occupied the campground this morning. Alexis was better prepared this time. Her moccasins were sturdy, and she strapped a light to her forehead. The telescope bumped her knee as she hiked, so she moved it to a hip pocket. She had found her old climbers' gloves, as well, and tied a rope to her belt, just in case. She stopped, faced south, opened her arms, and prayed for faith and the ability to focus on the task ahead, not her grandfather's possible illness. He had taught her that to focus upon an illness empowers and increases the ailment, even in another. She allowed herself gratitude for the success of their mission and all the solutions she sought.

With an effort, she caught up with him, and the two nearly matched strides to the foot of the vertical red rocks that topped the mountain. Crickets sang and night hunting creatures scuttled out of their path. The air felt cool and crisp. Soon the sun would burden them. Perhaps by then, they would be seated at the top, recovering from their exertions, feeling the blessings of the Four Winds.

Few people she had ever known could climb the sheer face of a vertical rock as fast or as surely as Granddad, even in the pale light of breaking dawn. She had learned from the best, and he reminded her of that now while he scuttled up the wall as if related to a spider. She stopped trying to keep up with him and settled for doing as well, and not as fast. His gnarled fingers found tiny shelves and cracks she would have missed, except for watching him. They reached the top before the sun, and he helped her crawl over the edge.

He took her hand and led her to a place on the far edge of the peak. Stepping back from the edge one step, he spread his arms and waited for Alexis to do the same. She recognized the light of Venus, hanging low in the sky.

Chases Bear chanted a Cherokee phrase that sounded like: "oolee haley ess dee." He repeated the phrase again and again, standing very still. After a few repetitions, she joined him. They continued this until Venus faded, no longer brighter than sunlight, and tears flowed from her eyes. Turning, she saw that Granddad's eyes were as wet as hers. In contrast, joy flooded her being, a surge of delight like none she had ever felt. She wanted to ask about the experience, to discuss it with him, to thank him for it, but she could form no words.

Her grandfather turned from the rising sun and untied his pack. From it he took a prayer rug of exquisite beauty and a pipe decorated with feathers and paint. He sank down on one end of the rug, facing east, and crossed his ankles. With measured movements, he filled the pipe, lit it, drew air through it, handed it to Alexis, and placed his hands together. He repeated the chant with which they had started. Having never smoked anything, Alexis prayed she would not choke.

When she didn't, finding the herb surprisingly smooth, she handed the long-stemmed ceremonial instrument back with the same care as that with which she had received it. Granddad took the pipe, twisted his body to face north, drew in and released the smoke, and returned the pipe to Alexis. They continued the ceremony, facing all four winds, chanting the Cherokee words each time, then repeated the motions twice more. At last, they paused. Silence filled the space between them until the sun rose and the day's heat warmed them.

Without knowing why or stopping to question, Alexis rose from the prayer rug to stand facing the West wind, looking down on Trout Creek. She spread her arms wide, taking in the Breath of Spirit. As before, a great nest perched solidly on a high stone shelf, its materials—sticks, grass, and mud—poking out in odd directions, its bottom side stretching beyond the shelf it occupied. She had only a moment to ponder the significance of the nest's presence there before the wind blew in her face, fluttered her feathers, and lifted her from below. Looking east, she saw her grandfather far below, watching from his rug. To the west lay a rocky wilderness beneath a clear, blue sky. She

168

soared, higher and higher on the West Wind, until she felt at peace, a peace so deep, she could have dived into it. As never before in her life, she focused on this now moment, knowing no past, no future, no sense of time passing, only the great, incredible *now*. The warm sky and the clouds enveloped her in an overwhelming, breathtaking feeling of limitless, unconditional love. Higher and higher she soared, until the length of Trout Creek lay beneath her, seen clearly through the sharp eyes of the eagle. As quickly as she had taken flight, she landed on her feet, in the same position, arms spread, taking in the blessings of the West Wind.

There was not now, nor would there ever be, a reason for fear. As with all beings of the Earth, she was spirit, and spirit cannot be harmed. She had heard the words at her grandfather's feet, but had never understood them until this now moment. She had prayed for focus on the moment and it had been granted her in a way she could not have imagined. She faced her grandfather, unable again, to find words.

"And you would doubt your ability, daughter of my daughter," he whispered with a smile. Again, there were unshed tears in his eyes. "I believe our prayer has been taken on the wings of an eagle. She flies closer to the Creator than any other creature."

"My father will live," she said.

"It is likely he will," Chases Bear answered, "but he will get worse before he gets better. You and I must listen to the wind." For the first time in her life, she understood what he meant by "listen to the wind."

Chapter 16: Artifacts

**"*. . . you are only growing and evolving*
in your life with your tough decisions."**
~*Rachana Shakyawar*

Having seen Granddad safely home, Alexis spent early
afternoon exploring Kerrie's predicament. The FBI had served
proper warrants on the bank, following a random FDIC audit that
Alexis suspected had been anything but random. The pattern she
had expected seemed to be there: transfers out of the country in
amounts low enough to evade detection; electronic deposits back
to the states from the same offshore locations, though not always
into the same banks. From there, the banks made loans to local
executives, charging exorbitant interest rates. A little research
into the companies in question left her with no doubt that their
businesses either did not exist at all, or were so deeply buried in
multiple corporate levels it would take a bloodhound to sniff
them out. Finally, deposits from these companies made their way
back to the bank of origin—the bank managed by Kerrie's
husband. By then, they appeared to be legally acquired funds,
and withdrawn by account holders.

Alexis wondered what—or who—had tipped Federal
Deposit Insurance Corporation and the FBI to go fishing in the
books. She had to hand it to John. She could not guess how, but
he had provided her with every scrap of information she might
have asked for. Now she had to fit it together and find a way out

of the mess for John's daughter. Alexis could point to Kerrie's husband as the sole perpetrator and file appropriate paperwork with the IRS claiming wronged spouse status, but she didn't know if Kerrie was ready to take such a drastic step. How did she feel about her husband? Did she want to see him in prison? That would come out in their interview later.

The day had been long and demanding of her time—"the tail wagging the dog," her father would have said. She decided to sleep on the mass of information she had read. After she spent some time ruminating over the remarkable events of the morning.

"Don't overthink daylight visions any more than dreams," Granddad had warned. "Our messages are lost in overthinking."

How did she avoid thinking of taking flight from a high bluff and soaring through the heavens as one with the eagle? "That isn't the only way we lose our messages," she had answered. He smiled.

"No. Many, we do not hear in the first place."

Alexis had agreed. "I don't know how to recognize a message unless it hits me over the head. It appears that the Grandfathers have decided to get my attention."

"They always do, eventually. Sometimes, we don't like the way Spirit lets us know we have taken a wrong path."

Her bedroom window, the one over the den, faced the West Wind. No wonder she loved to sit there and let still-warm desert air dry her hair. Had the house designers understood the relevance of the Four Winds? It was hard to see how they could have made a better plan. The front door faced east, the way of new beginnings, of inspiration and new life. The kitchen opened to the South, the way of life, the way of the heart and innocence. There, wisely, Mary had planted the kitchen garden, in the full, strong, life-giving light. Beneath sheltering evergreen trees to the north lay the Bishop family cemetery, to celebrate the power of wisdom, of looking back on life and what one has learned from the North Wind.

Alexis had remembered the meaning of the Four Winds when she planted her rooftop garden and used the private, soothing space for prayer. She had faced what seemed the appropriate direction at the time she prayed, depending upon circumstances. Considering that, she understood now why, having lived with him for nearly two years, she had never invited Terry to her garden, nor even told him about it. He knew nothing of her heritage and did not value the earth and nature as she did. If she went to a stable to ride a horse, he never joined her. Instead, he would be more likely to climb aboard his motorcycle and race over paved roads. He had hated her cat and chuckled when it disappeared. She could think of no instance when Terry had demonstrated an interest in nature or in being away from the city. He was not drawn to the sea, the woods, or the mountains. His idea of a vacation was a weekend at gambling tables in Atlantic City. He liked to dine and dance and see a movie, but would not take a walk in the park or go to the zoo. A self-proclaimed atheist, he scoffed at religion and those who believed in "superstitious myths." What they shared was a passion for the practice of law, and little more. It seemed far from enough, now. Alexis faced the West Wind at her window and breathed deeply of it for several minutes.

Feeling refreshed, she went downstairs for dinner at her father's bedside. Mary brought them soup made from cauliflower and thick, rich cream, both produced here on the ranch, together with crusty, fresh rolls spread with real butter. Having grown up on such fare, Alexis wondered how the family escaped the obesity that seemed to have the country in an epidemic grip. A question to ask Granddad, as lean as any man half his age.

Dad fell asleep before he finished the soup, mouth open, snoring softly. Alexis roused him for his last dose of medicine of the day. He groused, but drank it. She adjusted his bedding, kissed his forehead, took their dishes to the kitchen, and went upstairs for a long, thoughtful soak.

Her bathwater cooled. She donned pajamas and returned to the bedroom window. The high plains night would be chilly, but cold was preferable to stuffy.

The moon sprayed pale, silvery light over low rises west of the house. On one of these, in sharp silhouette, stood a horse, head high, mane flying. A wild Mustang. His herd would be grazing in the valley over the crest.

Alexis slept fitfully, listening for sounds of Dad's stirring that did not come. Once, she slipped downstairs to look in on him. Moonlight penetrated the tall windows and seeped into every corner of the room. By his preference, no drapes covered them. She moved a rice paper screen to soften the light, fearing it was bright enough to wake him. Then she felt the even throb of his pulse and touched his forehead. He felt warm and damp to the touch. Nothing to worry about, she told herself. He was sleeping, breathing evenly. Nothing to worry about. She returned to bed and finally, slept.

A pale hint of light shining into her room teased her awake. With the window open, the room felt chilly, tempting her to stay in bed. Then she remembered the graceful Mustang of the evening before. He would be gone now, but the memory of his majesty drew her. In jeans and a sweater, she went down to find her father sleeping, and still too warm. She turned back his comforter, leaving only the sheet, and watched him in silence, striving to sense messages from Spirit. None came. When he seemed to have cooled to normal temperature, she covered him.

Melanie tapped, entered, and laid a hand lightly on Grant's forehead. She smiled at Alexis and pressed her fingers against her patient's wrist. Alexis slipped away.

She ran to the barn. Saddling Cisco, she mounted, sensing his eagerness to run in the cool, pre-dawn breeze. Cell phone on her belt in case they needed her, she trotted Cisco toward the hill where she had seen the Mustang. He was gone, of course. By now, he and his mares were drinking from the stream on the other side of the knoll, hidden in the trees.

The morning smelled fresh, like after a rain. The earth held yesterday's warmth, and a clear sky sprinkled with fading starlight promised another sizzling summer day. A shadow soaring overhead drew her attention: a hawk, perhaps, or an eagle. The sky was too dark for her to discern anything except that it was a large bird. *Ask the eagle.* Granddad had said. *Ask him what?* She stilled and waited, with the breeze whispering over her cheeks, but no message came.

Dismounting, she turned Cisco loose to graze, and sat facing the valley. Shadowed mounds of sagebrush waving in the wind filled the valley, leaving precious little space for grass. Alexis made a mental note to have the pasture in this valley cleared and replanted. She couldn't guess when it had last been done. The sun's rays slid over the hill and Cisco stood out starkly against crimson color. A movement on the road below startled her. She lay flat and focused to see. A car without lights came from her left toward the highway. Who was leaving the ranch before dawn? The now-familiar sense of something evil surrounded her, close, robbing her of breath. Who would drive through their land without lights, and why? Straining to hear, she picked up faint engine sounds, not surprising from so far away. The sun edged over the horizon, throwing pale shadows and silhouetting gray shapes of stones and sagebrush.

As the vehicle drew even with her position, she saw that it was a topless CJ-5 Jeep like the one she'd seen at the old schoolhouse when someone had shot at her and Pat. A chill skittered up her back. What was he doing on the ranch? Was it Braithwaite? She thought not. Though it was hard to tell while he was seated, this person seemed to be taller, thinner than the squat, muscular Braithwaite. Alexis thought she had never seen this man. She was sure of it when he passed her position and she noticed long, straight, black hair flowing down his back, lifted by the wind. He was naked to the waist.

When the Jeep had gone out of sight, Alexis mounted Cisco and rode diagonally downhill toward the road in the opposite direction from where the Jeep had disappeared. Keeping her horse to a slow walk, she followed the road back to where she had first seen the Jeep and beyond, around the hill, until she saw a set of tracks on the dusty road shoulder. Footprints marked the dust and appeared to climb the slope. She shivered, though the temperature was comfortable. She followed, getting down a couple of times to relocate the trail, which ended in a dusty, scuffed area at the top of the hill. She knelt to get a good idea of what the intruder had seen and looked directly into her own room. Her father's window was screened as she had left it, but before it was, the man could have seen almost everything in both rooms. *Why?* She remounted and hurried home, eager to shed the grave sense that clung to her.

Changing in newly draped privacy, Alexis pondered what the spy could see from his perch that had driven him to enter their property and conceal both his arrival and his departure under cover of darkness. Nothing in her room could possibly interest a peeper except herself, if sexual perversity was his motive. That notion appeared farfetched at best, since she had seen the man nowhere else that she recalled. Her room harbored the usual furnishings: a bed, a desk and chair, lamps, a recliner for reading, a closet full of clothes, and two dressers. On her walls were a pair of hand-made native rugs, a photograph of her parents, a landscape, and a dream catcher. Nothing of value, nothing of note. She spent little time here. What she did was spent working or sleeping, occasionally praying. At least here, the sense of evil loosed its hold on her. Perhaps because the intruder was gone. Tomorrow, after her date with Granddad, she would have a chat with Pat. He was interested in these people with the battered Jeep. He had mentioned . . . forged artifacts. Like the ones that shared space with real antiquities on a shelf in her father's den? Like the forged items she had received and long since forgotten in the office? Brushing her hair, she paused and considered that thought. The shelf in question, near another window, was in full view from the hill, until she had screened it. Could the man tell from there what he was seeing? A glance at the small telescope she had bought for climbing trips answered: of course, he could. He could peruse the bookshelves and read the titles of books on their spines.

Tomorrow, she would find Pat and ask him why he was seeking this group and what they had to do with forged Native American artifacts. After she climbed a bluff at Trout Creek with Granddad.

First, she opened her laptop to her favorite search engine and typed in "artifacts of the Wasco, Paiute, Walla Walla," all three Nations of the Warm Springs Confederated Tribes. She found examples of beaded jewelry, basketry, moccasins and clothing, arrowheads, and rudimentary tools dating to the late 1800s, when whites began settling Indians on the reservation. She was unable to find a single example of pottery from the three tribes. She made a mental note to visit the Warm Springs Museum and Cultural Center.

One more task added to her growing list.

Chapter 17: Healing Prayers

. . . if you truly join your heart and mind
as One - whatever you ask for,
that's the Way It's Going To Be.
~passed down from White Buffalo Calf Woman

The distant sound of a coyote's howl teased Alexis awake the next morning. With the window covered but open, the cold room tempted her to cuddle up and stay in her comfortable bed. She couldn't; there was much to do. Once dressed, she went downstairs to find her father sleeping, and far too warm. She repeated the previous day's process of removing covers to cool him, and waited. The continuing fevers worried her. Worse, her cooling efforts failed, and his fever seemed only to rise. She went to the door and called Melanie.

The nurse arrived in a bathrobe with a towel wrapped around her head. She scurried into the den to Grant. She laid a thermometer strip across his forehead. With compressed lips and sympathetic eyes, she turned to Alexis, shaking her head.

"There may be nothing we can do," she said. "This may be the moment we've all been waiting for."

"What moment?" Alexis realized that Melanie meant the moment of Dad's death. "No! I will not give up!"

"I doubt it's really up to you, Alexis."

"Get out! Get—no, get wet cloths on his face and upper body." *Ouch. She owed Melanie an apology.*

Dad was running a high fever, for the third time since his return home. Chases Bear, she was sure, had expected this. He had prepared her to join in a healing ceremony he had thought would not be sufficient if he had performed it alone—or perhaps feared he could not finish when seizures threatened to occur without warning. His words had been both reassurance and warning. *Sometimes death is the healing we pray for.*

Alexis was not entirely sure she understood that. Did he mean that sometimes, death is the only way for people to find respite from pain? Did he mean that when we have passed through the gates of the afterworld, we are whole and well? Or did he mean death is the peace we seek?

Regardless, death was certainly not the result she sought for her fifty-eight year old father. She wanted him alive and well and part of her life for many years yet. That he would precede her in death was likely. But not yet. Not yet. She was uncomfortable with the amount of time spent away from him after Granddad's words. Yet, there had been few choices. Spirit must know the strength of her faith in prayers and her acceptance of whatever came. She ignored a niggling awareness that Spirit knew every snippet of thought that passed through her head, no matter what she did. Spirit knew there was no acceptance. There was only faith and hope, and both fragile.

We must hurry, Granddaughter. The words reverberated in Alexis' head and she knew her grandfather was coming.

"Do what I said! Put cold cloths on his head," she ordered and ran out of the room. She opened the front door to find her grandfather standing there waiting. Chases Bear brushed past her and hurried to the den.

Calmly, without speaking, he removed the wet cloths Melanie had placed on Grant's face and body. He folded them neatly and laid them beside the bowl of cool water. He drew Grant's covers up to his neck and tucked them close around him. Alexis watched, heart pounding, puzzled. Chases Bear opened his pack, removing a half-dozen prepared smudge bundles of sage and sweet grass. He lit them, one at a time, passing her two of them. Alexis' fear eased as she watched her grandfather's demeanor.

Mary came from the kitchen. He gave her two sticks as well.

"His fever spiked early," Mary said. "I called for Chases Bear, but he was already on his way."

Alexis nodded. Granddad knew when he was needed. The three of them waved the smoking sage bundles throughout the room to cleanse every corner.

"Thank you, Mary. Please go and prepare food while you pray to the Grandfathers. Food will be needed for my grandfather, late. Be near, in case we need you."

"Where else am I going?"

Alexis kissed Mary's cheek. Melanie slipped away, not bothering to express more feelings about the smudging. The scent of smoldering sage and sweet grass lay thick in the air. Alexis was surprised that it did not interfere with her own breathing. It seemed as smooth and mellow as the pipe tobacco they had shared on the flat mesa over Trout Creek.

She said nothing as Granddad lit more bundles of sage and sweetgrass and waved them around the room, spreading smoke.

"What a thing to do to a man dying of lung cancer," Melanie muttered. She emitted a noisy snort and stalked out, only to return a few moments later. No one acknowledged her.

Mary stood, arms crossed, a small smile on her face. She nodded at Chases Bear. Granddad laid the last sage bundle with others on a nearby tray. Sage and vanilla scented smoke still wafted from them. He opened his pack and spread on the floor the beautiful rug he had used atop the mountain. For the first time, Alexis noted that woven into it were a rising sun, a snow-capped image of Broken Top Mountain, and an eagle. Hand woven along its edges were several eagle feathers, illegal to possess unless as an inherited artifact. The medicine man sat cross-legged on one end of the rug and folded his hands. Alexis took the other end and followed his example. When he closed his eyes and chanted softly, she joined him. They sang together for several minutes. She had learned the few simple Lakota words when he stopped chanting and accompanied her with an Indian flute. The sound filled her and expanded her senses. Her body vibrated with it, as it had always done when tribal members sang or played. She imagined herself transported to another place, another time, in the far distant past. She remembered that the song was the more powerful when performed seated or standing on the earth, in contact with the life force of the earth. Still, the healing strength could not be denied. She lifted her voice toward the sky, which, though not visible, knew her prayer and carried it to the Creator. She felt her heart fill with the power of the prayer and the power of love, as taught by her mother and her grandfather and the tribes. If anything could generate healing, then surely it was this.

Chapter 18: Healing Ceremony

"Prayer is the divine key that unlocks
God's pathway to healing in both natural
And supernatural realms of life."
~Reginald Cherry

Alexis' fear faded. *Sometimes death is the healing we pray for*. Perhaps—for someone whose life was complete, someone who had done all that he needed to do. Someone no longer needed. That did not apply to Grant Bishop.

Her Grandfather caught her eye and nodded toward the cabinet near the door that held Grant's medical chart.

Folded there was a white garment embroidered with beads. Chases Bear's ceremonial medicine pipe lay on an open leather wrap. She felt blood rush from her head and bent to keep from fainting at sight of the dress. Granddad's strength supported her, though he had not moved. When she revived, she stroked the garment, removed her shirt, and donned the soft, pure white deerskin dress that had belonged to her mother and which Alexis had not seen since her mother's death. Adoni had married in it, and had worn it on the day she left Alexis at the ranch to live with her father. The day she walked away to die.

Alexis tied the dress at her waist and slipped out of her jeans and shoes. The closer to earth she was as she performed a Ghost Dance, the more likely Mother Earth would know her desires. It would be better to perform the ceremony outside, but Dad looked in no condition for a trek outside. She approached

185

his bed and passed her hands through the smoke Chases Bear blew across her dad's body, holding them there for several seconds. Chases Bear nodded approvingly.

Dad's face burned, so red she feared a heat stroke might give them their result. She touched his cheek and did not need the thermometer to tell her his fever ran dangerously high. Chases Bear nodded assurance: this was as it should be.

"The fever will burn the illness out of his body, if he survives."

"If he . . .! Granddad!"

"Have no fear. He is in the hands of the Grandfathers."

Chases Bear turned from the bed. He handed a smudge stick and the feather fan to Alexis. She poked her thumb through a hole in the center of it and fanned sage and sweetgrass smoke over her father. Chases Bear opened a wooden box and removed a small brazier, which he set on the floor. He blew gently on it until tiny flames leaped from the coals. Then he unrolled a pallet and placed it on the floor beside the brazier, extending the rug's length. He placed the woven rug across the pallet.

Chases Bear stood, braced his legs, and lifted Grant, blankets and all, from the bed and knelt to place his emaciated form on the pad. With a glance at Alexis, her grandfather took his pipe and sat, ankles crossed, on one end of the rug. Alexis sat in the same fashion, facing him. Chases Bear gave her a cluster of long sage stems tied together with a thong at one end, which she held to the brazier flame until it lit. He tamped brown leaves into the pipe. The pipe held deep symbolic and religious significance and was treasured by the People. She knew they must handle it with honor and care. Decorated with paint and feathers, carved of a single piece of wood, its stem was long and narrow, hollow all the way through. A small bowl perched an inch or so from the end. Air could be drawn into the pipe either from the stem or from the bowl. After Chases Bear filled it, he held a finger over the hole at the bowl end and sucked air through the tobacco. She held burning sage to the bowl until he raised a finger to indicate it was enough. Then he drew deeply of the resulting smoke and turned the pipe sideways, offering it to her with both hands. She took it the same way and drew smoke into her lungs, again half expecting to choke on it. Instead, the smoke soothed and coated her lungs and she knew he had filled the pipe with more than tobacco. Her head swam as she gave it back with the same ritual care as he had given it to her. He turned to his left to face west, drew smoke, blew it out slowly, and returned it to her. She turned west, smoked, and passed him the pipe. There was a flavor she did not recognize in the smoke. They repeated the ritual until they had faced all four sacred winds, and then he placed the pipe across the pallet at Grant's feet. The brazier's flames had died to glowing embers. Chases Bear laid his fingers on Grant's forehead and his eyebrows met in a concerned frown. He threw the covers off, leaving Grant nude to the waist.

Mary must have been watching. She entered the room with a bowlful of water and crushed ice. Alexis watched while Mary knelt and sprinkled small amounts of ice water from her fingers onto Dad's chest. She left the room as silently as she had entered, leaving a cool, wet square of leather behind. The old man laid it across Grant's forehead and checked his skin temperature frequently with his fingers for several minutes. When he seemed to think Dad had cooled enough, he covered his patient, crossed his arms, and chanted. To Alexis, her father still seemed too hot. She joined the chant, but after a few moments, her voice faded, as did the room before her, and she was drawn to look up toward the scream of an eagle calling overhead. Where there had been a white ceiling, blue sky shimmered, appearing to ripple as if powered by the rising heat from Dad's body. The eagle soared, flying a choreographed dance in wide circles. It began to soar lower and lower, until finally the bird landed on the back of a white buffalo calf Alexis had not seen before that moment. The eagle stared at her expectantly, his eyes sharp and piercing. He seemed to be asking if she had found her faith, and she searched within to find the answer. The eagle and the sky disappeared. She felt a loss when it went and wanted to call it back. The buffalo calf stood in the den, chewing stolidly, looking at home among shelves of books, overstuffed furniture, tables and a white hospital bed.

Alexis rose, rolled the bed away to clear a path around her father and danced the gentle, foot-stomping, torso-rocking ghost dance around his pallet. Chases Bear followed her example. The calf lifted first one front hoof and then the other, still chewing, watching. The dance continued for seconds, minutes, or hours. She never knew which, nor did she feel tired. All the while, a distant thrum vibrated in her senses. The calf watched, occasionally snorting to show it was alive, and chewed. She could feel that it lent the dance medicinal power. Grandfather's chant rose and fell, rich and strong, but at last, she found little air in her lungs for singing. She felt crowded by the fear that lived and stirred deep inside her, fear that the heat in her father's body was more than his weakened frame could bear, fear that wearing her mother's ceremonial dress would call her ghost to take him home with her. She wondered whose death shirt Granddad wore.

As Alexis danced past the foot of the pallet, the calf assumed a translucent quality. She could have read the titles of books through its body. As soon as the animal disappeared, the medicine man gathered his supplies and carried them toward the porch. Before his last trip, he lifted Grant's shoulders, struggling this time. Alexis lifted his feet and they put him to bed. Tenderly, Alexis covered him. His skin felt normal to her touch. The fever had burned itself out. As he left, Alexis kissed her grandfather's cheek, whispered a simple, "Thank you," before sitting on the bed with her father's head in her lap. Shortly, she heard the hum of the Cadillac in front of the house and knew Harm was driving Granddad home.

She sat that way a long time, long past the time her back began to ache and her head throbbed, perhaps from whatever substances her grandfather had added to the tobacco. She sat stroking his forehead with cool fingers, until he began to sweat and then she laid him gently down and went for a washcloth for him and food for herself.

Mary waited in the kitchen with a salad, a cheese omelet and toast for the tastiest meal Alexis could remember for a long time. Simple, and perfect, as always. Alexis was ravenous.

"Did you send food with Granddad?"

"Need you ask?"

"Of course not. How silly of me. Have a good night, Mary. Thank you for being here."

"Where else would I be?" She embraced Alexis and left, looking as exhausted as Alexis felt.

Her father moaned in his sleep as she sat beside him and washed his face, neck and hands with the cool cloth. His fever spiked and went. Relief filled her. His breath came without effort, without pain.

She sat back in the chair and closed her eyes, exhausted. There was barely time to reflect that she was grateful for the previous morning's energy ceremony with Granddad before she was asleep.

Hours later, the chill of the room woke her. She removed Adoni's dress, put on her jeans and shoes and found a blanket. She was still awake when Dad stirred and murmured, "Alexis?"

She jumped up and hurried to his side, aching with weariness.

"I'm here, Dad."

"Hot in here. I'm sweating."

"Yes. It's better now. Your fever broke."

"I had a fever?"

"Yes. For a long time."

He was silent for a long moment, then, "I dreamed Adoni was here, dressed in white."

Alexis pictured the white buffalo calf. "I think she was, Dad."

He took her hand in both of his. She had to lean down to hear him.

"I was wrong. I married an Indian woman and tried to make a white woman of her. So she left me. I will not do that again. Be who you are, Alexis, no matter who that is."

"Thank you, Dad. I will."

"You would, no matter what I said."

"What? Make my own choices? Yes. But it's nice to have your blessing. Dad, the truth is I do not yet know precisely who I am or who I want to be. All I know right now is that if I don't sleep, I'll be the first to meet my mother again. You're okay, for now, and I'm going to bed."

"Was he here, too?" His voice sounded stronger, but still tired.

"Yes."

"I don't believe I've ever seen you exhausted before. You go mountain climbing today?"

"Something like that."

"Good night."

From her bedroom window, Alexis looked out at the dawning day, wondering if she was again being watched, if their ceremony had been observed by the evil that haunted her life lately. She felt no sense of it, and thought perhaps that her senses were as exhausted as she was. It hardly mattered. Evil had only watched, so far.

Alexis went to bed and dreamed of living in a world with white buffalo calves, green grass, and serene mountains populated by Indians, bison, elk and deer; rivers full of fish, pure, clean air, and eagles soaring high in the sky. Feeling at home there, she ate from a bowl carved of strong Myrtle wood, drank from the horn of an elk, and gave thanks to the animals for their meat and bone and skins. She used a stone knife to cut herbs and berries and to dig wild roots, and she fell in love with a handsome young man who bore a striking resemblance to Patrick Collins.

Chapter 19: Newcomers

***Discovery consists in seeing what everyone else has seen
and thinking what no one else has thought.***
~Albert Szent-Gyorgyi

Morning came late for Alexis. She stretched luxuriously and remembered, with delight, the dreams that had accompanied her sleep. Scenes from them were as clear in her mind as if she had lived the life she had dreamed. In her weariness, she had forgotten to cover her window, and wondered if their voyeur had watched her sleep. How much could he see in the dark? She had fallen on the bed fully dressed, peeling off her clothes only later. The hell with the voyeur. She would think about him later, after coffee with Dad, after breakfast, after feeding Cisco. She felt no weighted sense of evil this morning, and her dreams had left her feeling immune to evil.

There would be no coffee with her father after all, not yet. On sock feet, to avoid disturbing him if he was not awake, she had poured two cups, carried them with her, and found him sleeping. His breath came easily and quietly, his face calm. Setting one cup down, she left as quietly as she had arrived.

Breakfast awaited her in the kitchen with Mary, who looked as rested as Alexis felt, sitting in the sun from a window, looking out on her kitchen garden. Scrambled eggs, potatoes, and sausage pieces, with gravy topping it all. Alexis slid into a chair opposite Mary and smiled.

"You look rested," Alexis said.

"They tell me the best sleep is dream sleep, and mine was full of them last night."

Alexis laughed. "Mine, too, about life before the Reservation, about wide, open spaces full of animals and tepees along the river. Horses, and kids playing, and a happy Mother Earth."

"Birds in the sky and plenty of food and laughter in the villages," Mary said.

"Amazing. Were you in my dream, or I in yours?"

They laughed, but Alexis felt an odd excitement, as if they had, in fact, shared not only the dream, but a knowledge of some early time when the world was a different place.

"He's resting," Alexis said, turning her attention back to her father.

"Yes. I expect he will for a while. His body has suffered a battle."

Mary had seen and taken part in more of Granddad's healing practices than had Alexis. "How long is a while?"

Mary shrugged. "Live your life, Alexis. It may be hours, days, or weeks, before he stops sleeping away most of his days. Melanie and I will be here and keep you aware."

"What would we ever do without you, Mary? You have been my safety net as long as I can remember."

"Not that it ever kept you from climbing mountains anyway. I have never known a girl so determined to get herself into trouble, you and that Chili Wenway and Patrick Collins. You were the wildest teenagers on the rez, and *you* didn't even live there."

Alexis laughed again. She felt full of hope, almost elated. "We survived, but I'll grant you that there were slim margins. I think we are talking about different kinds of safety nets. You did not keep me from riding wild horses and swimming fast rivers and exploring dark caves. You kept me from losing my way. You still do."

"Then why have you lived in faraway places for so many years?"

"You're right. It will not happen again. I have been wondering what I have seen in that life, and the man there."

Mary lifted one eyebrow. Alexis ignored the unspoken question and rose to carry her dishes to the sink.

"Your father will be pleased if you choose to stay home."

"Maybe. I think that depends on what I do while I'm here, don't you?"

"You will do what you are called to do. Your father will make peace with your choices. Now go, and let me get my work done. We have frittered away half the morning."

"So we have. And I have much to do, too."

Where to start? With John's daughter and her husband's bank? With Casey Johnson and the bad company he kept? With a man driving a vehicle through the ranch without lights? A vehicle she knew had been involved in her grandfather's assault.

In the end, she decided to let mysteries simmer for a few hours and go to her father's business office in Redmond to give Wade Corey a long overdue day off. She could catch up with some of the work that must be falling behind. First, however, she ran to the calving barn to check on the newborn and his mother. Casey was forking dirty bedding out of the calving stall. A pile of fresh 'fines,' small wood chips from a nearby mill, lay ready in the aisle. He had turned mother and baby into the next box while he cleaned the birthing pen. Alexis leaned over the rail to watch the little calf nurse. He was clean and fresh, his red hair set in dry whorls where his mother had licked him clean. Huge, fringed, brown eyes stood out in his stark, white face. His baby fur shone in dappled sunlight.

"Beautiful, isn't he?" she said to Casey.

"Yeah. They are. I try not to get attached."

"I just try not to think of them as future steaks. How many breeding cows do we have now?"

"Enough, I think."

She shook her head. "We don't need more right now." The calf would, indeed, be steak one day. She hoped that would occur in some faraway kitchen—not theirs.

In her office clothes, Alexis chose not to assist Casey. Instead, she took advantage of the moment of privacy. "You know who attacked you, don't you, Casey?" Deliberately, she softened her tone.

He gave her a quick, sidelong glance and reddened more than his exertion warranted. He stood straight and faced her.

"It won't happen again, Miss Bishop. I thank you for taking care of me."

"I'm not chastising you, Casey. I'm concerned about you."

"No need. I'm all right."

"You are more than all right in my book, and I want to know why someone would want to assault you. Is it your friends? The ones in the canyon?"

Casey's jaw dropped. He gave a furtive look over his shoulder. "How do you know about that place?"

"There is little my grandfather doesn't know. I was on the bluff with him. You and Harley Braithwaite, and Lila, and someone else. There is a kiln there, and it has been there a long while. Who is the man with long, black hair, the one who takes the Jeep at night?"

"How—" Casey clamped his mouth shut and returned to his work. Clearly, he was not going to share more with her now.

"You're keeping bad company, Casey."

"Not any more, Miss Bishop. That's why they . . ."

"Beat you up? Because you broke away from them? Good. Keep it that way. We value you. Take care of yourself, and tell us if you need help."

Casey said nothing. Alexis sensed fear. She guessed he risked another attack if his friends found out he had talked to her.

"Take care of yourself," she said again, and left him.

Morning was more than half gone, the office bustling. Alexis felt guilty for being late. A young, timid-looking couple entered the lobby. Two people waited there already, seated on opposite sides of the room. Bonnie fielded call after call. She covered the mouthpiece and nodded at the people waiting. The young woman seated wore a black skirt that stopped above her knees, white polyester shirt, and an abundance of makeup. Her long hair looked freshly trimmed and attractive. A briefcase that Alexis guessed still had the price tags inside lay across her lap. She fingered the leather as if she did not quite know what to do with it. The man, a little older, wore a suit that could have used pressing, and highly polished shoes. His bearing suggested former military, despite the rumpled suit. Alexis smiled at them both and went into the office she had taken for her own.

She put her things down and called Bonnie.

"Are they both applicants?" she asked when the secretary answered.

"You're a mind reader," Bonnie answered.

"Send in the one who got here first."

The young woman, Bethany Joseph, was from Eugene, a recent graduate of the University of Oregon. Her handshake was firm and dry. Her glance darted over the room, and then settled on Alexis.

"Have you ever worked in a busy office, Bethany?"

She nodded. "My brother is an associate at Morton Bern in Eugene. I clerked there for college money."

"Why didn't you apply there?"

"I did. I decided I didn't want to work with a brother as my superior."

"I can imagine the scenario, though I've never had a brother. Unless you count Wade, my father's partner."

"Your father?"

"Grant Bishop is my father."

"I heard he's a good attorney."

Alexis smiled. "Very." She questioned Bethany about her education, her work history, her readiness to work, and her attitudes about such things as guilty clients. She promised a speedy answer to Bethany, shook hands again, and called Bonnie to send in the other person.

Paul Marion was a local boy, a former Marine who had earned his law degree in the service, preferring that to using his parents' money. He had seen combat service in Afghanistan and been deployed to Iraq, Kuwait, and Southern California before coming home. He was married, expecting a child, and more than ready to work. He had worked in a Judge Advocate General's office and had courts martial litigation experience. He apologized for the state of his appearance, having just flown to Eugene from Los Angeles, grabbed a rental car and made it barely in time for the appointment. *He would do. He wants the job, and he is coming home.*

Alexis repeated the questions she had asked Bethany. She dismissed him with the same promise to give him a quick answer. He said he and his wife would be at his parents' home for a few days.

"Bonnie, set up a time and invite both our applicants for an interview with Wade," Alexis said as Bonnie left for lunch.

Alexis turned her attention to the job, her own mind made up about the both of them, if Wade agreed.

The work took hold of her, and she found herself drawn deep into each human story the cases represented, thinking of ways to do her best by them, making decisions, setting arbitration, depositions, and court dates, with Bonnie's help. She dispensed advice to those who needed little more, and set dates to see those she needed to interview. After last night's sleep, she felt energized. One case drew a sharp response from Bonnie.

"Good grief, Alexis, don't you ever slow down? You have reviewed and made decisions on five cases in an hour. If you don't need a breather, I do!"

Alexis laughed, accustomed to hearing similar complaints from clerks and assistants in her last office. "You need a little more help, too," she said. "Get on that, will you?"

"I already spend too much time on payroll," Bonnie groused, closing Alexis' door.

Alexis slowed, not her work, but the amount she sent to Bonnie to type, record, and file. Later, Alexis heard her on the phone making an appointment for an interview with a candidate.

Wade stepped out of his office and leaned on her doorjamb. "Bout time," he said.

"Good. Then you won't mind that I set up interviews for you with the two applicants who came in today."

"Me? You want me to interview applicants?"

"You have to work with them. Unless you're planning to desert us."

"You're stuck with me. You couldn't pay me to leave your dad. Maybe not you, either. You're as good as he is."

"Thank you. Go away." Alexis buried herself in the work again, until Pat's voice startled her.

"What happened?"

She looked up from her desk. She had not heard him come in. He stood in front of her desk, grinning at her.

"What do you mean?" she asked.

"You look like you could slay dragons today. Bonnie says you're a slave driver."

She smiled. "Dragons, zombies, vampires—bring 'em on today. I've never felt better in my life."

"Your dad?"

"Mary says he'll sleep the rest of the year. But he's resting."

"Chases Bear saw him."

Alexis sat back, turning a pen in her fingers. "We had a Healing Way ceremony for him last night."

"We? No wonder you feel lively today."

"What does that mean?"

He shrugged his shoulders, grinning again. "If you ever find out what he smokes in that medicine pipe, share it with me."

"It sounds like you know more about it than I do," she answered.

"I had a taste of it a few years ago, after I got shot."

"You did *what?*"

He shrugged again. "Story for another day. I came to pick up the relics and drive them over to Oregon State in Corvallis. Friend there says he can authenticate them."

Pat looked as if there might be more he wanted to say, but, instead, tossed her a lazy salute and left. A moment later, looking sheepish, he came back and retrieved the box of relics.

She watched wistfully after him, wishing she could catch up and tell him the decision she had made, but she had other things to do first. Honest things. She'd lost the mood to work—

and no wonder—it was past sundown. In Redmond, in the summer, that made it nine o'clock or later.

Gathering her things and organizing her desk, she called Mary.

"He's sleeping," Mary said by way of hello.

"Still, or again?"

"Still. He has not wakened since you left this morning."

"Does it still appear to be restful sleep?"

"Not always. He stirs and groans now and again."

"I'm on my way, Mary. You can take a break."

"I have slept, as well. There is nothing to do for him but wait."

Alexis hesitated. "See you soon." There was nothing else to say.

The air outside had cooled somewhat, and the drive home soothed Alexis. A clear sky, a million stars, the reflective white of snowcapped peaks to soften the gathering darkness, all made her grateful to be here and to be alive. The day had been a productive one, with a dozen items scratched off her 'to do' list, including adding two promising staff members to the office. She knew what her father had meant about leaving the matter of dress codes to existing staff. Bethany would quickly learn the difference between clerical garb and business wear. Alexis would bet Paul Marion would appear sleek and well-groomed when next she saw him, when he had not traveled all night to get there. She was almost at the ranch turnoff when she noticed that the car behind had one headlight dimmer than the other. The same car had been behind her in town. She made her turn without signaling and slowed to watch what the other driver did. He sped past without a pause. It was an old WWII Jeep with the cloth top down and a driver with long, dark hair. Her heart pounded. She pulled over and turned off her lights to wait. When he didn't return and no one else passed by, she continued on, worried. Who was watching again? Why?

She turned into the drive as Jerry stepped off the porch.

"Everything all right?" She called out.

"Yep," he said. "Here, I'll put your car away. She tossed the keys over the roof to him and hauled all her work out of the back seat.

"Thanks, Jerry."

"Yes, ma'am. No problem." He grinned, and she caught an air of mischief in his manner. He was gone. An object in front of the door drew her attention as she climbed the steps. She dropped her papers on a deck chair, and squealed with delight.

Chapter 20: Spirit of the Eagle

Wind was blowing, time stood still
Eagle flew out of the night
~Peter Gabriel

Alexis dropped to her knees beside the basket, oblivious of damage to her clothes, and gathered the warm, chubby little puppy up in her arms, nuzzling and cooing soft noises. The puppy wakened and tried to suckle her chin, which made her giggle. She lifted a leg and checked before turning its male parts away from her, not knowing when he had last peed. The pup wriggled and tried to turn toward her, licking her face. Alexis noticed a bag of puppy food tucked in the basket beside a soft pillow, as well as a small supply of absorbent wetting sheets for training. She would get more of those tomorrow. A pair of dishes sat on the floor beside the basket, which might last a month as a bed for the pup. By then, he would be too big for it.

He looked much like Jerry's blue heeler, with a perfect bandit mask over his eyes and a small black spot on the end of his nose. As evidence of the breed's Dalmatian forebears, a few more spots appeared; one on his belly, another covering his rump, a black tip on his tail. Otherwise, his coat was white, a condition Alexis knew would change over time, as black hairs grew in and gave him the attractive salt-and-pepper, blue appearance that was common in the breed.

Pleased, Alexis noted Jerry had not cut off his tail, as was common among heeler owners. She thought it inhumane, like cutting a horse's hair short in winter, which left it defenseless against bad weather in the event the animal escaped from his stall.

She hooked the basket over her arm by its handles and went inside, still snuggling the little dog. She set him on the floor, where he promptly sidled up to a chair and peed all over the floor.

"I guess I know when you peed last now, don't I?"

"I guess you know where to find the cleaning supplies, too, young lady." Mary picked up the puppy and cuddled him as lovingly as Alexis had done.

"He's a sweetie," Mary said. "But you know you can't take him to the city."

"No. Heelers and cities do not go well together. He's a working dog."

"Do you have time for him?"

"I'll make time. How's Dad?"

"Not well enough for you to introduce him to this little monkey," Mary said. "He's sound asleep, as he's been this livelong day." She handed the puppy back to Alexis.

Alexis put him down in his basket and hurried to her father's den, annoyed with herself for barely having thought of him all day. The puppy followed her. Her father hadn't stirred, nor even crumpled his covers since she had seen him that morning. If this continued, she was concerned they would have to exercise him to keep him from losing his ability to move and to prevent bedsores. She laid a hand on his forehead. It was as hot as summer sun on a rock and wet with sweat. The black and white puppy licked at her ankles.

"You little dickens," she said.

She turned her dad's covers down and sat beside him with the puppy exploring her lap until Mary came to say dinner was ready and to ask if Grant would want something. Melanie had gone to spend the evening at home.

"Not unless he wakes. Has he been feverish all day?"

"Yes. I am worried. There are some of those new-fangled thermometers over there, the kind you just lay on his head. They've been reading about a hundred to a hundred and two all day."

"I think it's higher now. Where did you say they are?"

Mary nodded toward a table by the door. "On the table."

His temperature was over a hundred and three. She frowned, considering whether to bring Granddad, and decided to wait. Her grandfather would know when they needed him. He would come or he would summon her.

Mary brought her dinner. Alexis finished the last bite as her father opened his eyes and grumbled.

"Why is it so goddamned hot in here? Open a window or something. Have you got the air turned off?"

"You're running a fever," she murmured. Since he was awake, she wet a washcloth in cool water and washed his face, neck, and arms, leaving his nightshirt open at the throat. A small, bright red circle of color on each cheek worried her.

"Did that old man's concoction give me some new problem?"

"I doubt it. You haven't taken any since yesterday."

"Yesterday! How the hell long have I been asleep?"

"About 27 hours. Longer than before. Are you hungry?"

"No. I want a shot of whiskey."

She puckered her brow. "I don't know. That doesn't sound like a good idea."

"I haven't taken anything since this time yesterday, and you think it's going to interact?"

"Good point." What was the harm in being a little intoxicated when you were flat on your back in bed? She poured a shot of scotch from a bottle in his bar, arranged his pillows and helped him sit up. He sipped it, coughed, and leaned back, smiling. Moments later, having emptied the glass, he snored, and the glass slipped from his fingers. She took it and touched his forehead. His skin felt clammy and damp, and he shivered in his sleep. She covered him, turned off the light, and drew another chair close to rest her feet. Puppy curled up in the crevice of her thighs beneath the blanket and slept. Dozing, Alexis hardly noticed when Mary covered them both.

Deep in dream sleep, she stirred when cool air blew over her face and motion stirred the skin on her outspread arms. Feathers riffled. She soared over a vast landscape, hundreds of miles of it in view. Noting movement here and there, she diverted her glance for fractions of a second, and dismissed each as unworthy of attention, except, for a moment, a beetle, black and tan vertical stripes, black eyes, as long as a twig on which he perched, eating an evergreen needle. She passed a river, dark in the shadow of a tree-lined canyon, blue moving water reflecting her flight. A fish stilled under the surface of a river, hugging a rock. She dove. Air whistled past her body and she woke remembering the image of a June bug eating a pine needle, and a fish lying still in a dark river.

"I like my steelhead baked," Alexis whispered. Peace filled her. Whatever message the eagle brought, she had seen it. Eventually, its meaning would become clear. It was four in the morning. Her father's fever had broken, his chills were gone, and he slept again. Upstairs, Alexis dressed in jeans and boots. The unnamed puppy slept soundly in his basket.

She slipped outside, saddled Cisco and rode to the Sacred Cave. She had yearned to be there since her last visit. Inside, she seated herself, waited for stillness, and drank from the vial of herbal mixture. After a moment, the sweet coffee flavor filled her mouth and she waited quietly to leave her body. She waited much longer than usual and feared the vision had eluded her. Lifting only her eyes, she saw blood red hieroglyphs depicting the horse and the buffalo. She looked higher, into depths of shadow, until she could barely make out the familiar, simple lines of an eagle, carved deeply, and stained with the indigo juice of blueberries. The eagle soared so far above the horse as to be nearly invisible. As she gazed, she asked silently for the spirit of the great bird to revisit.

The cave faded. She slipped out of her physical self. Mother Earth opened beneath the tree. She passed through its roots to the light sky of some other place, clear, blue, and warm. She soared into blue reaches of sky and looked to the field below, where she could see the creatures of her past visit, white buffalo, horse grazing, and a field mouse skittering into a hole. Beside her, an eagle cried, his hooded eyes piercing, his white feathers stirring with the passage of air. She felt wind in her face, the exhilaration of flight, the eagle's warming, reassuring love, and morning sun in her face. Her gaze followed his. They flew out of the other world, over the crags and scattered boulders of Trout Creek. This time, the kiln remained, but not the shelter, and no one occupied the space. Yet, Alexis sensed something, some presence, not evil as before, but innocent. Nevertheless, the presence brought fear she did not understand. Returning to the place of the buffalo, she soared to ground in the open field, walked beside the horse with her arm over its neck, and stretched out a hand in greeting to the white buffalo calf. The calf ambled forward and allowed Alexis to scratch its head. The feeling that bathed Alexis was one of warmth and intense love. When she reached to wrap arms around the calf, the animal faded and disappeared. Alexis returned to the cave. With a *ping,* she arrived in her body, shivering in the cool of the Sacred Cave. She rose and hurried out of the cave, then waited until the scent of the other world faded from her. The desert heat drew the chill from her body and soothed her while she waited. Peace filled her spirit. Finally, Cisco allowed her to mount and ride toward home, her mind fixed on scenes now gone. One piece of the message was clear: the white buffalo calf had greeted and blessed Alexis. She would ask her grandfather to repeat the ancient story to her, to help her better understand its message.

Nearing the house, she detoured to the place where she had found the tracks of the voyeur on the hill. She examined the area. He had been back at least once. What did he want? Nerves twitched all over her. Whatever his motivation, it was not innocent.

Alexis picked up Cisco's pace and lost the nervous feeling by the time she arrived home wet with sweat, as was her horse. Casey took him from her, after she checked for abrasions or cuts. She had ridden him hard and fast.

"Thanks," she said, meaning it. In the house, her new pet was under her feet so quickly she almost stepped on him. He squealed, his tail wiggling so fast it nearly faded out of sight, and his butt wiggling with it.

"Ah, hah," she said. "Great timing." She opened the door to let him out, but he just looked up at her, expectantly.

"Okay, okay." She stepped out and he followed eagerly, bounded down the stairs at her feet, and sniffed around the grass and plants near the door.

"Let's not take all day."

Finally, he found a satisfactory place to do his duty. When he was done, she praised him lavishly. He trundled along at her side, climbing the stairs to her room.

"Precocious little bugger, aren't you? Those steps are taller than you are," she said.

Mary appeared in the kitchen doorway below, watching the pup, laughing. He was part of the household already. Her father would love him, as well. But he was hers, and she knew the puppy had to choose if that were to be true.

She showered, dressed for work, and hurried to her father's side. He sat up in bed, looking disheveled, sipping coffee. A half-empty plate of scrambled eggs and sausage sat on the tray beside him. She smiled.

"I hope a shave is on your agenda today," she said as she kissed his cheek.

213

He rubbed his face. "Guess it is. Where the hell have you been?"

"Riding. Cleaning Cisco's stall."

"Somebody's cleaning Ranger's, I hope."

"No, Dad, we've let your horse languish unattended while you were out of your head."

"Hmmph. Anybody exercising him?"

"What do you care? You're not going riding any time soon, are you?" she teased.

"Might just surprise you, young lady. Might just surprise you."

"Someone rides him. I assume it is Casey. In any case, Ranger's in great shape."

"Mary tells me Casey has been away a lot, until someone beat him up. Since then, he's been here every day."

"That's true. I think he had a falling out with some unsavory companions, and they were responsible."

"Who?"

"He won't say."

This was the father she knew. Consumed by a need to know, demanding to be kept up to date.

"Dad?" She hesitated. A lump filled her throat.

"What? Now don't go getting all sappy on me." That was Dad, all right.

"Not a chance. But welcome back to the land of the living."

"Hmmph. Go to work. And keep me posted."

"You bet." As she turned to leave, he stopped her. "Tell Patrick Collins I want to see him."

"All right. Do I tell him what it's about?"

"I'll take care of that. Go on and get some work done."

Her father slowly swung his legs over the side of the bed and sat up. He shook his head as if to clear it, covered his face with his hands and fell sideways, onto the pillow.

"Whoa, Dad. Maybe not so fast. Maybe we need to put some food in you first." Alexis dashed to his side and lifted his legs back onto the bed.

"Get Melanie and get the hell out of here," he growled. "Wait! What's the little beast traipsing around your feet like he's attached to them?"

Alexis picked him up and carried him to the bed. The puppy sniffed at Grant and ran back to Alexis.

"What's his name?" Grant asked. He smiled. His eyes gleamed.

"He hasn't got one. I'm still thinking."

"Well, think fast. You have to teach him to like it."

"Yes, sir."

"Now get Melanie."

Alexis obeyed, wondering why his pride extended to preclude his daughter from his private needs, but not his housekeeper's daughter. Glad it did.

As she crossed the Deschutes River on her way to work, she called Pat from her cell. Her puppy curled up in her lap and fell asleep. She grasped his loose skin in her fingers and rubbed him, already loving him.

"You're up early. Are you out of your jurisdiction again?" she asked.

Pat glanced at his watch. "How long have *you* been up?"

"Since four. Dad's awake."

"I know. He called me an hour ago. Said you were off somewhere 'doing God knows what' at this ungodly hour."

Alexis laughed. "So you're the one who filled him in this morning. He was full of questions when I got back from my ride."

"I didn't tell him a lot. I didn't know how much you wanted him to know while he's sick."

"As much as he asks. But if you didn't . . ."

"He said he was going to call Wade since I was so close-mouthed. Where *have* you been?"

"Looking for messages."

He sighed, his voice resigned. "You're learning too much from Chases Bear. Now you're talking in riddles. Speaking of your grandfather, how is his medicine working on your father?'"

216

"He has slept around the clock two days in a row, he's lost his appetite, and he falls asleep two minutes after waking. This morning, he seemed better, but it is hard to remember what normal *is* for him. He tried to get up and was lightheaded."

"I would expect that, after taking a cleanse for three days and sleeping for two days," Pat said.

"I think he's lost fifteen pounds since he came home, and after weeks of chemotherapy, he didn't have any to spare. I can get by on a few hours of sleep, but last night I didn't get that much, so maybe I'm overreacting."

"Yes, you are. Chases Bear has a handle on it."

"How can you be sure? He's been having those seizures ever since . . ."

"Not when I saw him yesterday. He told me they were gone."

"Then why . . .?"

"Why, what?

"Why did he need me to help with Dad's healing?"

Pat burst into laughter. "That will be the day."

Alexis frowned. Pat was right, but she didn't pursue the matter, since she was pulling into the parking lot at the office.

"I'll see you for lunch," she said. "And we have to eat outside." She rang off, grinning, letting him puzzle about that.

Chapter 21: Dark Moon Kane

"If we could read the secret history of our enemies,
we should find in each man's life sorrow
and suffering enough to disarm all hostility."
~ *Henry Wadsworth Longfellow*

Alexis determined that from now and for the near future, Puppy would be at her side, learning manners gently and steadily by repetition and his desire to please her. His reward for every correct behavior would be her pleasure and praise. Food came at appropriate intervals, not from treats, and she would practice the correct commands at all times, giving him much love and attention. After all, he had been taken from his mother and siblings. She kept trying on names for him in her mind Puppy. So far, none seemed right. He was loving and loveable, making clear from the start that his preferred position was at her feet, though, true to his breed, he was as active as jumping beans on a hot stove. His energy seemed boundless, as did his curiosity.

Early in the day, before the weather became too hot, Alexis had taken him out to relieve himself in the courtyard at the office. She sat in the shade of the umbrella and worked while he played. He demonstrated his propensity for chasing things by ferreting out a three-inch June beetle and chasing it all over the courtyard, until the creature tired of his game and scuttled beneath a slightly raised table pedestal at Alexis' feet. He barked and looked to her for approval. She smiled and spoke softly, but did not praise. He would learn what she wanted him to chase, and it would not be June beetles.

"You tricky little dickens, you think you're smart, don't you?" *I am not mad at you, but this is not your best work.*

He lay down at her feet and soon fell asleep, weary from his efforts. The day was approaching the point of too much heat for comfort when Puppy snapped alert, struck a threatening pose, and growled. Pat Collins bent to kiss Alexis on the cheek, set a tall paper cup with ice and liquid in front of her, and laughed.

"So this is why we eat outside in this heat," he said, nodding toward the pup. When he sat down at the table with Alexis, Puppy single-handedly surrounded his feet and bit his booted ankles, catching all sides.

"Good boy," Alexis said, petting. "Quit!" She reached down and picked him up, took Pat's hand, and said again, "Good boy. Good friend." Holding onto the pup, she allowed Pat to pet him, knowing her life-long friend loved animals as she did. The pup knew it, too, immediately. He snuggled into Pat's hands and licked him. Alexis laughed. The pup, with the well-developed memory typical of his breed, had begun learning two things: the meaning of friend, and that Pat's presence was permitted. He had also shown willingness to be protective. For his age, she found that interesting and satisfying. Pat set the wriggling bundle of fur on the ground and opened the bag he had brought, spreading fried chicken and coleslaw containers on the table.

"Mmm. Smells good," Alexis said. "Want to go inside and wash your hands?"

"Nah. What's a little puppy slobber?" He passed her a packet of wipes and opened one for himself, chuckling. "He's cute. What are you going to do with him in Washington?"

Alexis put her chicken leg down on a napkin and regarded him seriously.

"If I go back," she said, "I'll leave him with you or Dad, whomever he likes best."

Pat looked up from his lunch with interest. "If? If you go back?"

"I haven't decided where I'll be when Dad's well. I could be in Portland. First, I have things to do." She tore off a piece of fried chicken and nibbled at it.

"Such as?"

"Discovering who our voyeur is, for one. Making sure that Dad has a business to go back to. Finding out who beat the living stuffing out of Casey. Replacing him or making sure he's here to stay."

"Here? He's—wait. What did you say? Voyeur? You have a peeper?"

"Slow this morning, aren't you? Yes. Someone has been up on the hill overlooking the house, facing my window and the den, where Dad is sleeping. He doesn't mind leaving evidence behind, or he thinks no one will ever go up there."

"So you haven't actually seen him?"

"Yes. I have."

"Who is it?"

"Probably Indian. Young. Very long, straight, black hair. He's driving the Jeep that was at the old schoolhouse where we found Granddad."

"Is he watching you, your dad, or Casey?"

"I hadn't thought of that. But, no, not Casey. The man can't see Casey from there, and I think he's only been there at night. It's either my room or Dad's."

"Close your curtains," Pat suggested.

"Curtains? What curtains? I hung something over the window, but I don't think that matters."

"What do you mean?"

"What is most visible from that vantage point are the bookshelves in Dad's den. That's where—"

"I know. It was where your father was keeping the vases he got from Lillian Red Sky."

"Was?"

"He asked me to take them away this morning."

"Oh. That's why he wanted to call you."

"Partly. He didn't mention that you had a stalker watching the house."

"Dad doesn't know, unless he saw him. That's unlikely, considering the limited time he's been awake. What else did he want?"

"To know more about Casey Johnson. He's worried about you, if Casey's into something dangerous."

"Did you tell him I can take of myself?"

"No. I told him I'd keep an eye on you, and find out who assaulted Casey."

"Well, as long as it's only an eye." They laughed together, comfortable again as they'd always been with each other. Pat touched her wrist with his fingertips, and then pulled his hand back. Alexis swallowed the lump that gathered in her throat.

"Your stalker sounds like our third man from the schoolhouse incident," he said.

"I didn't see him there." She forked a bite of cole slaw into her mouth.

"I didn't, either, but I've seen him hanging around the res, driving that Jeep. Where did you see him?"

"On the ranch, leaving in the Jeep at night, without lights. I backtracked, found where he had parked, walked up the hill, and watched. He left a lot of tracks, and more since then."

"He sounds like Dark Moon Kane."

"Lillian Red Sky's nephew? I thought he was in prison."

"He was. He served his time and got out."

Alexis drew a breath, sharply. "It's what? Six years since he killed his father? That's not very long for murder."

"Manslaughter. Eight to fifteen, time off for good behavior."

"It's hard to believe that kid could behave long enough to get out of jail. He's been trouble since he was a teenager."

"He was twelve the first time I arrested him. He and Harley Braithwaite burgled the casino office."

"I don't think I heard about that one."

"You were in school, or Europe. I forget. Braithwaite was maybe ten, and they both got juvie time. But they didn't get away with anything and neither one of them could talk fast enough, so the Court was easy on them."

"That's unfortunate."

He nodded. "I've been trying to catch up with Dark Moon for a few weeks now. He shows up, buys a few supplies, and disappears again. I hear about it later. When your grandfather told me there were people camping out on Trout Creek, I figured it could be him and some friends."

"Mostly relatives," she answered. "Braithwaite is his cousin and Casey is Lillian's grandson. Lila is somehow related to them, too."

He finished eating and cleaned his hands on another wipe.

Puppy scratched at Alexis' leg, begging to be picked up. Knowing he wanted to share her meal, she ignored him.

"That's right. Gayle's mother, Lila's grandmother, and Braithwaite's father were cousins," Pat said.

"That explains a lot." The puppy circled away from Alexis' feet and ran at her, scratching his way into her lap.

"Why, you tricky little dickens," she exclaimed.

Pat laughed at the puppy, but he remained focused on his job. "Yes, it does. It's probably why Lila won't talk to police about the assault on your grandfather, and why Casey won't tell us who attacked him."

She nodded. "They were all together in the canyon."

"Tricky Dickens is going to be on the table in a minute," Pat said, and gathered up their waste to throw it into the trash near them.

By the time he returned, the puppy was trying to climb on the table. Alexis set him on the ground. "Quit," she said, realizing how many times she had called the pup tricky dickens.

Tricky had a name.

Chapter 22: Baby Watchdog

"The worst part of it is you don't know if
he's barking at an owl, the moon or a burglar!
That's one of the drawbacks
of a limited vocabulary!"
~Charles M. Schulz

Alexis called home from the office the next afternoon. Dad was sleeping, and not feverish, for a change. Mary assured her there was nothing to worry about. She wrote a letter on behalf of the young couple who had arrived as she did the day before. She called their number. The wife answered.

"Lisa, I've written a letter to your former landlord, and sent you a copy. Let me know if you get any response."

The girl sniffled. "He . . . He called this morning. He says if we don't fix the bathroom, he's going to have it done and charge us. Miss Bishop, I swear—"

"I know, Lisa, the plumbing is dilapidated. I could tell by your pictures. I reminded him he had a duty to maintain a rental home in livable condition, and that he was liable for his failure to do so. I don't think you'll hear from him again." After a few more reassurances, Alexis hung up, marked the file pro bono, and left it in her outbox. She processed mail, and completed other work stacked on her desk. Finally, she called Pat.

"Hey!" he answered. "How's Tricks?"

Alexis laughed. He had never asked her that in his life. "*Tricky*," she said, "is fine. Want to say hello?"

His turn to laugh. "Naw, I'll pass. He's your shadow now?"

"Until he learns he belongs to me." The pup in question sat on her lap, stretching to show her where to scratch him.

"Or you to him," Pat said.

Alexis was totally in love with the little rascal. "Could happen. Did you learn anything from your friend at OSU?"

"Nothing we didn't already know. There were a few legitimate pieces—the carving, which was walrus ivory; a couple arrowheads; and a piece that was used for flint."

"Did he test the age of the ivory?"

"No. From its style, he estimates it is more than four hundred years old."

"So only that piece has some value."

"Pretty much. The containers—pots—are patterned after those made by Plains Indians, and no older than the last decade. Twenty, twenty-five dollars at any gift shop."

"What about the ones from our house?"

"Again, not old. Maybe half a century at best, and worth a few hundred. Lillian said she paid thirty-two thousand for the pair. She got them in Summit Lake, Nevada."

"Summit Lake is Paiute. They are related to one of our tribes. There is a vast difference in our cultures between Oregon and Nevada. Wait. Are you sure she said Summit Lake, Nevada? Not Summit Lake, Oregon?" Summit Lake, Oregon was part of the Mount Hood National Park. Removing artifacts there was a federal offense. In places, the park's borders touched those of the Warm Springs Reservation. Pat's silence said he was not sure.

Then, he spoke. "We had been talking about her life in Las Vegas, but now you mention it, she didn't say that, specifically."

"So the few relics that *are* real could as easily be from Mt. Hood National Forest as from here, as could the bowls Lillian Red Sky gave Dad. And our culprits could also have slipped over the border after they left the canyon."

"What makes you think they've gone from Trout Creek?"

"Trust me. They're gone."

Pat fell silent again. She could imagine him rubbing his chin as he did when he was thoughtful.

"I guess it's time for a close-up look at Trout Creek Canyon, then."

Alexis had arrived at the office parking lot. "Let me know when," she said. "I'll truck along."

"Tomorrow after breakfast."

"I'll meet you. Say where."

"At the Gateway," he answered. "You can bring your little dickens along. He can chase bugs." She knew as well as he did that heelers will herd anything from a cockroach to a whale. Under control, it was their greatest attribute.

"In that canyon, he's liable to chase snakes. I will keep an eye on him." She laughed. "See you tomorrow." She rang off and opened the car door for Tricky. He jumped onto the floor, to the seat, and then moved over when she slid in. "Good boy, Tricky," she said, patting his head.

When she started the car, he jumped into her lap. "No," she said firmly. "Move."

He lay down in the other seat, big, sad eyes watching her, and whined softly.

Alexis pursed her lips to avoid laughing. "Stay." She repeated the order several times before they were home, and stepped out of the car quickly when it stopped, before he could climb in her lap again. He followed, jumping on her leg, looking for attention.

"Heel," she commanded. He lay down and whined. "A lesson in heel commands is in line for tonight, kiddo," she said, using her okay-but-not-satisfied voice, firm and a bit chilly. He trotted along at her feet to the house, where she sat on the porch steps to let him sniff around the yard for a few minutes before he took care of business. She plucked several tissues from her purse and tossed the result in a trashcan on the porch. Finally, she let him come to her for a reward of affectionate words and pets. She washed up, grabbed a fresh pear from the kitchen, and went upstairs to call Chili, who promptly invited her to dinner the next evening.

"Unless you think you still need to hang close to your dad," Chili added.

"Dad's fine, still sleeping most of his time between meals. No, I am going up Trout Creek with Pat to see what our friendly neighborhood forgers left behind in the way of evidence. I'd love to spend a little time with you and your boys."

"What if those people are still there?"

"They aren't."

"Grrr. I won't ask you how you know that, 'cause you won't answer me anyhow. It'll be good to see you, now that all my brood are well. Okay?"

"Promise, Chil. See you tomorrow."

Dinner with her father was quiet and companionable. He was wide awake and had an appetite for the beef and vegetable soup, fresh rolls with homemade butter, and tall glasses of milk. Mary brought them slices of blackberry pie topped with whipped cream and sprinkled with cinnamon. Alexis recalled a lecture received from a fellow attorney in Washington. With Terry, Joan Rowe, and Will Stone, also from their office, they were lunching at a diner across from their building. Will had gone on about the benefits of organic milk, milk products, and grass-fed beef. "Conjugated linoleic acid," he had said, "and trans-palmi—something or other, from organic milk products and beef."

Terry had derided him. "There is no good reason for an adult human to drink milk. It does nothing but raise bad cholesterol."

"Shows what *you* know," the other attorney had snapped back, "CLA boosts metabolism, reduces the size of fat cells and supports the growth of muscle cells. Trans-P boosts the immune system, supports the gene marker for longevity, and supports overall good health. And the best source is organic milk products, from pasture-raised cattle."

Alexis could not remember the rest of the conversation, but it was a talk she would now have with Granddad. He said that poor nutrition is at the root of over half of our illnesses.

All their beef was pasture-raised, sans poisonous additives, free of growth hormones, as natural as it could be. If her friend had been correct, these were the best foods Mary could feed a man fighting cancer. Or anyone, for that matter. They were foods Alexis had consumed all her life before leaving home. She drank the rest of her milk. It tasted rich and creamy. Delicious. She recalled wondering if her Will had any notion what he was talking about and dismissing the matter from her mind. Now, she wanted to talk about it with her grandfather. He had always used foods and herbs as if they were medicine. Alexis had been thinking a lot about his medicine these past weeks.

Her father fell asleep within minutes of finishing dinner, and Alexis went upstairs with Tricky at her feet, saying "Heel," whenever he took the correct position, almost certainly by accident. He just was not big enough to leap tall buildings in a single bound. The stairs must have seemed like tall buildings to him, but he did not give up. At the top, she bent, picked him up, and rewarded him with much affection. In her room, she let him rest, talking nonsense to him, allowing him to explore every corner of the room and her bathroom, where she set out a dish of water. At last, he stretched out on the rug beside the tub and fell asleep while she bathed. She stepped over him, chuckling, and crawled in bed, leaving the bathroom door open.

Alexis slept soundly that night, deep, dreamless sleep— or dreams she never recalled. It was as if weariness had caught up with her, and both mind and body needed a break.

Tricky, growling, woke her sometime past midnight. A moment later, the tinkle of breaking glass somewhere far off stripped her of sleep cobwebs. She listened and switched on the bedside light. Tricky growled again. He peeped from the edge of her covers, nothing visible but his nose, which was wrinkled in another growl, teeth bared. When she sat up, he turned and buried his head, crawling under the covers to her lap, hiding his head in her curves. She petted him, listening hard for whatever had wakened her. The familiar sense of evil pervaded her senses, and Tricky barked, every part of his furry little body quivering.

With that, Alexis reached into the nightstand drawer and withdrew the Smith & Wesson revolver she had begun keeping handy. She threw back the covers and stepped out of bed. At her bedroom door, she stood very still, listening. At her feet, Tricky gave a little yip.

"Hush," Alexis whispered. She knelt and held his mouth closed. He buried his head in her pajamas. She stood up, whispered, "Heel," and started down the stairs. Mary appeared in the dim light at the foot of the staircase.

"Shah," Alexis mimed, holding her finger to her lips. A light flickered in the den. Someone was there with a flashlight. She stepped downstairs, her bare feet silent. Tricky seemed to know he needed to be quiet, as well—until he reached the door of the den. Then, with Alexis beside him, he ran like a deer toward the slender man with the flashlight, growling as loudly as his weak little voice could manage. As Alexis switched on the light, pointing her gun at him, Tricky sank his sharp, small teeth into the burglar's ankle. The man spun around to face Alexis. He was native; slim, muscular, narrow waisted, dressed in snug blue jeans and a red flannel shirt. He kicked, and Tricky was bowled across the floor, yipping. Then, the man spun and jumped through the window, shattering glass. Long hair spread out behind him, blue-black, shiny. Alexis fired, but he kept moving, so she guessed she had missed. She was sure he was losing a lot of blood anyway, from shards of glass that flew everywhere. She looked around the room, making sure he had been alone. Her father leaned on his elbow, watching.

"Your little dog is a keeper," he said. "See he's not hurt." His calm voice seemed normal, as strong as it had ever been. She pocketed her gun and went to Tricky.

"Good boy," she cooed. "Good boy." Gathering him into her arms, she held him close. He trembled and whined, but she could find no injuries. Broken glass on the front of the display case that held her father's pots and other items explained the tinkle of glass that had wakened her.

"Bring him to me," Grant said. He reached out and examined the pup with gentle hands. Alexis had forgotten how capable he was with sick or injured animals. Tricky stopped trembling and quieted. Grant held him close. Mary hovered at the doorway.

"That's a good boy, Tricky. That's a good boy," Grant said.

Alexis had left her cell phone upstairs. She lifted the desk phone receiver and called Jerry, no doubt getting him out of bed.

""Bring some help and some materials and come to the house to cover a large broken window, please." The night air sifting into the room chilled her. Mary wrapped a spare blanket around her shoulders.

"How long were you awake, Dad?" she asked.

"Since he came in," Grant answered. "I heard him open the window—the one he didn't go out. I figured my best move was to wait until he realized that what he was looking for was gone, and went away."

"Are you so sure he would have gone?"

"On the contrary, I was pretty sure he'd wake you. Hoping he wouldn't hurt you to get what he wanted."

"But for Tricky, I doubt if I'd have wakened. I was sleeping like a hibernating bear."

"As I said, he's a keeper. Good boy." He petted the puppy. He held Tricky out to Alexis and lay back on the pillow, looking tired. Mary covered him to his neck.

"You haven't asked what he was after," he said.

Alexis shook her head. "Pat thinks it is Dark Moon Kane. I imagine he was after the pots Lillian Red Sky gave you. He's been watching from the hill."

"Why didn't you tell me?"

"It never occurred to me he'd break in."

"Pat's right. It was Kane. I'll never forget that worthless little bastard."

"Harsh words from a defense attorney," she answered.

"Some people are born evil. He is one of them. I don't know which is worse, him or Harley Braithwaite." He was looking tired, his voice waning.

Jerry and Casey had the window securely covered in no time. Casey looked grim, his mouth drawn into a straight line, his forehead creased. He glanced toward the bookcase shelves two or three times. Mary hung another blanket over the covered window space to keep night chill from seeping through the cracks. Grant was already asleep. Minutes later, so was Alexis, arms around her precious little savior. She had tucked the gun under her pillow.

Tomorrow, she would wear it on her hip when she went up Trout Creek with Pat.

Chapter 23: The Wall

The murdered do haunt their murderers.
I believe--I know that ghosts have wandered the earth.
~ Emily Brontë, Wuthering Heights

Alexis slept deeply, but briefly. She woke before dawn, knowing Pat would expect her to be early, because she always rose early. The fact that she had lost more than two hours of the night was irrelevant. He did not know that, and there was a job to be done.

The day would be hot before they reached their destination. She dressed accordingly, in knee-length shorts and moccasins, and covered the gun and holster under a loose tee shirt, so as not to alarm her father and Mary. She needn't have worried. Mary had not come down, no doubt making up for her own short night, and Dad was still soundly asleep.

Alexis wandered around the den, carefully touching nothing, looking for things out of place, evidence of any kind of their intruder. He had tried her father's desk drawers, no doubt looking for money, but had not succeeded in accessing any. As would any good attorney, Grant Bishop kept private papers and anything relating to his practice under lock and key. Two glass door panes over display shelves were broken. One was where Dad had kept the decorative, native-style vases. They were there, out of place, but intact. Dark Moon would have known they were of little value with only a glance. In any case, they were not what he wanted. That he had not broken them was most likely due to his need for silence. The question was why did he want the forgeries? Did he believe what Lillian had likely told him, that they were worth the thousands of dollars she had claimed she paid for them? Or did he know they were forgeries? If so, did he want to get rid of the evidence? That didn't make sense. Dark Moon had been in prison for killing his father at the time Lillian gave the relics to Grant. He certainly did not have a hand in forging them. To protect someone else? No one was ever going to accuse Dark Moon Kane of empathy. Everyone on the reservation and not a few away from it knew his history. The child of a pair of seriously addicted alcoholics, Dark Moon had probably suffered fetal alcohol syndrome from birth. Teachers, neighbors, family, and acquaintances had long since concurred that he was born without the capacity to feel anything for others. As a child, he had tortured small animals; as a teenager, he had assaulted and was convicted of the first-degree assault of his then girlfriend. Given another three minutes before the girl's brother broke up the attack, he might have killed her.

Alexis found nothing of evidentiary value in her perusal of her father's den. She would leave everything untouched and call police and crime scene investigators to examine more thoroughly later. She glanced at her watch and decided to go. The sky softened outside those windows that were still intact.

Her father's voice startled her. "Did you find anything missing?"

"Only the forged pots you gave Pat yesterday," she answered.

"My handgun?"

"No. He didn't get any of the desk drawers open."

"Bring it to me," he said.

Alexis hesitated. He seemed alert enough now, and had during the night, at first. She decided that arming him was wiser than not. Kane might be carrying a gun the next time he broke in. She brought her father the weapon and let him stow it in the nightstand, noting that he was able to reach it easily.

"I'm going to ask Jerry to put a man outside for the next couple of nights," she said.

"Make that two men—well armed. Tell them to watch each others' backs, as well as ours. Where's Tricky?"

"In my room, whining to be let out. I'm taking him with me today, but I didn't want him to wake you."

"When I'm up and about, tell Jerry I want one of Tricky's brothers. It has been too long since I had a dog around the house. I'm seeing the value of having one." Their last dog had expired of old age, complicated by arthritis, several years ago. Grant had loved him, and had not wanted another, not then.

"I can do that, Dad. I am glad you're thinking of getting up. We need you at the office."

"You just hired two attorneys, didn't you?"

"I've never seen the day that two green kids could take your place."

"Huh. Don't get carried away, here. A man might get to thinking you like him a little."

She laughed and kissed him on the cheek.

"Where are you going in shorts and moccasins?"

"Rock climbing, Dad. Along Indian Creek."

"Trout Creek, you mean."

"If you say so. But I'll be inside the reservation, so I guess it's a matter of opinion," she said.

"You stay far away from Dark Moon Kane, young lady."

"I plan to do just that."

"And make sure your cop knows you're carrying that weapon. He might not want you to have it on the rez."

"I will." As if his sharp eyes might miss it, regardless of what she wore to cover it. "How do you know Pat's going to be there?"

"He told me yesterday he wanted to get in the canyon, but he didn't want to chase that rat pack away. He just wanted to take a look around."

"Did he say what he thought he'd find?" she asked.

"I didn't ask. Figured it had to do with forged artifacts."

She dashed upstairs, let Tricky out, and returned to the first floor. A sharp whistle sounded. Tricky yapped and ran between Alexis' feet into the den, where he stood barking at Grant's bedside, wanting up. Dad was smiling at him.

Laughing, Alexis said, "Maybe I'm the one who needs to get another sibling of his." When she turned away, Tricky gave two short barks and raced after her.

"Ah! So you *do* know where your bread's buttered, kiddo." She bent to give his chubby sides a vigorous rub and led him outside. Minutes later, he stood on hind legs and looked out the car window, his tail wagging excitedly. Periodically, as she drove faster than the speed limit toward the Rez, Tricky dropped down, and jumped instead on her lap, washing her face liberally with a sloppy tongue, disregarding her curt orders to sit.

"Am I making a mistake, bringing you out on this trek too soon? Am I going to be able to control you?"

Finally, she pulled over to the side of the road and put him in the back seat. Getting back in the car, she felt an onslaught of goose bumps all over her. Tricky growled, as low and menacing as a two-month–old puppy can sound. She glanced back at him as she slid into her seat. His short hair stood on end the length of his back. Alexis locked all the doors and peered out at the hills and dips around them.

There was nothing. Yet, Alexis might be able to deny her own senses, but there was no denying Tricky's. She started the car and glanced over her shoulder at him. He whined and buried his nose between his two front legs. Was he picking up her sense of a presence, after all? Or was he, young as he was, able to feel the presence of something alarming?

She patted the seat beside her as she turned off the shoulder onto the highway. "Come on, boy. Come on."

Tricky whined. She glanced back at him. He stared at her, his eyes wide, whites showing. He scrambled over the console to the front seat, lay down on his belly beside her, and hid his face again. His behavior magnified Alexis' nervousness until she felt silly. He was, after all, a puppy. He crept closer to her, crawling across the dividing console, and buried his face in her lap. She scrutinized images in the mirrors, peered out the windows. Nothing. Tricky's hair still stood up, and his body trembled.

"I did not speak to you harshly enough to justify this, Tricky. If anyone wanted them, I'd give my eyeteeth if you could speak English." She petted him. He whined.

They pulled into the parking lot at the Gateway, just inside the reservation border, expecting to wait for Pat. He stood leaning against his patrol truck, two large cups on the hood at his elbow. She reached him and rested her hand on his for a moment.

"Thanks," she said. "Is that coffee?"

"What else?" He handed her one. "Did you bring Junior Mutt along?"

"I did."

Pat stepped to the truck bed and came back with a generous length of hay string in hand. "Thought you might need this," he said. "Kid wearing a collar?"

"Of course, and a leash. Thank you again. I was worrying that I might be rushing things."

Pat nodded. "He'll be tired before we get back."

They climbed into Pat's vehicle and while he backed out of his parking place, Alexis tied the hay string securely to Tricky's collar. Tough enough to contain two hundred pounds of hay in a tightly packed bale, such strings were handy tools for controlling horses in a pinch, never mind a pup. She felt better.

Settled, with Tricky falling asleep in her lap, Alexis noticed that Pat had turned, not out of the Rez to the state highway, but deeper into it, toward the back side.

"You're taking us to Granddad's back trail, aren't you?"

"Yes. I believe they were gone when you told me they were, but there's nothing stopping that gang of hoodlums from returning. I'm glad you're carrying, but before we go up the trail, I'll have to deputize you. Your gun permit on the Rez is too old. It's invalid."

"What does that entail?"

"You do what I say and back me up."

"Sounds reasonable."

"Want to tell me why you suddenly think you need to carry a gun?"

"Dark Moon Kane broke into our house last night. I've put a couple of hands on guard around the clock now. Worse, I am getting increasingly paranoid."

"Damn! I knew I should have hunted that bastard down. Anyone hurt?"

"No. If anything, Dad's better."

"Glad to hear that. What aren't you telling me?"

"Even Tricky had an episode of rising hackles and fears on our way here. I'm beginning to think I have a psychic dog. I couldn't see a thing, but I suffered some lively goose bumps."

"All animals are psychic, to a degree. It's their protection against us."

She laughed. "And one another."

"Well, yeah, there's that." He grinned at her. "Nobody likes being someone else's lunch."

Well off the road, they stopped at the foot of the path Alexis and her grandfather had taken off the bluff. Tricky wakened the instant the truck stopped and stood on hind legs at the window, yapping. When Alexis opened the door, he was off and running before she could clutch the hay string. Pat checked the position of his handgun and jogged after him.

Alexis followed his example, but felt no sense of danger. Whatever had tickled Tricky's senses, she felt no hint of malice, until she heard the pup growl. Then she thought of rattlesnakes that occupied the cool shade of rocks in high desert country. Tricky would have little knowledge of their danger.

Pat's steps slowed as he rounded a rectangular slab of rock almost as tall as he, balanced against a pair of other, similar boulders. He whistled. Tricky continued to yap and growl. There was someone, or something, around that corner. Alexis hurried. Her grandfather sat there on another stone, eating a piece of jerky that Tricky seemed to want in the worst way.

"Granddad, what are you doing here?"

"Seemed like a good idea. Who is our noisy young friend, here?"

"Tricky Dickens," Pat said, chuckling.

"Hmm. Name's bigger than he is. Does no one feed him?"

"He eats very well, as I'm sure you know." Alexis picked up the hay string Tricky had pulled from her hand, and tied it to her belt before shortening its length by winding it around her fist.

Chases Bear grinned, stood up, and strode among the boulders up the sloping trail he and Alexis had traveled down on their last trip. Alexis deliberately brought up the rear, so she could maintain better control of Tricky. For a distance, each time he moved ahead of her, she turned toward him, forcing him to get out of her way or be trampled. After several episodes of this, Tricky decided the best place for him was beside or a little behind her.

"Heel," Alexis ordered, each time he got it right. By the time they faced the choice of climb or return downhill, he was doing a fair job of walking at her side. He was panting hard. Pat came behind her to lift the puppy into a sturdy bag she carried tied over her shoulders, and secured the dog by tying him in position with the hay string. Chases Bear was already a third of the way up the sheer, cracked wall before Pat finished. He stood back to let Alexis go first. They had covered less than half the distance when Chases Bear hauled himself over the rim. As Alexis reached the top, her grandfather took her arm and helped her over. His amazing strength, undiminished by years, reassured Alexis. The two of them did the same for Pat. He motioned for them to wait there, drew his service weapon, and crouching, hurried to the other side of the bluff. There, he moved along the edge and stopped, stretching out full length on his belly. From a holster on his belt, he took a pair of collapsible binoculars and looked through them into the canyon. Chases Bear and Alexis crossed the bluff with the same caution and joined him, one on either side. Both had brought their spyglasses along.

The camp lay in a natural dip in the sloped land, which made it invisible from the creek, where kayakers and people in tour boats might have seen them. The creek spread wide and shallow at this juncture, edged and interspersed with trees and shrubbery that could easily have provided safe cover when

Braithwaite and his kin went for water. The real question was, what were they doing here? What was this place to them?

Chapter 24: Dugout

"Heaven lent you a soul,
Earth will lend a grave."
~Christian Nestell Bovee

Alexis rounded the giant, rectangular stone leaning across their path. Tricky stood in battle mode, barking at Chases Bear, who eyed Tricky and nodded approval. "When he is grown, it may be that he will resemble his namesake a little." Alexis chuckled, knowing he referred to the mythical Tricky Coyote of Native American tales.

"He'll have a long, pointed nose," Pat said. "But there'll be more of him than there is of a coyote. Especially the way Alexis feeds her animals." He was right. Tricky would grow to look like his sire, shaped more like a sturdy pit bull than a lean, sinewy coyote.

"We must go down," Chases Bear said, his voice suddenly urgent. He turned and strode a path around the upper edges of the sheer bluff that crowned the mountain. Weather had cleaved stones from the vertical, cracked sides of the mesa, piling them chaotically at its feet. Alexis clung to Tricky's haystring in case he wriggled his way out of her backpack. Pat stepped aside to let her pass, grinning behind the older man's back. He seemed glad to see her grandfather. She was pleased, as well, feeling somehow safer in Granddad's company,

247

although, unlike them, he was unarmed. Unless she considered the amazing power of his mind. At a narrow promontory, he stopped, held up his hand, and dropped to his knees to look through the spyglass, this time pointing it down the length of the creek that meandered from its headwaters in the forbidding, rocky, heavily forested Ochoco Mountains to the north. Alexis and Pat knelt near him. Tricky whined and wriggled in an attempt to free himself. Alexis could feel his toenails digging into her back through her shirt. Pat moved the pouch to her front and snugged him down under Alexis' chin.

"We must go now," Chases Bear repeated. He pointed toward a distant curve in the canyon, beyond which they could not see. Alexis squinted through the monocular she had bought after seeing Granddad's. An eagle soared over the mountains and disappeared. After a moment, she saw what Granddad had seen: a distant, faint dust cloud in motion. She could not tell if the cloud moved toward or away from their position overlooking the remnants of the campsite, and wasn't sure she wanted to know. If she did, she might be tempted to back out of going down there.

Chases Bear had started down along a narrow crack between vertical stones lined up from top to bottom of the crowning bluff.

"He's right," Pat said. "If we're going to learn anything from the site, we need to move. It will take a long time to get down there and back." Again, he started before her. If he was being protective of her, it was uncharacteristic of their history, during which they had sparred and competed far more often than he had gone ahead to help her if he was needed. Maybe Tricky's presence made the difference. She was glad he had moved the pup. She found herself leaning against the opposite side of the crack to pause and quiet the little dog's anxiety more than once. They made it down safely. There, she and Pat untied Tricky's pack and freed him to explore the grounds on foot, with the hay string stretched as far as Alexis felt comfortable letting him go.

Tricky wasted no time. He found first one, and then another of the mounds Alexis and her grandfather had seen on their first visit to the bluff, when they had guessed the gang used them as buried latrines. Tricky scratched and sniffed the length of each and quickly lost interest, moving on to other fascinations: half-buried fire coals, a grocery bag, a beer bottle. He seemed inordinately interested in a flat rock that might have been used over the fire, perhaps for cooking.

"What's that?" Alexis asked, pointing toward one side of the slope in the ground that surrounded them on three sides. She had spied some sort of rough wooden construction covered by dead and dying tree branches, about twenty feet above on the side of the hill, and protruding no more than a foot from the earth behind it. There appeared to be an opening into the slope.

"Stay here." Pat drew his gun and hurried toward the structure. Chases Bear followed. Alexis watched, crouched

249

behind a thick huckleberry bush, holding Tricky close, with her own gun loose in its holster. Only a few minutes passed before she heard Pat call, "Clear!"

She ran across the rough space and climbed part way up the slope with Tricky on her heels. The structure was an entryway, constructed of rock and wood, covered by brush. She ducked and entered an opening which someone had lined with the volcanic basalt stone found all around outside. The air inside was stale and dry. Pat and Chases Bear took up nearly half of the available floor space. Tricky squeezed between their legs and explored, sniffing everything in sight. He seemed perfectly comfortable. Alexis cringed when the pup sniffed at rodent feces and ferreted out beetles and spiders to chase. The scent was not only stale, it was musty and heavy.

"It's a dugout!" Alexis said. "I've never actually seen an old one." A dugout was a hole dug into the earth or into the side of a slope like this one, and covered, providing shelter or, in some cases, storage for those who dug the hole.

Pat nodded. "Very old," he said. "Except for additions to the door." Alexis looked to her grandfather for confirmation. He stood still, staring, as if seeing something far away, or as if in a trance. She touched him. He seemed not to notice.

The small room held bowls carved of stone or wood, tools made from rock; bows, arrowheads and remnants of a quiver; pieces of baskets, dry as dust. Pieces of leather clothing hung high on the wall. Low shelves carved from stone lined the walls. Bits of skins lay on the shelves, more holes than hides. A pair of stone carvings hung from a stick or bone poked into cracks. Alexis fingered them with awe. These were of different stone that that found all around them outside. One appeared to be a coyote, the other an eagle. They looked authentic and very old.

"These," she said, "are worth a fortune. Why are they forging pots when they have these hidden away?"

Pat touched her arm and motioned for silence. "Tell me what you feel," he whispered. He nodded toward Chases Bear, who stood still, with that faraway look in his eyes.

"Calm. Comfortable. As if I am in the presence of someone or something . . . soothing. And yet . . ."

"What?" Pat urged.

"The ghosts in this place are disturbed." Chases Bear said. "We must leave."

Alexis could not agree more. She tugged Tricky's line and left the stale, underground room cut into the side of a mountain. The men followed her.

"That was . . . strange," Alexis said. "How could it feel comforting and angry?"

"The ghosts are angry at someone else, not us. Their space has been violated, their world disordered," Chases Bear answered. Alexis shivered.

"Could you see them?" Pat asked.

"Only in my mind. I felt their presence. There is something here that was left behind by those who desecrated this holy place."

"In the dugout?" Alexis asked.

He shook his head. "I don't know."

"Pat, what made you ask me what I felt?"

"I was watching your grandfather. Did any of the relics we have seen before come from here?" he asked Chases Bear.

"Some objects were taken. Of the relics you have shown me, perhaps tools, arrowheads, ivory from the walrus that sometimes swam up the Big River to the north. Those were minor ones. There may have been more important pieces, like the argillite carvings."

"Argillite?"

"Indurated," Pat said. "Hardened sediment or clay. It undergoes pressure for long periods and becomes hard. The way diamonds are, but not as long. As rocks go, they are still quite soft."

"Is it common here? And how do you know so much?"

"While you were taking pre-law, I was taking geology," Pat said, grinning. "It's more fun. Argillite is more common around Vancouver and the northern islands than here. The storage place could be older than we can imagine."

"Why do you say that?"

"It could have been dug by people making the trek down from Alaska.

"You said big river, Granddad. Do you mean the Columbia?" Alexis asked.

"Walruses are rarely seen even there," he said. "The carving from such a tusk would have been a great treasure. It could have been from there or from further north."

The dugout could explain why she thought a few of the relics Pat had brought to her office appeared authentic. Kane, with or without others of the group, must have taken them from the dugout. There was no question in her mind about why they had kept the place secret. It would have been declared sacred by the tribes, and the gang would have been barred from it. Tribal archeologists might have been allowed here, but no one else.

Pat had stopped listening. He was examining the nearby kiln. From here, it appeared of much more recent vintage than the dugout. Constructed with some skill from pieces of the ubiquitous stone that had fallen from the sides of the mesa, it was rectangular, with evidence of fire scarring its interior and edges. It might have been used as a cooking place, or to bake clay objects, or both. If its builders had baked clay, she wondered where they had found it. The nearest clay deposits she knew of were south of Cottage Grove, miles away. She was not aware of deposits in this area, which she thought might be why archeologists more frequently found dishes and utensils carved and shaped from stone or wood.

The area boasted plenty of both materials.

Tricky scratched at another of the odd mounds in the rocky soil, this one apart from the others, closer to the bluff and more even in appearance. Tricky behaved differently, too. He scratched with more energy, at the end nearest the wall, and his hair stood on end as it had earlier, in the car. He growled and resisted when Alexis tugged him away. Hairs were standing up on her neck, and goose bumps grew on her arms.

"Granddad?"

Chases Bear frowned. "Sergeant Collins, it is time for you to call someone to support us. They will need to bring those who examine crime scenes. It is also time for us to remove ourselves from this place, quickly."

"What is it?" Pat asked, his voice higher than usual.

"The invaders of this place of spirits are returning. And the little dickens has found a mound we must explore at another time." Chases Bear helped Alexis catch Tricky and place him back in the pouch on her chest. Together, they tied him in securely. Pat picked something up from near the oven and dropped it in his pocket. He returned to the dugout, frowning, and came out a moment later, carrying a camp shovel that was of a much more recent vintage than anything she had noticed there. It had a flat, sharp blade and a short handle. He took it to the mound where Tricky had been digging. Watching, Tricky barked and tried to escape from his pouch, twisting and turning to see in Pat's direction.

Pat dug for a few minutes in the area surrounding one end of the mound, which was about six feet long, two feet wide, and perhaps a foot high at the center. Someone had covered much of it with rocks, and footprints marked the ground around it. After a bit, Pat stopped thrusting the shovel into the soil and instead, scraped gently. He turned to Alexis. "Take my radio," he said, "and go up where you can get a signal. Tell my office we need a crime scene tech, an ME, and backup. Lots of backup."

"No," Chases Bear said. "You must come. *Now*." Alexis stared at him, unable to remember ever hearing him speak to anyone in such a firm voice. She did not question him. Alexis, too, felt a powerful urgency to get away from this place. Pat glanced over his shoulder, and started to dig again.

"*Now*." Chases Bear said. He pulled Alexis toward the side of the bluff. "Patrick! Waste no more time!"

Pat looked up, tossed the shovel aside, and followed them. Tricky whined and covered his head, increasing Alexis' sense of urgency.

Together, they hurried to a location out of view of the campsite and began their climb from a different angle than the one they had used to get down, to avoid being seen by the returning campers. This climb was more arduous. Alexis found fewer hand and toe holds, more places where she need to push herself up, supporting her back against one side of the narrow crack and her feet against the other. At the top, she breathed a great sigh of relief as her grandfather helped her over the edge and they both reached to help Pat.

Her relief was cut short by the sharp zing of a gunshot echoing from the stone surrounding them.

A bright red flower bloomed on Pat's back and he lost his hold on the wall. Alexis, ignoring Tricky's squeals of protest, grabbed and clutched his uniform shirt. Chases Bear had a strong hold on his left arm. Together, they brought him close enough so she could grab his extended right wrist. Alexis cringed inside as he screamed in pain, but they pulled him over the edge and far enough from it to be invisible to most places below. Lying on his belly, Chases Bear looked through his spyglass. He tapped Alexis and pointed across the canyon, handing the glass to her. Shaking, she stretched out, keeping low, and looked. Light gleamed from something concealed in a cluster of boulders. The shooter hid across the river from them with a high-powered rifle. She scooted further back from the edge.

Chapter 25: Bushwhacker

The dead cannot cry out for justice.
It is a duty of the living to do so for them.
~Lois McMaster Bujold

Chases Bear and Alexis pulled Pat away from the edge, until they were all out of sight from a lower-level pile of boulders across the river. If they moved far enough from the edge, the shooter hiding over there would be unable to hit them. Chases Bear made a quick, cursory examination of Pat and told him to lie still.

"You will be well," he said. "Do not try to rise." His firm voice carried absolute certainty. Alexis was reminded of the doctor who had said with equal certainty that her father would die and understood how much weight such assurance carried.

Tricky whined. Alexis held him close and crept toward Pat. He was alive. He moaned in pain every few minutes. How long that might be true, she couldn't guess. She touched his neck, felt a pulse, and carefully tugged his shirt away from the wound. The bullet had struck him a little right of his spine. She looked around the mesa for Chases Bear. He was not there. Panic threatened to overwhelm her for the time it took common sense to prevail. Chases Bear would never leave anyone alone in trouble, least of all his only kin. If he was out of view, it was for a reason.

Pat lay on his side, his back toward her. Blood seeped from his wound, soaking his shirt. Edging on frantic, she cast around the bare mesa top for anything that would help, and spotted a sparse handful of wind-dried sage growing from cracks here and there. Holding onto the struggling, protesting puppy, Alexis crept to the closest bush and broke off several branches, taking care to get as many young leaves as possible. Returning to Pat's side, she reached into his jeans for the knife he had carried in his pocket since they were children, and used it to cut away his shirt. Of good quality, the knife was razor sharp, as always. She worked gently to avoid hurting him any more than necessary. Blood oozed steadily. Alexis was grateful for the growing heat of the sun that warmed him, and perhaps delayed the onset of shock.

She crushed several leafy branch tips between her palms until they were nearly dry dust. She packed it into and over the wound, pressing firmly. His breath whistled between his teeth and he moaned. She felt the sound of his pain deep in her own chest, and ached for him. Crushing more sage, she added to the dry poultice until his blood stopped seeping through it. Then, she added intact leaves. Finally, Alexis covered the sage with a square of his shirt and pressed to be sure his bleeding stopped. It eased, as had some of his pain; he had quieted. Checking Pat's pulse, she barely noticed when Tricky succeeded in wriggling out of his pouch. His heartbeat was strong enough not to frighten her. Pressing her ear against his back, she heard a faint rattle, but no whistling of air. Had the shot missed his lung? It had missed his spine, perhaps breaking a rib. If they could get him off this mountain in one piece, he would recover; she was sure of it. As she pulled away from Pat's back, a bare, brown arm reached over her shoulder, pouring some unknown liquid over the dry poultice from a canteen.

"Oh, thank God!" Alexis said, letting out a breath.

"For the capability of my granddaughter? Yes, thank the Spirits of the Grandfathers. Well done, Alexis."

"Where did you go?" she asked, and then she knew. Chases Bear reached beyond her and replaced Pat's radio in its holster. He had gone to call help. He was nude to the waist.

"How far did you have to go to get any reception?"

"Not far." For Granddad, not far could be three miles or thirty yards. She let it go. She ducked as another shot rang out, well over their heads. Pat stirred. Chases Bear spread his own shirt over Pat and tucked it in around him. Alexis wished she had brought more clothing.

"Where is your little dickens?" Granddad asked.

Alarmed, Alexis looked around. Tricky was nowhere to be seen, and she had not even missed his squirming and yipping. Had he fallen? If he had, his lifeless body would be a hundred feet or more below them. She spotted his hay string slipping toward the edge of the cliff and crab-walked toward it until she felt safe enough to stand up and grab the string. He stood on a ledge not far below the top of the bluff, the string wrapped around his feet. His attempts to free himself had drawn it across the rock behind him, and he would soon have dragged the lifeline over the edge with him. From there, wide-open space separated him from the next landing. Alexis ached for the possible loss of the adorable puppy she barely knew and already loved. She lay on her belly and reached for him. He was too far away. She tugged at the string, rolling him over in her effort to untangle it. Her action moved him closer to the edge.

Alexis looked back at her grandfather. He squatted beside Pat, hands on Pat's back beside the wounds, chanting softly. She tried whipping the hay string away from Tricky's body. Limply, it hung there. Tricky stood up and gazed up at her, whining. She saw a chance in the midst of his struggles and tugged again. The string moved up from his feet to wrap around his body. Could she pull him up, or would she succeed only in dumping him over the edge to his death? She looked back again. Her grandfather nodded in her direction: *Rescue the puppy,* he seemed to be saying, *we are fine.*

Experimentally, Alexis tugged at the string again.

Tricky turned aside and scrambled up the side of the rock like a mountain goat, up and over her as if she were part of the landscape. A loop of the string dragged behind, still wrapped around his belly, catching on stone protrusions.

"You little devil!" Alexis said, tempted to smack him. Instead, she picked him up, freed the string, and tucked him back into the pouch hanging from her neck. She scrambled back toward Chases Bear and Pat, holding Tricky tightly. The rescue had taken no more than three or four minutes, but she felt guilty for having placed the puppy's welfare over her attention to Pat. She squatted in front of him, facing her grandfather over Pat's body. Chases Bear's nude chest gleamed with Pat's blood and his own sweat. Pat opened his eyes.

"You found him," he whispered.

"I did. I'm sorry. I should have been taking care of you."

"I'm good," he whispered, and lapsed into silence, closing his eyes again.

"How do we get him down?" she asked Chases Bear.

He held a finger to his lips and then a hand behind his ear.

"*Listen*," she heard in her mind. She listened.

A motor started in the canyon. The group below was leaving. An eagle flew south, high in the sky. She felt wind in its feathers for only a fraction of a second.

She laid her hands on Pat's back and spread her thumb and first finger so that they encircled half way around the wound. Her fingertips met Granddad's, completing the circle. Chases Bear chanted in words she didn't recognize. She closed her eyes, focusing on the injury, seeing it knit together in her mind. Her fingers tingled. She breathed deep, measured breaths, in sync with the sound of Granddad's voice. The energy in her fingers expanded, traveling up her arms, and filling her body with a vibration in tune with the chant. Pat's breath steadied. She felt his body relax. Tricky gave a series of odd little sounds. Could he feel the energy singing through her body? He didn't seem afraid, only restless. Alexis felt alive in every pore, every cell. She could feel her heartbeat, energy flowing through her as if to fill her up, every part of her. Chases Bear removed his hands and the energy disappeared, taking her focus with it. She had no idea how long they had sat there. She felt alive, strong, and completely at peace.

She heard a distant whir and whack and recognized the sound of helicopter blades. She glanced around at the stony, rugged surface. How and where would they land?

Pat grasped her hand. She leaned close to hear his words. "No hospital," he said.

Chapter 26: Holy is the Earth

Where I sit is holy
Holy is the Ground
Forest, mountains, rivers
Listen to the Sound
Great Spirit circling
all around me
~ Native American Chant

Spewed from the caldera of a volcano eons ago, the surface of the bluff resembled rectangular posts upended and bundled together before being broken off at uneven heights. From the air, Alexis guessed it appeared that an irregular line of separate bundles had risen from the desert floor.

The helicopter hovered over the surface of the bluff and made no attempt to land. Instead, two uniformed men lowered a collapsible gurney on wheels and followed, in harnesses. The whirring of its blades raised a cloud of dust from the uneven surface of the bluff. Afoot, the medics grabbed the gurney and raced, bent over, toward Pat's prone body. He opened his eyes. His face visibly relaxed, and he closed them again. Chases Bear rose and stood back. Alexis cleared their path as well.

"Stay away from the edge," she warned.

"We saw him," one of them said. "He beat feet as we got here. Your grandfather warned us to watch out for him."

Careful to avoid adding to Pat's pain, one of them strung a bag of clear liquid from a folding rack attached to the gurney and pressed a needle into Pat's out flung arm. The other examined Pat with his hands, glancing up at Chases Bear with a question in his eyes.

"He has suffered only the bullet in his back," Chases Bear said.

The man, young, handsome, with long, black hair tied in a low ponytail at the back of his neck, noticed Alexis and grinned at her with even, white teeth. His brown skin, free of blemishes, complemented dark, fringed eyes. He flashed Chases Bear a warm grin.

"You always do half the work for us, don't you, old man?"

Chases Bear smiled back. "I do mine. You do yours, young warrior."

Alexis remembered that camaraderie her grandfather had shared with many members of the tribe for as long as she could remember. She had taken it for granted: everyone loved her grandfather. No surprise in that. *She* loved him. Now, however, it seemed to have taken on deeper meaning. Chases Bear was not this youth's grandfather. She watched as the pair of medics strapped a now-sedated Pat onto the gurney, hooked it up, and supervised its rise to the helicopter. Then they strapped themselves in lowered harnesses to follow him.

Another thing she remembered: when interviewing first responders in an injury case, without exception, they had reported that medics arriving on the scene had ripped off bandages or any other attempts at first aid. In their world, they trusted no one to do their work. As the chopper lifted, she thought about their own upcoming descent from the mountain.

"Oh! The keys!" Alexis cried. Chases Bear dangled Pat's car keys from his fingers.

Alexis laughed. When had she ever seen him fail to think ahead?

Tricky, restless again, clawed at the pouch strapped to her chest and wriggled. His claws scratched her through the thin fabric of her shirt. She turned to face her grandfather, feeling confused. Having gone some distance to conceal themselves from the hoodlums before scaling the wall, they stood on a section of the massive bluff far from where they had climbed up this morning. From here, she did not know the way down. Granddad beckoned her to follow and stepped over the edge. Apparently, he did know.

Relieved, Alexis followed. Worried about Pat, she lost track of time and could not begin to guess how long it took them to reach the rock-strewn foot of the wall. They made their way to sharply sloped, lower ground, covered by sage and grass instead of boulders as big as picnic tables, and turned north.

Alexis paused to release Tricky from his prison. Chases Bear gave him a piece of venison jerky to chew. The pup forced them to pause for a potty break and to pick up his jerky when he lost it, but otherwise, surprisingly, kept up with them. When they found the car and set him in first, he curled up and fell sleep before they settled themselves. Granddad surprised Alexis by taking the driver's seat and exceeding reservation speed limits until they reached populated areas.

"I didn't know you could drive," Alexis said.

"I am not moved to do so often," he answered. At his home, they found the helicopter parked in his front yard, its blades halted. The pilot and the two medics awaited them. Chases Bear parked and jumped out to open his front door, which most people knew he never locked. He returned with a mat, pillow, and blanket. The two men seemed to know what to expect. With gentle hands, they straightened Pat, now sedated, on the gurney, covered him securely, and strapped him in place. Alexis watched, puzzled. She understood his desire to avoid hospitals, but these men acted as if they were leaving him outside, rather than taking him into Granddad's home for care. They each took one end of the gurney, lifted it and carried it to a grassy common area containing a circle of stones and cut logs, where they set it down in the center of the circle. There, they removed the IV from his forearm and packed it up. Alexis had no doubt they had performed this entire process before and knew exactly what to do. Chases Bear ran inside his home and returned within minutes with a large, decorated leather bag hanging from his shoulder and a rolled mat under his arm. He beckoned Alexis to follow and ran to the circle. Chases Bear laid the soft mat on the ground beside the gurney and spread the other on top of the first.

Alexis understood his reasoning. Mother Earth imparts much healing power. The closer to the earth one is, the better for healing. Yet, her 'civilized' western half rebelled. Grass and soil instead of sterile sheets and railed beds? No computers to track pulse, blood pressure, blood gases, and who knew how many other factors? With an effort, she held her tongue.

Chases Bear, the medics, and a couple young men of the tribes gently lifted Pat from the gurney and laid him face down on the mat. A crowd was forming around the activity. Chases Bear sank down beside the mat at Pat's head and the medics left with the gurney. Moments later, Alexis heard the helicopter lift off from Granddad's yard. Tricky, free from his confinement in the car, pressed close to Alexis' ankles, shivering and emitting tiny squeals. Other people began arriving. The moccasin telegraph—news spread by word of mouth—had done its job well. Even a few visitors to Kah Nee-Ta Resort, on a hill nearby, stood along the outer edges of the circle. Alexis crossed her ankles and sank to the earth beside Pat, facing Chases Bear. He chanted:

> *Where I sit is holy*
> *Holy is the Ground*
> *Forest, mountains, rivers*
> *Listen to the Sound*
> *Great Spirit circling*
> *all around me*

Alexis had not heard the song before, and thought it came from a different tribe. Nevertheless, by the second time she heard it, she knew the words, and joined Granddad. One by one, those who had joined the circle learned the chant and sang with them. Drummers and flute players entered the circle and played to the sound of the chant. Outsiders joined their chorus. Vibrations coursed throughout her body from the sounds. A few of the singers broke loose and left, returning with bundles of smoldering sage, which they waved around the entire circle to cleanse the area.

Following Chases Bear's example, she placed her hands beside Pat's wound. Once again, she felt the profound sense of life that accompanied feather-touch heartbeats at the tips of her fingers. She closed her eyes and breathed deeply of the clean desert air, feeling the pulsating throb of music that enveloped them. That Spirit walked among them, she had not a doubt. She felt the passing of the Presence in the incredible rush of love that filled her senses. Chases Bear carefully removed the blanket and dressing from Pat's back, opening it to the warmth of the afternoon sun. Dancers rose from their places and began a gentle, swaying movement to the rhythm of the chant they still repeated.

Chases Bear unrolled a packet he took from the leather bag carried over his shoulder. From it, he withdrew a sealed packet, opened it, and laid out a neat row of surgical tools. He removed a pint jar of liquid from his bag, opened it, set it down, and dug in his bag for a paintbrush, its end wrapped and sealed in some sort of wrap backed by plastic. Alexis jaw dropped. With not less than a hundred or so witnesses, the native medicine man was about to perform surgery. She watched, keeping quiet, praying no one in the audience knew or better yet, cared, that a surgical procedure performed without a medical license on a reservation violated federal law, and therefore left him open to prosecution in the event that Pat's condition took a turn for the worse. In fact, as an officer of the court, she had an obligation to arrest her grandfather for this offense. She considered leaving, but could not. She could not even remove her hands from their position on Pat's back. He stirred. Alexis realized she had lost her focus on prayers for Patrick's well-being. She centered herself again. Chases Bear poured the liquid over his hands, rubbed them together, and waved to air dry them, before removing the sage poultice that had so far protected Pat's wound. Chases Bear used the brush, which looked soft, to paint Pat's entire back with the liquid. Pat shivered until it warmed. Alexis caught scents of tea tree oil, lavender, cinnamon and cloves, and perhaps a little alcohol. Her grandfather poured more of the strong-scented preparation on her hands. Now, she was not only witnessing a crime, she was participating. She thought it unlikely Pat would arrest her when he woke. A couple of uniformed officers had joined the crowd and now pushed them back, clearing a wide space between the patient and the singers.

Tricky, Alexis noted, had disappeared. Chases Bear opened two packets containing sterile bandage squares and handed several to Alexis. The rest, he put within reach of both of them.

At last ready, he chose one of the instruments, a curved scalpel, stood it point down in the sterilizing liquid, waited a few minutes, and withdrew it. With it, he scored a vertical line on Pat's back that crossed the center of the wound, then scored another that crossed the first in the exact center. He wiped the tool on an antibacterial wipe and dropped it back into the solution. Then he chose a tool that vaguely resembled a garlic crusher, sterilized it, and spread the wound gently. Alexis placed her fingers on the other side and spread the ragged edges, too. The bullet gleamed in sunlight an inch or so below the surface of Pat's well-muscled back. He did not stir. Chases Bear removed the bullet and dropped it on one of the bandages. He beckoned toward a tribal cop and pointed at the projectile. The officer bagged and marked it and carried it away, thus preserving the evidence, not only of the shooting, but of the crime of unlicensed surgery as well. Alexis felt herself ready to explode with inappropriate laughter and controlled herself with difficulty. She cleansed her hands again, and used bandage squares to wipe away blood that now seeped faster than before. Chases Bear took a few of the squares and applied pressure directly to the wound. When the bleeding slowed, he sterilized a curved needle and waxed thread and stitched the wound from inside out. Still sedated, Pat slept throughout the procedure. Around them, people brought flashlights and torches to light his work as the sun drifted toward the horizon. Singers and dancers continued their performance.

Someone brought beer and the dancers, still keeping a safe distance from the patient, imbibed and danced with even more energy. Pat slept through it all.

Alexis, feeling the strain of muscles long in one position, longed for a drink, and grinned gratefully at the young, handsome medic who had swapped his uniform for casual dress. He handed her an ice-cold beer and slipped away among the singers and dancers. Later, she saw him beating a drum. Chases Bear grinned at her over Pat's still form, his white teeth gleaming in gathering dusk.

"He will walk in beauty again."

Alexis could feel Pat's heartbeat under her fingers and knew he would recover. Her entire being felt full of the joy of life, both hers and his. She smiled back at her grandfather. Discussion about his illegal activities—practicing surgery and driving too fast without a license—could wait for a private moment.

As if he read her mind, he burst into laughter. When he had tied off the final stitch, he packed the wound with a dry, powdered substance from another container. Alexis caught the scent of sage, and others she was too tired to recognize. Her

271

grandfather gave her tape and more gauze. Someone handed him a beer. He rose to join the dancers. A crowd of onlookers clapped and cheered. Some clapped him on the back. Alexis set her drink down and bandaged the wound with gauze squares and white tape.

Chases Bear did not eschew all things white in medicine.

Chapter 27: Miracles

Believe in miracles
and cures and healing wells.
~ Seamus Heaney

The sun had long since set before the music stopped, the dancers slipped away, and spectators returned to their gambling and their sumptuous hotel rooms at the casino. Some went away to talk, eat and drink, others to call it a night and listen to whatever sounds continued to fill the air on the Rez, and some to catch a few hours of sleep before morning.

With only one beer and a stick of jerky from Granddad's ample store in her belly, Alexis helped settle Pat in her grandfather's spare bedroom and drove home to check on their other patient. Tomorrow, they could discuss what needed to be done about what might—or might not—be a sacred place on the reservation. Tonight, all she wanted was real food and lots of sleep. She prayed her father rested as peacefully as Pat tonight.

The night felt cool for a change, once she had left the adrenalin and frenzied activity of the dance behind. She rolled down the car window and smelled clean, fresh air, brushing her cheeks with a soft, sensuous touch. Her entire body tingled with the activity of the evening, keeping her wide awake until she stopped in the ranch's circular drive, stepped out and let Tricky jump to the ground. Jerry materialized out of the shadows on the porch, startling her.

"Glad you're home, Miss. We were getting worried."

"We?"

"Me 'n' Jim." He nodded to indicate something behind her. Jim Fraser, one of the hands, gave her a careless salute to his hat brim.

"Yes, Ma'am. We was wondering if we should maybe send someone looking for you. Then Jerry called a cop on the Rez and he told us you was at a medicine way for one of the cops. He gonna be all right? We heard he got shot, and you and your grand pop come into town with him in a helicopter."

"Heard your granddad was driving a car," Jerry added with a laugh. "That I'd like to have seen."

"Not if you were in his way," Alexis answered, sharing his laugh as she went in the house with Tricky at her heels.

Inside, she kicked off her dirty shoes, picked them up, and stopped to look into the den. Her father's covers lay thrown back, his dented place in the white sheets empty. She felt her heart pound as she scanned the room, well lit by moonlight from the windows. She stepped back out on the porch to speak to the guards.

"Has everything been quiet here tonight?"

The two men looked at each other as if debating whether to tell her something or not.

"More or less," Jerry answered. "There was some little bit of movement up on the hill overlooking Mr. Bishop's den, but my Dink started barking, and whoever it was took off in a hurry."

Alexis felt goose bumps on her arms. "How do you know that?"

"Once he started running with Dink on his heels, he didn't worry none about making noise or being seen. He just skedaddled," Jim said.

"Good. Where's your dog now, Jerry?"

"Aw, he'll be back pretty soon. Don't know how far he chased the guy. But you can bet the fellow kept flying until he got where he was going."

Worried, Alexis stepped back inside the house. This time, her father stood at the newly installed window, looking up the hill. He chuckled. Tricky sniffed around the entire room, as if checking everywhere Grant had walked.

"Dink must have liked the taste of Dark Moon Kane's flying feet," he said without turning around.

She relaxed. "I'm glad Dink and the men were here. Windows like that one are hard to find. How do you know it was Kane?"

"Do you know anyone else with that long black hair that flies out behind him?"

Alexis shivered.

"Should have the other window cleaned," Grant went on. "In daylight it looks dingy by comparison." He turned to face her. "Four o'clock in the morning?"

"Our friend out there shot Pat in the back this afternoon—yesterday, now. He wouldn't go to the hospital, and Granddad held a Healing Ceremony for him. I stayed to take part in it."

Grant grunted. "So why did I have to fight you tooth and nail to get away from the hospital?"

"Pat wanted his personal physician from the start. You required a little brow-beating."

He ignored the jibe. "How badly was he hurt?"

"He took a rifle bullet in the middle of his back, an inch from his spine. Badly enough."

"Are you sure a healing is the best way? That sounds serious."

"It is. And we could lose him yet. He was resting and free of pain when I left."

"With your grandfather?"

"And Chili. She's spending the night to tend them both. Granddad had a long day. He wants to be fresh if he's needed tomorrow."

"You're up pretty late, yourself. Go to bed. I'm fine. If I need anyone, I'll call Mary." He came away from the window, walking without apparent difficulty, and embraced her. She could feel his bones through his shirt.

"Dad! You are dressed! You are up at four o'clock in the morning!"

"A little slow at this wee hour, aren't you? Since you didn't ask, I feel fine, at least for the moment. You had a phone call while you were off gallivanting around."

Alexis shrugged. "If it's important, he or she will call back. I'm more interested in how long you've been up."

"He will call back. He sounded irritated that you weren't here. He said his name is Terry."

"He'll call. How long have you been up?"

"Since he called from Bend, around eight in the evening. He sounded possessive, so I got curious and invited him out."

"You didn't!"

"I did. He arrived a little after nine and wanted to know all about what you've been doing. He seemed to expect me to be ready for embalming and burial. Apparently, you didn't tell him about your grandfather's wizardry."

"Did you?"

"No. We discussed the law and his career. We even talked a little about yours. He seemed as curious as I was. How long have you been seeing each other?"

"I told you, Dad—a long time ago. We live together. For about a year."

"You don't seem eager to see him again."

She turned her back on him. "No. Not very. I haven't taken time to miss him."

"Then dump him. If you can be away from him for months, and feel nothing, he's the wrong one."

"You're right, Dad. When I left here, I missed Patrick, and we had no commitments. If I don't even miss Terry when we've been living under the same roof, something's out of kilter."

He drew a deep breath, hesitating. "Have you made a decision I should know about?"

"Several. And if you've been up for eight hours and impressing Terry, it's time you went back to bed, which is where I'm going, right now."

"You're erstwhile—uh—friend—will be here for lunch at one. Wade will manage the office."

"Oh, hell. You invited him back? Thanks for the heads up. I have a cell phone."

"Which, according to Mr. Wells, you neglect to answer. Which may be why he's irritated."

"Yes, all right. I've no one to blame but myself. But I'd have chosen to see him alone, for the first time in months. Good night, Dad. I'll see you in a few hours. Get some sleep."

Passing Mary on the way, Alexis dragged her tired feet upstairs. She had been up 22 hours, climbed a mountain—twice, chanted, and danced for hours after the ceremony.

"Is he still up? I heard voices," Mary asked.

"Yes. Go hit him over the head, or something, so he'll go back to bed."

"You get yourself to bed. You'll be busy by noon."

"I know. Good night, Mary."

"And don't forget your dog. He's liable to keep your father awake."

Alexis whistled and Tricky came running, falling over his own feet in his haste to catch up.

Since Kane had come and gone and probably guessed they were posting guards, Alexis didn't bother covering the windows. She showered quickly, stood for a moment looking out at clear, dark sky dotted with bright stars. She was asleep within seconds after snuggling into her pillow with her gun nearby in the night stand, the murmur of Mary's and Dad's voices dying away. Her last thought was of Pat sleeping in Granddad's spare bedroom, fighting to stay alive.

She'd completely forgotten about being hungry.

Chapter 28: City Visitor

It is in your moments of decision
That your destiny is shaped.
~Tony Robbins

Alexis woke as high desert sunlight flooded through windows and warmed her room to the point of discomfort, even with her bedding on the floor beside the bed.

She groaned, recalling that Terry would be there for lunch. He had sounded irritated, according to Dad. Alexis knew that, for Terry, irritated was controlled anger, often as not moving toward a full-blown tantrum. She had never been treated to his temper, directed toward her, perhaps because she knew how to talk him out of it, distract him, or give him an alternative view of whatever made him angry. That ability to sense what the other party wanted and work with it was what made her good at her job; it was possibly the only true people talent in her arsenal. Otherwise, she counted on straightforward honesty and solid knowledge of the subject at hand. It was the reason she got along with John Stockman. A roughhewn, blunt man, he liked to know where he stood with others, good or bad. She had always been straight with him.

It wasn't a characteristic Terry appreciated. He had spent a lot of time at work telling her to "keep her own counsel, unless what she said accomplished a purpose."

Musing over how well she knew or didn't know Terry Wells was an exercise in futility. She shook it off and surveyed her closet, considering the impression she wanted to make: definitely not sexy; not too casual; not too professional. Rejecting outfit after outfit, she finally settled on a straight khaki skirt with a sleeveless white silk shirt and sandals. Simple, straightforward, casual. Still, she hadn't entirely avoided sexy. Her red-brown skin looked its best against virgin white, as did her chocolate hair with its streaks of gold, which she caught up in a ponytail. No makeup. Let her brown eyes stand on their own. She settled for a little concealer to cover the lack-of-sleep shadows under her eyes and turned her back on the image in the mirror, no longer sure whom she wanted to see there.

Whistling to get Tricky's attention, she giggled when he rolled down as many stairs as he walked, following at her feet. From the foyer, she led him outdoors.

Jerry sat by the door, his long, thin, booted legs stretched out in front of the chair.

"How long have you been here?" Alexis asked him.

"Since sundown," he answered, trying to stifle a yawn. "I'll have David Henry and Baker here in a few to take the day shift." Baker was barely out of his teens and David almost as wide as he was tall, though he managed to work as hard as the next guy. Jerry hadn't found many horses David could ride, so his work was primarily confined to repairs, walking fence lines, and barn cleaning. Neither would have been Alexis' first choice for a bodyguard, but choices were limited, and they were less likely to be bothered during daylight hours in any case.

"See if you can pick up a few more capable hands, Jerry. We'll be needing them for roundup anyway. They might as well get an early start. We'll want range horses and men who can ride. And keep two guards on at night until further notice. Dark Moon Kane broke in and I saw him shoot Sgt. Collins."

Jerry whistled, sat up, opened his mouth to speak, and seemed to think better of it. His eyes glittered and his mouth became a straight, firm line across his jaw. His eyebrows knit together.

A pointed snout poked up over the edge of the porch and two dark eyes sought Jerry, who noticed immediately.

"About time you got your butt back here, Dink. Where the hell have you been all night?"

"He's been gone since I came back? That's over three hours."

"Yeah. He's a hard-headed mutt. Doesn't give up easily. Count on that being one of your Tricky's faults."

"When is a heeler not persistent?"

The question was rhetorical, and he ignored it with a grin.

"How many men is a few, Miss?"

"Let's call it four, Jerry. You can tell them through October, at least."

"Yes, Ma'am. I got enough work around here for all that, and more."

The puppy finished his business and appeared at Alexis' feet, begging.

"He's hungry. Wait here a few and I'll feed them both." She brought food and water from inside, and set it out for the two cow dogs. Tricky tried to sneak a bite from his sire and earned a growled reprimand.

When the pair had finished eating, Alexis told Jerry she'd be at the rez for a few hours and whistled for Tricky.

Jerry nodded. "Kane be there?"

"Not likely, but if he is, I'll be among people." She would be safe from the devil himself on the Rez among people who loved her grandfather.

The puppy scrambled into the car floor and Alexis lifted him to the seat and hooked a leash to his harness. He lay down, his belly full and bladder empty, and went back to sleep. Alexis chuckled. He was already beginning to lose the clean, white fur between black spots as dark hairs grew in among them. Before long, he would look as blue as the breed name dictated. White hairs would not encroach among ebony spots. He would keep his black patches, including the bandit mask around both eyes.

The drive to the rez seemed long today, worried as she was about Pat. This time, she waited outside her grandfather's house to be invited in, as was the custom. Her grandfather would forgive her the past oversights, but now he had guests. She wondered if Chili was still there and as the thought struck her, Chili opened the door and waved her inside. Fresh coffee and breakfast burritos awaited her. She sat at the table with Chili, to eat and wait for Granddad.

Chili's normally sparkling eyes looked serious and tired.

"It is good to see you, Chili."

"And you as well, my friend. I have missed your adventurous spirit leading me into trouble."

"How does one get into adventures with three boys under ten on her heels?"

Chili laughed. "Carefully, if at all."

Alexis sobered. "How was his night?"

"He had some pain, but Chases Bear stayed on top of that to the best of his ability."

"Granddad's ability is impressive."

"It is. Patrick did not suffer greatly, and he slept. I expect him to awake hungry. I have quail broth cooking and eggs to soft cook in the broth, sieved huckleberries with cream. Your grandfather's instructions."

"Eggs and cream for an injured person?" Alexis asked, forking a bite of a perfect egg and sausage burrito with guacamole sauce into her mouth.

"According to Chases Bear, garlic, salicylic acid, omega 6 and CLA. Do not ask me the purpose or meaning of any of them. Ask him. He added crushed garlic and clove oil to the sage poultice."

"No wonder it smells like a culinary school in here." She sipped hot, fresh coffee and wondered why Chili's always tasted better than any she found elsewhere, no matter who made it.

Chili nodded ruefully. "The stronger the house smells, the happier he is. It always smells of herbs and plants, but the last time it was this powerful was when David Decker sliced the length of his arm with a fileting knife."

"Did it work?" Alexis asked.

"He barely has a scar."

"Did Granddad operate on him?"

"Of course. Who else would he have?"

"Chili . . . You don't mention things like this outside the reservation, do you?"

Chili burst into laughter. "Alexis Lee Bishop, is it possible you do not know everything about your grandfather?"

"What do you mean?"

"Maybe he wouldn't want me to tell you."

"Oh, don't you dare say that just to tease. What do you know that I don't?"

"Well, you already know that Chases Bear was a medic in Viet Nam, of course."

"Yes, he spoke about that long ago."

"Turn around and look on the wall behind you."

Alexis turned. A framed document hung there. Why had she never seen that before?

"It wasn't here before you left us for the big city," her grandfather answered her unspoken question.

"Oregon Health and Sciences University Medical School," she read aloud. "Doctorate Degree in Medicine, General Practice. Granddad! When did you do that?" The school was a little over fifty miles away across the rez, in Portland. She knew he had graduated from Oregon State after four years in the Army. She had not known about this.

"I believe it is dated," he said.

"A dozen years ago! I was still in college. How did you keep a thing like that a secret? More important, *why* did you keep it a secret?"

"I keep no secrets, daughter of my daughter. A man allows others to learn his value. He does not act the crow. You have never asked if I attended medical school."

"Why would I? You were already the finest medicine man I knew."

"I did," Chili said. "But I was here on the rez all that time, watching him go away for weeks and even months at a time. So I asked. He didn't go away in the summer when you were still here."

"And you never thought to mention the fact to me."

"I thought, but I mostly thought you already knew," Chili said.

"And, though you deemed me so capable, you feared that I might be arrested for caring for our friend, Patrick. He is asking for you."

Alexis jumped up. "Granddad, you couldn't lead with that?"

Chases Bear smiled. "I thought it best you wait until he was out of the bathroom, in bed, and decently covered."

Chili laughed. "Aunt Gail is with him."

Alexis was already on her way to the spare bedroom.

Pat leaned against a stack of pillows, looking quite relaxed, but out of breath. The bathroom run must have taxed him. She leaned over his bed and kissed his forehead. He took her hand. Chili's aunt slipped away.

"Doesn't it hurt to lean on your back?" she asked.

"No. The soft pressure seems to help. And your grandfather takes care of my pain."

She wrinkled her nose. "I can tell."

"I can't smell it, any more. The scent grows on you after a while."

"I know. How are you, really?"

"I'm good. I'll be up and around in no time."

"I don't doubt that. But let Granddad say when, please." She pulled a chair closer and sat down, without letting go of his hand. She leaned in and kissed him again, this time full on the lips. He responded, his mouth warm and soft against hers. His touch made her consider how close she had come to losing him. And how she didn't look forward to seeing Terry.

When she sat back, he said, "Chili tells me the council has ordered all entrances to Trout Creek closed and guarded. The US Forest Service has closed the other end to the public until further notice."

"Will they spare guards to watch it?"

"No. They chained the road in and locked it. Patrols will check to make sure the chain's intact. Elders are talking about whether to let University of Oregon Archeology in to examine the dugout. There's talk of dating some pieces before making any decisions."

"That makes sense. How important it is depends on how old it is."

He fell silent and closed his eyes.

She kissed him. "Rest. All that can wait for you to get well." She sat holding his hand for as long as she guessed she could, if she meant to greet Terry on his arrival and not leave him at her father's mercy. Maybe she should. That would be one way to be rid of him.

Maybe she'd be lucky and her father would sleep through the entire visit.

Chapter 29: Enough is Enough

Breaking up is the hardest thing we do.
It's the most important thing we do, in a way.
You've got to embrace rejection,
or you'll maintain a very limited life.
~Laurie Helgoe

The rental vehicle parked in the driveway was a dead giveaway. A compact Toyota, it wouldn't have set Terry back more than $40 a day, if that. He didn't rent a car to impress anyone, he rented it to get where he was going. He wouldn't have seen a need to impress a small town lawyer from an obscure and distant state that was on his personal horizon for only two reasons: Alexis was here; and the Oregon Ducks came from here. An avid football fan, he always followed the good teams, wherever they originated.

She parked beside the rental. Tricky sat up and yipped expectantly when the car stopped.

"Heel," she said, stepping out. The pup attached himself to her ankles. She had no illusions that he knew or understood the command yet. He was young enough to harbor some timidity, and David Baker, a stranger, had walked out of the cool shade of the porch.

"Hello, David. Everything okay?"

"Far as I know, Miss. Your dad appeared to know the driver of that car. He let him in."

So much for Dad sleeping through lunch.

Alexis nodded. "I know. We were expecting him. Thanks." David opened the door for her. Tricky growled. They both laughed.

"'Thinks he's tough, doesn't he?" she said.

"He will be, one of these days. Have a good day, Miss."

"You, too, David.

Inside, she followed voices from the den. Her father stood silhouetted against the light at the new window, facing a tall, shadowed figure who could only be Terry Wells. As her eyes adjusted, she saw that they both held Old Fashioned glasses, and a bottle of Dad's good whiskey stood open on the secretary beside his desk. The hospital bed and all its accoutrements were nowhere to be seen. Her heart took a joyous leap, giving her smile more welcome that it might otherwise have had. If the bed was gone, it would not be back, regardless of his motives for banishing it from the room.

"Dad! You look great today!" She approached him, arms out.

Terry stepped into her embrace and held her. "You look like you've spent a week in the tropics," he said. "All this open air and sunshine must be good for you."

Alexis looked over his shoulder at her father and grinned. His color looked strong, his eyes bright, and she knew full well it had nothing to do with the whiskey. "Lunch is ready," Mary announced from the door of the den. Alexis wrestled out of Terry's embrace and thanked her. She took a moment to hug her father and held his hand on their way to the dining room. "Stay, Tricky," she said to her pup, closing the door behind them. Tricky whined once and was silent.

"How is Patrick Collins?" Grant asked as they arrived in the dining room.

"He will survive his injury, thanks to Granddad."

The table looked set for a king. A bouquet of their own flowers in a glittering, multi-colored vase graced the center. There was no casual stoneware here; fine china marked their places, with folded linen napkins on each plate. Alexis restrained the urge to giggle and held her father's chair at the head of the table. Mary had prepared the room as if for a state dinner. Terry unsuccessfully masked a look of surprise and puzzlement as he glanced at Alexis and held her seat at Grant's left before taking the chair facing her. Mary brought a tureen of soup and set it within everyone's reach. Alexis caught a scent similar to the odor of Chili's quail broth and smiled to herself, wondering if Granddad had prescribed both Pat's and Grant's meals. Wondering who had hunted quail recently. Floating in the broth were strings and flakes of egg, like Chinese egg flower soup, baby red potatoes, onions, and minced garlic. Alexis decided not to mention that the eggs were probably quail. Mary set a plate of garden salad beside each of them, full of fresh vegetables. She left them fresh sourdough rolls in a basket.

She wondered if anyone else felt the unbearable level of tension in the room. Both men were adept at concealing emotions. It was the nature of their occupation. Of hers, as well, of course. So, did she appear as poised as they did? She dropped her fork and blushed. Mary was immediately beside her with another. Alexis listened to the men.

Alexis poured tall glasses of milk for herself and her father and offered one to Terry. He declined, reminding Alexis of his long ago, firm statement that there is no reason for an adult human to drink milk.

She wondered if anyone else felt the unbearable level of tension in the room. Both men were adept at concealing emotions. It was the nature of their occupation. Of hers, as well, of course. So, did she appear as poised as they did? She dropped her fork and blushed. Mary was immediately beside her with another. Alexis listened to the men.

"The food is superb," Terry said. "Alexis, I think you should poach your Dad's cook and take her back to Washington."

"Over Mary's dead body and mine," Grant said.

"Well, I can't say I blame you."

"We're not so uncivilized we don't know a good thing when we see it," Grant answered, smiling at Mary.

"How long have you lived on the ranch, Mr. Bishop?"

"Call me Grant, please. I was born here."

"Ah," he said, as if that explained something. "Is it really half the state, or does it just look that way, getting here?"

"It isn't as big as several other ranches in the state," Alexis answered.

"And were you born here, too?" he asked.

"No. I was born on the reservation. Mom was under my grandfather's care."

"Oh, is he a doctor?"

She opened her mouth to answer, having decided it was as good a time as any.

"Yes," Grant interrupted, "He's the best man of medicine in the state, bar none."

Alexis gasped. Dad's eyes twinkled at her.

"How lucky you are to have such a person in a rural area."

"It's not as if we're on the moon," Grant answered mildly. "Oregon Health and Sciences University in Portland is just over a hundred miles from here. It's world famous."

"So it is. I recall hearing about it," Terry answered. "You really aren't far from civilization at all, are you?"

Alexis counted off cities on her fingers. "Redmond, Bend, Madras, La Pine, Salem, Eugene, Sisters. Warm Springs."

"Sisters. I think I passed through there. It's kind of a quaint little town, isn't it?"

"You should see it in winter, under four feet of snow."

"Snow? I thought this was desert country."

"High desert," Grant answered. "Mary, may we have some coffee?"

Alexis frowned. Grant ignored her. Mary brought cups and fresh coffee for them all.

"Why don't we retire to the den with our coffee?" Grant asked.

When they were seated on more comfortable chairs, facing the windows, Alexis responded to Terry's comment. "We're at about 3,100 feet above sea level and surrounded by mountains. Sisters is higher, but it snows on occasion here, too. And gets very cold in winter." Tricky demanded to be lifted into her lap and curled up there.

"But not today. It must be past ninety outside now," he answered. "I don't hear any air conditioners here. How does it stay so cool?"

"The original house is built of stone," Grant said. "The walls are a foot thick. One of my ancestors tired of stone and covered it up with siding. I went one further and used Hardieplank a few years back. It's concrete and wood fiber. It should last the life of the house."

"So you don't need air?"

"Oh, it's here. It's just very quiet. And sparsely used."

"Alexis, I expected to find you at your father's bedside and he ready to leave this world. Where are you spending your time?"

Grant, his voice slightly edgy, answered for her. "She's been at my bedside more than I needed or wanted most of the time. The rest of her time, she keeps this place and my business office running smoothly."

"Or I'm on the rez, with my grandfather."

"Is that where you were this morning?"

"And yesterday, during which time, a police officer who has been my friend from childhood, was shot and seriously injured."

"Is that the Patrick Collins your father mentioned? How did that happen?"

"The three of us were climbing back up Indian Creek bluff after examining a campsite that appears to have been occupied by someone raiding an archeological site of possible cultural importance. Patrick was last to climb over the top of the when someone shot him in the back with a high-powered rifle."

"It sounds as if I need a little updating, too, young lady," Grant said. "I didn't hear that you were in danger."

"I'm unscarred, and so is Granddad. We did a healing for Patrick. The drummers came, and everyone danced. Granddad applied his miraculous hands and herbs through the night, with Chili's help. And Pat was sitting up this morning. He was resting when I left. Gail Wenway was there by then."

"A Healing! Is that what I think it is?" Terry asked.

"Highly doubtful," she answered, "but it is a Native American ceremony, complete with medicine man, drummers and dancers."

"I've never seen one of those. Were they all in feathers and moccasins?"

"Most of us wore jeans or shorts, and yes, moccasins, the most efficient footwear for such an occasion. There might have been a few feathers. It was a bit impromptu, so we weren't much concerned about costumes. All that mattered was praying our friend well."

"Us? You took part in this?" Terry had an odd look on his face, appearing made up of interest, slight distaste, and surprise. If Alexis had not made her decision about Terry long before, this moment

294

would have made it up for her. She excused herself, went to the kitchen and opened a bottle of Willamette Valley White Zinfandel wine, her favorite, taking it and three glasses back to the den, where Grant demurred, asking for whiskey instead. Tricky protested. He wanted her to present her lap for his comfort again. Terry tasted the wine with a look of approval, and she poured a full glass for herself.

"Does this . . . ceremony . . . actually accomplish anything?" Terry asked.

"Ask my father."

Grant answered. "You expected to see me wasting away on my deathbed, suffering through my last days? Just a few weeks ago, you'd have seen just that. Today, I am in no pain, feeling my energy returning, and awaiting the results of new tests. My doctor in town is amazed at my remission, but making no judgments yet. My doctor on the res. Says I will live to pester him forever."

Terry's smile seemed a little condescending, but he made no comment. Alexis decided she would not waste very good wine by throwing it in his face. The thought was tempting. She wondered when he was leaving.

Grant finished his whiskey, found a cane, and called Mary to walk with him to his bedroom. Mary grinned at him. He had not been in his own bedroom in many weeks. It had been months since he had climbed the stairs, with or without assistance. Clearly, her face said, he would live.

"A word?" Terry asked Alexis, as Mary and Grant left the room.

She took her attention away from her father and the strong evidence that he had beaten his disease. "Let's go outside," she answered lightly. Even Terry could not ruin her happiness at this moment.

"They won't be back down, will they?"

"I imagine Mary will. I've never known her to retire while dirty glasses sit on the furniture."

"Is she your mother?"

"I told you my mother died when I was twelve."

"Stepmother, then."

"Outside," Alexis said. She had a strong feeling that he would say something hurtful about Mary and didn't intend to stay where they might be overheard.

On the porch, she led him to the far end, away from Jerry's two new hires, nodding at them as she passed. The day guards had retired for the night.

"Who are they?" Terry asked.

"I don't know yet. Our foreman hired them today." She took a seat in one of the wrought iron garden chairs and indicated another for him putting a table between them. She was past wondering what she had ever seen in him, and was on to how best to get rid of him.

"And you let them hang out on the front porch? How do you know you can trust them?" He sat down facing her.

"I trust them because our foreman does."

"Is he Indian, too?"

"How is that relevant?"

"I just think you might want to be careful who spends time on your porch when people are shooting at each other."

"They are my people," she said very softly.

"I got to that, all on my own," he answered. "You might have shared it before now."

"Yes, I begin to see it would have been a good thing to do." Their affair would have ended before it began. It was over now. As if he read her mind, Terry switched gears.

"You're not coming back, are you?"

"Is that just a touch of relief I hear in your tone?"

"Alexis, don't be an ass." His tone had become harsh, grating, and angry. "Everything we planned, everything we meant to each other, and you'd just throw it all away for this— this wilderness. Your world-class education, your career, *our* careers. For this uncivilized pile of sagebrush and rocks!"

"My career has nothing to do with yours, Terry. My *life* has nothing to do with *you*. I don't even know who you are any more.*"*

"You know exactly who I am. I never kept any big secrets. I told you where I came from, how I got where I am, *everything*. You didn't even tell me your race, for God's sake! Who is the guy who got shot, the one you spent all night and all morning with before I got here? Your new boyfriend? What is he, some uneducated savage you met on this reservation you talk about?"

"That's enough!"

"Not by half, it isn't. Answer the question. Who is he?"

"I don't owe you answers. And I don't answer on command. But he is my friend since childhood, who worked his way through college, working right here on this ranch. He's a police officer, an honest and hard-working man I *respect*."

"Respect? Is that what you call it?"

297

"I have been faithful to you, which I suspect is more than you can say. Give me your keys. I'll have your car brought around." Apparently, the hands had taken it to the garage. It wasn't here anymore.

"Are you all right, Miss Bishop?"

"Yes. What's your name?"

"I am Tony."

"Yes, Tony, I'm fine. Thank you."

"You sure? Cougar went to get his car already, Miss. Does he need any help getting off the place?" Tony's tone of voice made the terms of the offer clear. No one would threaten his employer.

"No, thank you. He got here. He can get away from here."

"Away where? Where am I going in this godforsaken desert?"

"The modern cities of Redmond and Bend are south. The rez and all its savages are north, so be sure you turn the right direction, or I can't speak for your safety. They are liable to bury you up to your neck in an ant hill or strap you to a wagon wheel and let you fry in the sun. Of course, if you get by the wild Indians, the metropolitan city of Portland is northwest of the rez. They have airplanes and everything—not to mention world class schools, hospitals, and attorneys and the Portland Trail Blazers."

"All right. I deserve the sarcasm. But if you'd told me ahead of time, I wouldn't have been caught by surprise."

"All three cities have first class hotels where you can spend the night. Just mention that you are a guest of the Bishops and they will send us the bill. I'll authorize it. Just let me know which one. And I am glad you were caught by surprise. I have never known you so well."

She brushed past her guards and marched toward the door, seething, wishing she could hit him.

"Alexis! That's unfair!"

She spun to face him. "Unfair! Unfair? Who are you to call me unfair? You are exactly the bigoted sort of ass who confined our People to reservations, took our children to boarding schools to strip them of their identity, and stole our culture. Get off this place and do not ever return. I *never* want to see you again."

"I don't give up that easily, Alexis. We'll discuss this when you come to your senses and get back to Washington." He stomped off the porch, keeping an eye on Tony and the other Indian.

"Well, do me a favor," she snapped. "Hold your breath!"

Chapter 30: Gone Guy

The Spirit Keeper of the East Wind is Wabun or Eagle.
Wabun shows us power through illumination and wisdom.
~Native American Wisdom

From her open window upstairs, Alexis heard gravel spray as Terry Wells spun tires on his way out of her life. Forever, she hoped. What had she seen in him? How could she have thought they had anything in common? They both loved their work, did it well, and shared certain career ambitions. Had shared. Nothing seemed to draw her back to the city and the hustle and bustle of people passing through the offices in which she had worked, like passengers on a train with no destination. She still loved the practice of law, but it was her father's kind of law she wanted in her life, not the assembly lines of people processing through the system as it was done in the city's justice system, and probably in every other big city in the world. Portland? She had an opportunity to find out if she wanted to accept what Mark offered.

Alexis slept restlessly that night, knowing she had burned at least one bridge in her life. Whatever Terry told others, she would not be eligible for rehire after taking off without warning and failing to give notice when the DA was running for reelection and needed all hands. She'd be lucky if her boss didn't blackball her throughout the city. He certainly had contacts and power enough to do it. He wasn't known as the most generous

300

and forgiving of souls, either, a fact that possibly came with his job of prosecuting felons.

Being blackballed in Washington was less than the most worrisome of her quandaries tonight. What did she want to tell John Stockton? Did she want to be her father's partner or join one of the most prestigious legal offices in the state? Did he even want her as a partner, now that she had hired two more attorneys, with John's business in mind? And what about John? She'd kept him hanging for weeks. Had he given up waiting for her to come around and accept his business? Did she want to be a small cog in a large machine in Portland? She knew she would practice more people-contact law in Dad's office than she ever would in Portland or Washington. She also knew that partnership in the larger firm promised more opportunity for both money and prestige. At her age, it was a stepping-stone to wherever she wanted to go—even politics if she ever considered that route.

"Sleep on it," her grandfather's voice said in her head. "The answers will await you upon awakening.

By morning, her bed looked as if it had hosted a wrestling match. Covers piled up in the middle, and her every extremity stuck out. Glad it was still summer, Alexis showered and dressed quickly, choosing a cream linen suit, heeled sandals and an olive silk shirt that complemented her eyes and hair. Two minutes to apply lipstick and blush; another two to draw her hair into a twist and tease loose a few curls and she was ready to face the professional world. Her grandfather, as always, was right, whether he was in her head or in her memory, tapped in the twilight between sleep and awake. Her psyche had fought a hard battle to reach decisions if the condition of the bed was any indication. But reach them, she had.

Alexis was eager to see how her father's night had gone. He had moved around more in one evening than in the prior six weeks. Climbing stairs, even on Mary's strong arm, was an amazing accomplishment when she remembered the weak, pale man, determined to die, who had come with her from the coast. She wondered how much being home had contributed to his apparent recovery. Being here made *her* feel alive.

He had beaten her to the breakfast table, fully dressed in slacks, a short sleeved shirt, and dark shoes. A sport jacket hung over the back of his chair. She stepped over his extended legs to reach the coffee pot, kissed his cheek and sat around the corner from him.

He looked her over approvingly. "What are you all dolled up for? You look like you're going to court in the big city."

Rather than answer his question, she gave him a once-over glance. "You're looking pretty good for an old dog, too. All we need is to get Mary to fatten you up a bit and you'll be chasing girls like a young dog."

"My days of girl chasing are long gone. But I'll admit to needing a little fattening. It took half an hour to find a pair of pants that didn't fall off, and I think they are older than you are."

"Why are *you* all dressed up?"

"I asked you first."

"So you did. I'm meeting with John Stockman with an outline of what I think four attorneys can handle of his business, and to refer him to other firms for the rest. Then I'll drop by the offices of Reinhardt, et al, and inform them of my decision not to partner with them, nor to bring John's business there."

"What brought you to that wise decision?"

"I am neither John's protégé nor his mistress and I have no desire to be seen as such. Your turn."

"I was rather hoping that I could hitch a ride to work with you today. Oh, and make that five attorneys in our office, not four. I may not handle a full load for a while, but I will foot a few of my own bills."

A grin spread wide across Alexis' face. "We will be happy to have you there, Dad, and I certainly will drive you to the office, provided you promise to call Harm if you need to come home early."

"Why? I can sit on my butt there as easily as here. And Harm's coming early this afternoon to take me to my doctor for the results of all his tests. Eat your breakfast. I'm not the only one who has lost a few pounds lately. And did you get rid of that jackass for good last night?"

"I hope so. I'm advising my landlord in D.C. that I won't be renewing the lease in January. Terry will be on his own after that. Or with the woman I suspect he's been seeing behind my back."

"For God's sake, don't tell me you've been paying the rent for both of you!"

"I'm not a pushover, Dad. He's been paying, but I seriously doubt he can afford $2300 a month on his income." She sliced a raw peach and added home-produced cream.

"Is that why you let him move in? So he could help you pay the rent?"

"No, Dad. I was doing fine without him. But he found himself homeless at a time when we were awash in cases and pulling all-nighters half the week, so I let him stay in my spare bedroom. Then friends turned into romance and we started talking about futures."

"You weren't thinking of marrying that ass? How could you if you hadn't even told him who you are?"

"Relax. No, we hadn't talked marriage. We talked about taking similar career paths and supporting each other along the way. And I gave a fleeting thought now and then to giving you a beautiful grandchild someday. My clock is ticking, after all."

He grunted. "Looks aren't everything."

"Uh, huh. The woman *you* married was certainly a beauty."

"Indeed she was, as is her daughter." He gave her a conspiratorial grin. "But I wouldn't mind having a grandchild or six to spoil rotten and return to you."

"That'll be the day." Alexis used her coffee cup to avoid letting him see how their conversation pleased her. He had not been so relaxed in months. They finished breakfast in companionable silence and she cleared the table. At the front door, Mary was telling Jerry to bring Alexis' car around.

"I'm leaving Tricky today, Mary. Please let him out of jail in my room after we're out of sight. Whoever's on guard outside by then will watch him take a walk and feed him. Dad and I will be home a little early."

"Good. You don't let him do too much."

"Like I could stop him? I'll do my best."

They had the road pretty much to themselves on the drive to Redmond from the ranch. Alexis used the time to brief Dad on the current cases awaiting them, including the *pro bono* matter of the young woman with landlord issues.

"I'll take care of that one," he said. "I know her landlord. I'd like to chase him out of the business. He's our version of a slum lord."

"So I gath—" Alexis stopped speaking, pulled off the road, and stopped.

Fifty feet ahead of them, on a low tree branch, an eagle had landed and sat facing them, as if she had something to say.

"He's beautiful, but why are you stopping?" he asked.

"She."

"How do you know that?"

"She's much bigger than the average male. And her face and beak are narrower, her eyes hooded. She looks meaner."

"Your grandfather teach you that?"

"No. Observation, with Pat and Chili when we were kids. We used to watch them for hours."

"Her presence here means something to you? What?"

"I'm not sure. Eagles are the keepers of the East wind, which signifies new beginnings. But for whom? You or me?" She faced him, brow furrowed. The eagle's message, as were so many, was unclear.

He took her hand from the wheel and smiled. "Or for both of us?"

"Without doubt," she said, wishing she could detour and find Granddad. "She brings illumination and wisdom and I think I spent the night wrestling with her."

Chapter 31: The Governor

"O Great Spirit, whose voice I hear in the winds
And whose breath gives life to all the world, hear me.
I come to you as one of your children . . ."
~Native American prayer salutation

The eagle seemed satisfied that her message had been delivered, or she gave up. With a flurry of her wings, she took flight and soon soared high, a dark shape in a clear, blue sky. Alexis shivered. Goosebumps flickered over her bare arms. She glanced at her father and saw an odd expression on his face, too, as if he had seen or felt something illuminating. Was the eagle's message meant for him, and not Alexis?

She started the car and, in silence, drove on to the office with a lump in her throat that defied explanation.

At the office, she left her father at the door and parked. As she got out, a pale blue Toyota passed by on the street, reminding her of the car Terry had driven yesterday. She hurried to watch the greetings her dad received.

Bonnie stood with her arms around Grant, crying. Wade, patiently waiting his turn, leaned on the wall. The two new hires had come out to see what the fuss was all about, and looked puzzled. Alexis smiled at them, indicating all was well.

When Bonnie finally released him, Wade stepped forward and eagerly shook his hand. They had been friends as well as partners for two decades.

"Man, Grant, it is good to see you on your feet again. I was beginning to wonder if old Chases Bear was losing his touch. Should have known." He winked at Alexis.

"Well, that makes two of us, Wade. It's good to see you, too," Grant answered.

What makes two of us? Alexis wondered. *Should have known about Chases Bear, or glad to see each other?*

When Wade released Grant's hand, he raised his eyebrows at Alexis.

"Go ahead," she said. "Introduce our newcomers."

While Wade introduced Bethany Joseph and Paul Merrion to her father, Alexis slipped into her office to gather information relevant to John Stockman's various on-going cases and stuff the papers in her briefcase.

As she returned, Grant disappeared into Wade's office and the others to their own, leaving her alone with Bonnie.

She smiled at Bonnie, whose tears still rolled down her cheeks. Bonnie blew her nose. Alexis grinned. His team had always loved Grant. Alexis was pleased at their reaction.

"He's back, Bonnie, but it will be a slow bounce. He's been through a lot. The cancer may be in remission, but his strength is, too, for a while.

"I have to be gone for several hours," she continued. "If he begins to look too tired, call Harm's cell phone. Knowing Harm, he's likely to be hanging out around the corner somewhere, waiting until he's needed. Don't hesitate, no matter what Dad says. If you can't talk him into going home, Wade and Harm can. He has a doctor appointment early this afternoon, so if he looks okay, let him wait for that. If he doesn't, let Harm decide what to do."

"I will keep an eye on him, don't you worry."

"I'm sure you will."

Alexis turned as Grant crossed the hall a few feet away and entered the office assigned to Bethany. Alexis would be interested in his opinion of her first ever hires. Now, however, she had a long drive to Portland ahead of her and needed to be on the road.

Two hours away on US Highway 26, she noticed another blue Toyota in her rear-view mirror, five cars back.

"Damn," she muttered. "It's like when you buy a new car. Suddenly it's the most popular vehicle on the road." She strained to see the driver, but the car changed lanes and dropped back into a cluster of other cars. She shrugged it off. Of course, Terry wouldn't follow her. She had been surprised that he had enough interest come to Redmond after her. She found it even more surprising that he had not called ahead to let her know he was coming until he reached the area, as if it would be too late to send him away without seeing him. He had probably taken the plane to Portland and was returning to D.C. the same way. She had never known him to demonstrate enough emotion to chase after her. She wondered why that had never bothered her before. Perhaps because she lacked enough feeling for him, to care? From this distant perspective, the relationship seemed dry and monotonous. Compared with the tingling excitement Patrick had aroused in her since they were teenagers, their affair left a lot to be desired.

John Stockman was staying at the Governor Hotel, less than a half-mile from downtown and the Reinhardt Building, the glass-walled edifice that housed Portland's top legal firm. Built in 1903, the Governor had recently been re-named The Sentinel. After seeing it, Alexis would never be able to think of it as anything but the Governor. The hotel is one of Portland's finest architectural relics, replete with pilasters and columns and robot-like figures circling the upper edge, far ahead of their time.

"I admire your taste in hotels," Alexis told John as he answered the door of his suite.

"My favorite anywhere in the world, so far," he answered. "And I've stayed in a bunch of 'em. I like to just sit here and soak up its history."

"It's elegant," she said. "I rather expected ostentatious, judging by the exterior." John showed her to a comfortable upholstered chair. He took a straight-backed chair before a small, carved desk, at a 90-degree angle to her. She gazed around the room: Dark painted walls, white molding, pale gray, upholstered, oversized chairs and sofas, puffy white linens and hardwood dressers and beds, visible from the room where they sat. The overall affect was one of affluence, peace, and comfort. As John had said, she could just sit here and drink it in.

Alexis opened her briefcase on her lap, and extracted her small, thin tablet. This she set on the end of the desk, angled so they both could see it.

"How is your father?" John asked.

Alexis' smile came with joy. "He is in the office today, getting to know two very promising new associates.

John burst into laughter. "The son-of-a-bitch is going to fool us all, isn't he? I'm glad, damn glad, for you, Alex."

"He'll fool a lot of people, John, but not our people. We knew he would recover from the day he returned to the desert and agreed to see my grandfather."

"Your grandfather? Is he a specialist, or something?"

"You could say that. Granddad is a Cherokee medicine man who joined the Warm Springs Tribes as a boy. He has spent a lifetime studying the medicine ways of indigenous cultures worldwide. He has a special talent that he's had from birth, and he did a 'Healing Way' for Dad."

"And you've kept that on the down low for obvious reasons. Indian magical healing could have an adverse effect on your credibility as a lawyer." He made it a statement, not a question. Alexis waited to see if there was more. None came. He wore a benign, pleasant expression as he, too, waited for more information.

"Native American medicine is anything but magic, John. It may, on occasion, give the impression of being miraculous, but it is the result of thousands of years of trial and error and shared knowledge by indigenous cultures around the world. Many of their practices depend upon nutrition, herbal remedies, and prayer. Prayer often takes the form of chanting, singing, drumming, and dancing. There is more, much more, but we don't have all year."

"I understand all of that, believe it or not. I also understand that we have done ourselves a gross disservice in attempting to eradicate the cultures, which carried so much knowledge through the world by word of mouth."

"I'm glad you understand, John. I have kept it on the down low not only for my career, but for Dad's. I hope you will honor my confidence."

John rested his hand on her arm. "On one condition, dear girl. If I ever have the need, you will introduce me to your grandfather, and ask him to ply his trade for me."

Alexis burst into laughter. "Done and done, John. Anytime. And you needn't wait for disaster. He is a licensed practicing physician, as well as a medicine man. Shall we get to work?"

They spent an hour and a half negotiating over what Bishop and Bishop would be able and willing to accept of John's prodigious legal affairs, and what would be better passed on to another firm. As for the other firm, Alexis recommended a capable young partnership, up and coming in Bend, just twenty miles away from Redmond. Since Stockman operations were worldwide and both domicile and company headquarters were located in California, the other firm would be no less convenient than their own. Best of all, Alexis knew she and her father could easily work with them if need be. In the end, Alexis had agreed to accept approximately fifty-five percent of the business and send the rest to Bend. With five attorneys, and more if needed, she thought they could handle this. John seemed doubtful at first, until she told him the two from Bend had graduated with her, both with honors, and their loyalty was assured by the fact that her father had contributed to the pair's education. She saw no reason to add that the two men were a couple, both Native American.

At last, they rose from their labor, shook hands, and called it quits, both pleased with the outcome.

"Come downstairs," he said. "I'll buy you a drink. You should get a good look at this magnificent piece of architecture."

"I agree. I've lived not far away for most of my life and knew nothing about the grand Governor Hotel."

"The Sentinel, now, and it's been beautifully restored. She's been here since 1903, and changed by adding two neighboring buildings, but restorers have been faithful to her history. She's a grand lady."

"I won't argue with that."

He guided her to the entrance of the Jackknife Grill and held a chair for her. As she seated herself, a man hurried out the other door to the street and disappeared. In a suit and tie, he was easily as tall as Terry Wells, and as slender, with sandy brown hair like Terry's. Shaking, unsure whether with anger or fear or both, she attempted to conceal her concerns from John. Why would she fear the man with whom she had shared a home for nearly a year? She glanced at her watch: the meeting with Reinhardt, Wilson would be short and unpleasant, and then she would go home. Meanwhile, a glass of white zinfandel from the Willamette Valley Winery south of Salem soothed her jitters. John ordered a BLT and ate with gusto, but she had lost whatever appetite she might have had. *Great. Nerves, an empty stomach, and alcohol. And a long drive home.* She watched the door where the man had disappeared and remembered gratefully the handgun in her glove compartment. *Uh, huh. No food, long drive, jitters, alcohol, and a gun. Perfect.*

Chapter 32: Shadow

There is a fine line between serendipity and stalking.
David Coleman

John Stockman escorted Alexis from the Jackknife through the hotel lobby and out the front door. They shook hands and he turned to go back to his drink in the Jackknife. She'd parked on the street not far away because it was closer to Sixth Avenue. She could walk the five blocks to Sixth, and two more to her right in less than ten minutes, even in her heels. A quick glance as she crossed the street told her no one loitered near her car.

With the sun high in the sky, the city felt warm now, but she moved quickly and stepped into the refreshingly cool lobby at the Reinhardt Building still feeling comfortable, perhaps because of the wine coursing through her system. The front desk receptionist had called a young man, an associate, to escort her upstairs, where she found that five of the nine equity partners awaited her in a conference room.

The meeting was neither as short nor as simple as Alexis had hoped. After brief introductions, Alexis quietly announced that she had made a decision: she was neither joining the firm in any capacity, nor was she bringing the Stockman Construction business to them. First, the partners attempted to persuade her to change her mind, then they tried to pressure her. Finally, the discussion became adversarial.

"Alexis," Will Reinhardt said, "We are not going to raise our exceedingly generous partnership offer for an attorney of your limited years in practice and your youth. We won't be increasing the annual compensation, nor your status here."

"Gentlemen, I am not here to hold you up for more money or benefits. If I were, I would simply state my requirements. I am here as a courtesy to advise you that I have agreed with John on a suitable arrangement with Bishop, Bishop, and Corey. We have signed an acceptable agreement. I know you would have taken steps to prepare for the work, and I didn't want to unnecessarily inconvenience you."

"When did you arrive at this alleged agreement?" Reinhardt asked.

"This morning, before I came here."

Another partner, an attractive black man in his fifties, spoke. "Is Mr. Stockman in Portland?"

"I am not in the habit of divulging the whereabouts of my clients," Alexis answered. Will gave a barely perceptible nod. The man seated beside her stood up and left the room.

"If John agrees to speak to you, you are welcome to try to dissuade him. I don't see it happening." She guessed that the man who had left the room was now calling all the better hotels in Portland, searching for John. Let them. She had signed contracts in her briefcase.

"The amount of work you are proposing to take on is far more than two attorneys can manage. The ethical thing would be to admit that and decline Stockman's offer," Reinhardt said.

"Five," she said.

"Five? You've hired three lawyers? Do they have enough experience to justify your decision?"

"That isn't your concern. We will do very well, I assure you. By the way, I hope you noted that we are now Bishop, Bishop and Corey.

"And with that, gentlemen, I will say good day. It is a long drive to Redmond."

"Grant is back at work? We had heard . . ."

"I know. You had heard he was dying. The key word is 'was.' Dad is waiting at his office to ride home with me. Thank you for your time." She left the room, her stride purposeful. Closing the door, she smiled at the angry babble of voices behind her. Next time they met, their attitudes night be unfriendly, but she was willing to bet they wouldn't be condescending.

She walked quickly, wanting to be out of the building before they stopped squabbling long enough to catch up with her and try again. With millions of dollars at stake, she doubted they would give up easily. John had approached them first, then called her for a meeting. They had thought his business was in the bag.

She hurried, exited the front door, and walked smack into Terry Wells, dropping her briefcase. He reached, but she was quicker.

"What are you doing here?" he asked. "Throwing me under the bus?"

Alexis expelled a breath. "What do you mean by that?"

"First, you dump me unceremoniously and kick me off your father's place. You have a two-hour visit with John Stockman in his room, followed by a cozy little tête-à-tête in the bar. Then you go to a special meeting with the hottest legal firm in the city, according to their receptionist, who thinks you are a 'rainmaker.' There's hardly any question how you raked in Stockman to buy a partnership with Reinhardt's team. What happened to us joining a big firm together some day?"

"You really, really don't know me at all, do you?"

"I guess I do now. But you don't have to dump me for this. I'll go along with your play for the Stockman account. Hell, what's a little nooky on the side if it's worth millions of dollars? It isn't as if you were a virgin when we met."

She slapped him. Hard. He backed up a step and tried to grab her hand. She ducked under his upraised arm and tried to go back inside the building. He grabbed her other arm and spun her around to face him. She stomped on his toe with her heel. He yelped and grabbed both her arms.

The door beside them opened. A beefy, tall security guard stepped out and planted a huge hand on Terry's chest, giving him a light shove. It was enough. Terry looked up at him and backed away.

"Mind your own business," he sputtered.

"A disturbance in front of this office *is* my business," the guard answered. He looked toward Alexis. "Are you okay, Miss?"

"Yes sir, thank you," she answered, and darted around him into the building, where she made for the ladies' room, across the lobby. Fortunately, the lobby was nearly empty and most people seemed to be ignoring them. Inside the bathroom, she was alone. She splashed water on her face, bright red with fury at herself for allowing the situation to deteriorate into a tawdry scene, and at Terry Wells for his asinine conclusions. She grabbed a towel and was dabbing at her face when the young receptionist entered.

"Are you okay, honey?" she asked.

"Yes, if you don't count dignity and anger. Neither is likely to recover in this millennium."

"Well, don't worry. I'm not going to tell anyone. Neither is Dave. That's our security guard."

"I wouldn't either, if I were the one who told my ex-boyfriend about a confidential meeting."

"Oh my God! He told me he was your partner, a lawyer from Washington D.C. and he was supposed to meet you here, but he got caught up in traffic! I'm so sorry! I didn't mean to get you in trouble. He asked me if they made a decision, and . . ."

"And what, exactly, did you tell him?"

"I . . .uh . . . I guess I told him you were our new partner, 'cause you were bringing in a really big client, and they were meeting with you about it today. I'm so sorry."

"Don't beat yourself up over it. The only thing he told you that was true is that he's from D.C. The only thing you told him that was true was that we were meeting about the matter. It's over."

"Oh, I'm sorry. Did the partners change their minds?"

"No. I decided." Alexis gripped her briefcase and left the room. She'd learned what she needed to know. Terry Wells had done a slipshod job of investigating and jumped to unwarranted conclusions which made him angrier than he was before. She hoped he wouldn't be waiting for her. She wished she had brought the car around to the parking garage.

Alexis stopped outside the door of the law offices and considered her options. If he was waiting for her, he was at the car or along the path she had taken to get where she was. To get back there, logic dictated she would return the same way. She crossed the street and turned left instead of right, to approach her car from behind. She concentrated on remembering what stores or businesses fronted the street beside the car. With those in mind, she turned right at the next block and walked three blocks, to the street one short of the one where she'd parked, and turned right again. At least three of the buildings she passed would allow through access to the street in front of the hotel. She waited for the fourth and entered a narrow restaurant with entrances on both streets. Searching the clientele as she walked through, she assured herself that Terry wasn't waiting for her there. Six feet from the glass front, she stopped. He stood leaning against her driver's door, watching the path she should have taken. He changed positions and leaned with his back to her. Traffic flowed sporadically, making moderate noise.

Alexis slipped off her shoes, and handed them to a surprised young woman seated at one of the tables and ran outside, key fob in hand, waiting until she was no more than two feet away before she pressed the button. She bent low, hoping he wouldn't hear the click. She opened the passenger door a few inches, pressed the lock on the fob again, and jumped in, squirming across the console. Seated, she started the car. Terry jumped, turned, and tried to open her door.

That's when Alexis saw John Stockman, standing near the door of the hotel chewing a toothpick. *Oh, goody, she thought, another scene.* When he waved, she grinned and waved back. Terry stood up and looked around. Not as tall as Terry, John was nevertheless an imposing man. Dressed in jeans, boots and a plaid shirt, he looked like a man who could take care of himself. Alexis backed up toward the car behind her and turned the wheel as if to leave the parking place. John said something and approached the street. Terry had to know who he was, and that if he crossed a line there would be no hope of ever being involved in business with him.

"I'll see you later," Terry called out to Alexis, with a careless wave and a friendly smile, and walked away. His blue Toyota sat near the corner, facing the wrong direction.

"I didn't know you were such a great actor," Alexis muttered under her breath.

Now, there were options again. There were a number of exits she could use to leave Portland. South on the I-5. East along the Columbia Gorge. West to 101, the winding coast road, and back to the Willamette Valley, then over the passes to the desert. If she lost him, he wouldn't find her again unless he beat her to Redmond, and there she would be among people she knew. He would arrive first if she took a western route. It was too wide a detour. This was her world now, and she knew every road. In the end, she went the one direction she was sure he would not follow. She drove east out of the city and then diagonally across the Rez toward Warm Springs and Madras, not even sure if there was a name for the road, which surely was not the fastest way home. The sign, when she turned off the Columbia Gorge Highway, said Highway 26.

There seemed nothing wrong with an opportunity to visit Granddad and Pat along the way. She thought it unlikely that she'd seen the last of him. But what there'd been was more than enough of Terry Wells for one day—or one lifetime. For as long as she'd known him, Terry Wells had been a mild man, even on situations when a little assertion might have been helpful. Now, however, they were at cross purposes, and she saw a part of him she had never known existed. Thank the Spirits she had never been tempted to marry him. This man seemed to her now, to be just the sort whose aggression was reserved for behind closed doors at home, with women and children as his victims. She glanced at her right arm, which still felt sore, and noted the purple bruises building there.

"Bastard!" she whispered.

Chapter 33: Stalkers

Tell me and I forget.
Teach me and I remember.
Involve me and I learn.
~Benjamin Franklin

The road seemed in better shape than she remembered, but longer. Alexis surmised the tribe saw it as direct backdoor access from Portland to Kah-Nee-Tah Resort, the tribe's casino hotel, so they had improved it. Much of it traveled through deep forest, which increased her jitters. In spite of this, she enjoyed driving, as it gave her rarely available time to ruminate over events, organize her thoughts, and consider options. She had eliminated several in recent days. She would never return to Washington, D.C. Check. She would contact her landlord to give away the few possessions in her apartment and cancel the lease as it ended, two months from now, and never mind Terry. He was on his own as of now. Eliminate Terry. Check.

She had settled John's notion of luring her into a partnership with the Reinhardt Group. Check. That decision brought more relief than expected. The notion of becoming a cog in a multi-story machine made her shiver. Alexis would feel trapped, imprisoned. Places like that required 60-80 billing hours per week of each lawyer. She could do it, and do it well, but such a commitment left no time for a life. More than she had ever imagined, she longed to be involved in other things as well as the law.

Her father would regain his health. Check. There was no room for doubt left. He was well on his way. She would work with him as long as she was needed and then walk the walk Spirit set in front of her, one step at a time, wherever it led. That decision filled her with a rush of relief, much more than had the decision not to become a partner in a huge, powerful legal firm.

The most powerful of all the restless questions Alexis grappled with arose when she recalled the wealth of emotions that had flowed through her body as she had placed her hands on Patrick's back. That question rested in the back of her mind like a hibernating animal, just waiting for her to wake it up and take a good look. It had always been there. She would address it when the time was right.

The incredible yearning to relive the satisfaction and joy she had shared with her grandfather over the injured bodies of her father and Patrick Collins was wide awake and racing through her mind. The energy that had filled through her entire being during those ceremonies had never been matched in her lifetime. She had felt filled to overflowing of a rich, unmatched bliss and unconditional love that she knew did not originate with her or even with her grandfather. Had she been capable of such fulfillment on her own, she'd have known long before now.

Somehow, she thought the abundance of this feeling was connected to her sacred cave and the spirits, or dreams, or visions—whatever it was she encountered there. Acting on Granddad's advice not to examine such things too closely, she had resisted attempts to intellectually analyze her experiences. When Alexis had asked her grandfather to help her understand, his response had always been that understanding was hers to see, that he could not explain what she already knew. Already knew? What did she already know? But when had he been wrong?

In years past, she had gone through periods of avoiding the cave because sometimes when the wonder of the visit wore off she was left feeling restless and anxious, not knowing the answers she sought. She had eventually come to understand that her prayers were always answered, if sometimes in unexpected ways, so when the yearning to be there returned, she made her trip through the tunnel to the other world again. Finally, she had simply come to accept the visits for whatever they were. Whether she understood or not, many times after a trip to the cave her thinking became clearer and her direction was easier to determine. During her years of absence from Oregon, she had secretly held the knowledge of the cave and its miracles in her heart and felt the knowledge strengthen her, but she had not seriously missed it, nor had she knowingly sought to replace the sacred space. Despite all these mixed feelings, she rarely felt confused, but more as if her life were on hold, and she patiently waited for the answers to unfold. Her grandfather had told her she was exactly where she needed to be at any given moment in her life. She took his words to heart and simply waited.

A noise alerted her and she glanced in the mirror to see a convertible WWII Jeep with its top down, driven by Harley Braithwaite, following her. She picked up her speed, reminding herself of her emotional disorder, the beer she'd drunk, and the occasionally rough road she traveled. Braithwaite sped up, too, but he'd be hard put to keep up with her car if she poured it on.

"911," she said, addressing the hands-free, voice-operated cell phone in a holder on the dash.

"Nine-one-one operator, what is the nature of your emergency?"

"I am being followed closely by a related suspect in the shooting of Sergeant Patrick Collins," she said, and gave her location.

"I have units in route. May I have your name, please?"

Alexis answered. She came to a curve that she recognized as preceding the turnoff to the home of a friend, and began to ease up, hoping a back shooting wasn't on Braithwaite's agenda for the day. She waited until she was almost on top of the driveway, slammed on her brakes, and barely made the turn. The Jeep skidded by, stopped, and backed up in the road, started to turn, and must have seen what she saw: her friend's entire clan was in their yard, men bare to the waist, women in shorts and tees and sneakers. The framework of a new structure was taking shape to her left. Men were all over it, hammering, sawing, fitting, and assisting. The women had laid out a board-over-sawhorses table and she could imagine it groaning under the load of food they were adding. Suddenly, Alexis was famished. Braithwaite backed up, and was gone in a spray of dust.

Alexis came to a stop and leaned over the steering wheel, nearly sobbing with relief. One stalker was dissuaded- for now. She wondered where the other one was. A large, overweight man whose jeans were slung under his prodigious, naked, brown belly, approached her car, a hammer in one hand. When he saw her, a huge grin broke out all over his homely face. A warm-hearted man, he carried laughter lines in his face deep enough for crop growing, and a mouthful of very white, false teeth.

"Alexis Bishop," he shouted, "There are better ways to come to my house than to spread dust enough to fill up ol' Broken Top. What'n' hell brings you to my barn raisin', anyhow?"

"I just realized I was damn hungry, Nathan Red Fox. And I see you've got food."

"And you had to bring that sneaky killer, Braithwaite, with you?"

"Not willingly, old friend. He got on my tail about a mile back, and I couldn't shake him, so I made an unexpected turn."

"You running away from him?"

"Yes, I'm running away." He's partners with Dark Moon Kane. I saw Kane shoot Patrick Collins in the back. I'm on my way to find out how Pat's doing. When I'm sure I won't be followed again.

Red Fox opened her car door and helped her out.

"Coming from the big city?"

Alexis hiked up her skirt, slid her wrecked pantyhose down over her hips and stepped out of them, tossing them back in the car. In the rough turf of Nathan's yard, she didn't miss her heels. "Yes. I was taking back roads to avoid another, equally unwelcome stalker who's following me."

"He drive a blue rented Toyota?" This came from Daniel Red Fox, Nathan's son, a young man in his twenties. Two children clung to his knees.

"Grandbabies, Nathan? What makes you so lucky?" Alexis asked, afraid to find out what they knew about the blue Toyota. There was no mistaking the familial resemblance among the clan.

"Aw, darn, Alexis, the Great Sprit has been smiling on me all my life, and it ain't no different now. I got me five of these beautiful young'uns, what with both sons and a daughter bringing them home."

"So that's why you have such a great smile, Nathan Red Fox. I always love to see your big, wide grin. Yes, Daniel, he drives a blue Toyota. Where did you see him?"

"Leaving the Gateway Café. I had Breakfast there. I asked the girls who he was, and they said they didn't know much, but he was asking all about you."

So he had the nerve to approach the Rez after all. She would keep a sharper eye on her surroundings. For now, she felt safely sheltered in the warmth of Nathan's big, happy, well-armed family.

The makeshift table did, in fact, groan with the weight of food upon it; fried rabbit, biscuits and gravy, fresh vegetables from someone's garden; potato salad, dried salmon, and braised venison; more food than Alexis had seen since the college cafeteria in Washington. She ate, not only because the family urged her to eat, and she was hungry, but because she was afraid to leave until she was sure Harley Braithwaite was not waiting on the road for her. She called the 911 operator again and was told the officer had been called off for a disturbance at the casino, which was along the way and he would be coming, unless he arrested someone. Hearing her conversation, Red Fox called his sons and other visitors together and told them the story. Several of them mentioned having had unpleasant encounters with Kane and his friends.

Half an hour after eating and helping the ladies clean, Alexis left the cozy comfort of the Red Fox clan with an amazing escort: pickups in varying degrees of condition from dilapidated to sleek; 4-wheel drive vehicles from ATVs to SUVs; and family cars, also varying in age and condition. In all, 16 to 18 cars surrounded her, front, back and on both side, and escorted her all the way to her grandfather's house, where two of them walked her safely to the door and said good evening, barely giving her time to express her thanks. Her grandfather met them at the door and handed a concoction to Red Fox.

"For your wife," he said. "And tell her to stop forgetting."

"Oh. My fault, Chases Bear. I will do better in the future." And as suddenly as they had all arrived, they all left her there.

Alexis turned to her grandfather and burst into laughter, as did he.

"Braithwaite will not come here," he said.

"No. I know that. I hope he doesn't find a way to take it out on them."

"If he does, they may bury him to his neck in an ant hill," he said, chuckling at her.

"Granddad! How did you . . . Did you hear me say that?"

"No. It has been whispered on the Rez today. I think by one of those who guard your house, first."

"Ah! The moccasin telegraph at its best." She stepped inside with him, laughing.

"I will prepare food if Red Fox's family did not see to that."

"Granddad, I will have no room for food for a week. Pat!" He sat in an upholstered chair in the living room, laughing.

"What did you do to deserve the parade?" he asked.

"Harley Braithwaite followed me shortly after I turned onto the Rez on Highway 26."

"You cut across? Why didn't you take the freeway south?"

"I will tell you all about it soon. How are you?"

By way of answer, he raised both arms, with a grin.

"Wow! No pain when you do that?" she asked.

"Some. But it's much better."

Alexis sat on the arm of his chair and laced her fingers through his. He released them, slid his arm around her waist, and pulled her, with caution for his wound, onto his lap, where he held her close and kissed her, a warm, passionate, loving kiss like none she'd ever known. She returned it with enthusiasm. He released her mouth and said, "You're done with him?"

"In spades," she whispered. *Check.*

Chapter 34: Spirit Bear

"In three words I can sum up everything
I've learned about life: it goes on."
— Robert Frost

Alexis eased her way off Pat's lap and regained her seat on the arm of the chair. Granddad beamed at them. He brought another chair and set it beside Pat's.

"While you may be the best medicine for my patient, I prefer you not reopen his stitches," he said.

Pat changed the subject. "Kane followed you on the Rez?" he asked Alexis.

"Yes. He picked me up just a mile or two from Nathan's place."

"Did you call the tribal police?"

"I did, but they were delayed by a disturbance at Kah-Nee-Tah."

"Damn! Why were you up north? And for that matter, I wonder why he was there?"

"I couldn't answer the second, and I think it was purely coincidence. Certainly no one expected me there. I didn't expect to be there. As to why I was there, I was avoiding any likely place Terry might think to look for me."

"Terry Wells! Why would he be following you?"

"It seems he had more attachment to me than I gave him credit for. I never imagined that he would follow me out west, never mind around the state."

"Tell me. What happened?"

"I had a meeting at the Sentinel Hotel with John Stockman, a client."

Pat whistled. "CEO of Stockman Construction?"

"The very same. We met. We spent a couple hours with the paperwork, completed our business, and I went to a second meeting at the Reinhardt Building a few blocks away. I finished up there and collided with Terry on my way out. He had poked around while I was upstairs and found out I was supposed to be signing a partnership agreement with them, and bring a big piece of business with me. He was angry."

"Why?"

"Because he expected that when we went into private practice, we'd be doing it together, and he jumped to some conclusions about how I was arranging to be a partner in the most prestigious law firm in Oregon." She glanced at her grandfather and saw concern in his eyes.

"So what happened?" Pat asked.

""I must admit, I didn't respond in a ladylike manner. I slapped him, hard. Then the security guard interfered and I ducked inside, where I found out from a receptionist how he knew so much. He left and I avoided him.

"Terry's car was parked half a block away, facing the wrong direction, so I lost him in the city, and I didn't think he'd risk catching up with me on the Rez, so I cut across to here. It was a good excuse to see you, anyway."

"Is your father expecting you home by now?"

"I would think so. Harm was supposed to bring him home. He went to work today."

"Saving the best for last aren't you? Grant went to work? He must be feeling a lot better."

"Very much so." It occurred to her they might be worrying at the house, so she used her cell phone to call home and tell Mary she was well, just delayed, and would be there soon.

Pat pulled himself up straight in his chair and faced Chases Bear. "I need to be out of here, too. I'll drive you home."

"No!" Alexis said.

"You are not ready," Chases Bear added.

"I need to go after Dark Moon Kane before he hurts someone else," he said. "And I guess I need to be around to keep an eye on Alexis."

"I will take care of myself," Alexis said. "If I need a security guard, I'll get one. Your job is to heal, so you'll be fit to do the rest."

"I'm not so sure it can wait that long," Pat said.

"It will wait," Chases Bear said. "When you are well enough, I will release you. Spirit will guide your steps to prevent further damage by Dark Moon."

"Another thing. We need to be protecting that dugout site until we find out exactly what it is and what they've already seized from it."

"That has been managed, son of my heart." Alexis started at the way her grandfather addressed Pat, having never heard it before. He must have been more deeply affected by the shooting than she knew. She was not surprised that he loved Pat Collins, only by the apparent depth of his feelings. She and Pat had spent much of their growing up time with her grandfather.

"Managed how?" she asked, curious.

"I spoke with the elders. Both ends of the canyon are closed. State police have agreed to watch the access that is outside the Rez. Guards and chains are enclosing the entry inside our land. Not many will enter the canyon as we did, over the bluff. If anyone gets past the campground, there are guards posted at the Rez borders."

Pat nodded. "I'm glad. There is more to find in the canyon. It is good to keep it safe."

"More than you know," Chases Bear answered. "And you will find it, perhaps with the assistance of the little dickens again." This time, his voice sounded grim. Pat frowned, but

Chases Bear had no more to say. Alexis bade them both goodbye, kissing Pat again, and left, watching her mirrors and any turnoffs she passed. The sun had set, arousing chills from more than cooler temperatures along her arms and shoulders.

The more common than usual presence of police cars along the way suggested that Pat had called upon not only tribal police, but his friends in state and local law enforcement, as well, to assure her safe passage. She smiled at the thought. She was not the only one with influence.

Dinner awaited her arrival. With relief, she dropped her briefcase in the foyer and whistled for Tricky. He was underfoot, jumping on her bare legs before she could take two steps. Carrying him, she hurried upstairs, wondering if she should pretend to enjoy Mary's cooking on her still-full stomach. The taste of Pat's kisses lingered on her lips.

Upstairs, she washed and sat facing the open window while she brushed her hair. She sensed no presence except that of her grandfather, who had not left her since she'd departed from his house.

Granddad? She whispered on the wind, understanding now what that meant.

I am here. She smiled and hurried downstairs, where her father sat at the dinner table, reading the newspaper from the office, as he had done every evening that she could remember before his illness. She kissed his cheek.

"How was your first day at the office?" she asked. Mary, setting a tureen of soup on the table, smiled.

"I'm tired," he said. "But not overly so. I will sleep well tonight."

"You must have found everything to your liking," she answered. She served them both soup.

"Did you doubt it?"

"I have never hired anyone."

"That, you did very well. What Beth lacks in experience, she makes up for in education and common sense. Paul combines all of those, plus an awareness of the area, having grown up here. His father is an old friend, a city councilor."

"Of course he is. I had a feeling I knew the name, but couldn't place it."

"I'm surprised he didn't tell you. His experience is military, which is quite different."

"So are public service positions, Dad, but court is court and rules are rules. If he can interpret the law and speak to a court, he'll be fine."

Mary brought more food, but Grant served himself another bowl of soup first.

"He will. You and Wade did a good job of holding the place together. A few matters put off, but we'll fix that. I'm glad you came home."

"So am I. I won't be leaving again, as long as you want me here. I'm closing the lease on my apartment and sending for my things."

"Will he give them to you?"

"Once, I would have said he wouldn't care. Now, I don't have a clue what he will do. I could always threaten to evict him. He's not legally a renter."

"Has he gone, then?"

"That's another thing I don't know. He followed me to Portland and to my meetings today. He accosted me outside the Reinhardt Building. I slapped him—hard—when he called me a whore. He said I had slept with John to get his business and used it to buy a partnership in the law firm."

"You might want to send for your things and have the manager gather them before he gets to D.C."

"Very little is irreplaceable. I'll send a cop if I have to, with a warrant and a list. I have lots of friends in high places, but moving fast is a good idea. Terry is highly unpredictable. I am surprised. I didn't know he had that much passion in him."

"We often take people for granted until it's too late."

She wanted to ask if that was the case with her parents and held her tongue. He was feeling well. Granddad had told her how important Pat's emotions were. It was no surprise that Dad's spiritual well-being was equally vital. She settled for covering his hand with her own for a moment.

"I cannot imagine a circumstance in which I would ever want you to leave again," he said. They finished dinner and retired to the den, which was back to its comfortable arrangement, *sans* hospital bed and its accoutrements. They chatted about goings on in the office for a few minutes.

"Mary!" Grant called out. She came to the door.

"Please get yourself a glass of whatever you want and join us for a few minutes."

Alexis clapped her hands. "Yes! Do, please! Come sit with us."

Mary grinned. It was rare that they invited her, and hadn't happened for a long while. Not, in fact, since Alexis had come home. Mary poured herself a glass of Grant's good whiskey, while Alexis decided to try the *Pinot Noir* from the Willamette Valley she'd heard much about in recent months, since it was in Dad's wet bar.

Just sweet enough and richly fruity, it was better than any French wine she'd ever tasted.

"Mmmm," she said. "That's perfect. They dropped the talk about legal business for Mary's sake, and spoke of the year's calf return, the grazing competition of the wild horses, and the waning summer. Mary laughed at Tricky's antics with Grant's shoestrings, and told Alexis she'd been glad to have his company. Alexis watched her with interest, noting that her father's eyes seldom left Mary's face. He respected and appreciated her for her good work. Was there a hint of more? She couldn't tell, and, tired, finished her wine and bade them good night.

A dream came to Alexis late that night.

Cedar trees towered high overhead. The sea lapped the shores outside the forest, and snow fell into the water. Branches sagged with it. They had stopped and built shelter quickly, while snow faded away before it could gather. Fear plagued them; they were only a day ahead of the Others, warriors from the north. Flat Faces, some of the People's warriors called them. The People had stopped in the cover of trees and hidden their shelters with fallen cedar boughs and shrubs. From outside, on the sand, they would be extremely hard to see, spread out as they were among the trees. In small groups inside shelters built far apart, they huddled together for warmth, sharing furs, afraid to build fires. If the Others came while they slept, perhaps they would find a shelter or two, but many would escape discovery. They slept, while a few kept watch, and counted on their hiding places to protect them. The Others had followed them for many days, having chased them from their homes to the north.

The Others came in the night, and made camp on the sand. The People trembled as some of the Others came into the woods to find wood for their fires. The scent of cooking meat wafted toward them and a few of the children began to whimper before they were shushed. They had eaten what they found along the way, and all were hungry. The People remained still and awake for the rest of the night, except for a few warriors, who sat together in one of the shelters, whispering. Then, toward sunup, they slipped out of the shelter and away into the woods. In her dream, Alexis saw a huge, white bear lumber out of the woods to the south, and to the water, where he began fishing, tossing many fish onto the beach, perhaps for later use.

The Others stirred and set about building fires and cooking breakfast. Some walked into the woods. Alexis heard a shout and through a peephole, saw the men walking over a large, white lump in the snow—one of the shelters. The men were laughing, shouting, stomping, jumping up and down on the shelter, now a foot under the snow. More of them left their campsite and moved into the woods. The People knew they were found, but remained still, even those injured under the relentless feet of the Others.

A great roar reverberated through the woods and bounced off the trees. A white bear, nearly invisible against the white snow, rose up, knocking snow off branches, and roared again. Behind him, the warriors who had slipped away in the night whooped and called out and chased the bear toward the Others, who fled, leaving behind everything in their hurry to escape the white bear, who followed, running ahead of a handful of the People's warriors. Hours later, the warriors began to filter back, winded but elated at their success, and the People left their shelters to gather up materials left behind on the beach. They found food, furs, weapons, and tools and collected them to disburse among the families according to their needs. Finally, the last of the warriors returned, to report that he and the bear had chased them very far north and they would be unlikely to return. As far as he knew, the bear was still chasing them. The People cleaned and cooked the fresh fish frozen on the beach where the great bear—Spirit Bear—had left them. Strengthened by the pink flesh of the silver fish, they set off on their southern march again, stopping when they reached a great river, too wide and fast to cross. A deep fog lay across the land, so they rested. When the sun burned off the mists, they saw a home and built permanent shelters. When their village was established, they held a ceremony to thank the Spirit Bear and named the longest running warrior Chases Bear.

Alexis woke up. The warrior in her dream was not the Chases Bear she knew, nor even his own earthly grandfather. Her grandfather was born to the Cherokee Nation in the east. Yet, she had no doubt there was an important message in this dream. Her heart beat faster, and she felt unsettled, as if there were something she must do, but she didn't know what. There was an urgency to the feeling, a power she didn't understand.

She had never seen nor heard of a white bear, other than the Polar Bear. She sat up, turned on the lamp, and opened her laptop. She learned that the First Nations of British Columbia had occupied a strip of land along the north coast, where one or two in 100 black bears has a recessive gene turning their fur white. One in ten white bears are found among those of Kermode Island, just off the coast. The First Nations revere them as Spirit Bears.

Why had she been given this dream? Granddad had said they could discuss dreams, but not visions. Was this a dream or a vision? Either way, she would speak with him about it.

Chapter 35: Mistaken For a Ghost

Earth teach me to forget myself
as melted snow forgets its life.
Earth teach me resignation
as the leaves which die in the fall.
Earth teach me courage
as the tree which stands all alone.
Earth teach me regeneration
as the seed which rises in the spring.
~William Alexander

The week passed without further incident. Alexis and her father traveled to and from work together each day. The office fell into a pleasant routine of informal conferences and focus on the work. The sound of laughter was common. Alexis had never been so happy. Most days, she left Tricky at home now, certain that their bond was strong enough to survive the separation. Mary confessed that she was glad of his company in the empty house.

On two evenings during the week, Alexis dropped her father at home and drove to the Rez to visit with Pat. They spent most of their time together holding hands, quietly chatting about the past, and filling each other in on the intervening years. Pat told Alexis he had gone to college, starting a couple of years after she did, and gaining a bachelor's degree in cultural studies. He had followed his interests and studied archeology and geology, as well. Both were of interest because of where he lived. Central Oregon's geology was so diverse and so often amazing that he had found the study entertaining. Anthropology

344

attracted him because their people had been in North America for thousands of years, and he wanted to know more. So, here he was, working in law enforcement. "Getting shot at," he added.

"I certainly hope that is not a regular occurrence," she answered.

"No, fortunately, most people are not murderers." Saturday, Pat called Alexis at home to ask if she wanted to go back into the canyon with him and a team from the University of Oregon to see what they thought of the dugout and its contents. She dressed quickly after the call and hurried to meet him at the Gateway Restaurant, bringing Tricky along on a leash. Spotting Pat's 4-wheel drive pickup in the parking lot, she left Tricky in the car and joined Pat, who introduced his companions: Professor Layne, Teacher's Aide Simon, and students Mark and Leon. Pat turned another cup upright for her and the waitress filled it. It was early and the Gateway was quiet.

"I hope Granddad released you," Alexis said.

"Do you think I'd have gotten out of his house alive otherwise?" He grinned. "Good to see you, too."

"It *is* good to see you on your feet."

Mark spoke, his eyes full of curiosity, "Sgt. Collins was telling us he was treated by your grandfather, who is a Shaman."

"Medicine man," Alexis answered.

"What's the difference?" Mark asked.

Alexis shrugged. "It just isn't used much here."

"Probably as much geography as practice," Professor Layne added. "Shaman is a term used more commonly among indigenous Turkish and Australasian populations. It is the medicine practiced for centuries and passed down by word of mouth as is that of the Native American medicine man or woman."

"For my grandfather, it is probably a combination of many practices. He has spent time traveling to a lot of places to learn, even Siberia."

Pat drained his cup. "If we are done with the lesson of the day, how about we get on the road? Alexis, where's Tricky?"

"Moping in my car."

They rose as one and filed out. Alexis freed Tricky from his prison in her backseat and climbed with him into Pat's pickup. Pat handed her a hay string, which she tied to Tricky's leash. The others piled into a small SUV and followed.

Pat used his police radio to advise guards stationed on either side of the creek that they were going into the canyon. A chain reinforced the signs that denied admittance to unauthorized persons. *No cars, no boats, no trespassing, no entry permitted* signs must have kept painters busy for a week. She wondered if there was a similar number on the other end. The tribes could only post guards preventing entry on tribal land.

The sun had not reached into the canyon walls yet. The temperature was still cool. Later, it would be blistering hot when light bounced off vertical rocks. Pat waited for one of the guards to unlock and drop the chain, then drove over it and followed the rut of a road to within a few hundred feet of the dugout site. They walked the rest of the way. Their university team stared in awe at the giant vertical stones, and the great piles of rock made by those that had broken and fallen at the feet of those that remained standing. Pat crossed at a low place and led them along the west side of the stream, rather than the east. Alexis, though curious, didn't question him.

"What did that?" one of the students asked, looking up at the bluff, high over their heads.

"A volcano," Pat answered. "Those stones are cooled lava from the center of it."

"Wow! How tall are they?"

"I don't know. I don't have a tape measure that long."

The others chuckled.

Alexis looked up. "I would guess it is at least a dozen times as tall as you are. You do the math," she said.

"Wait here," Pat said to the team of scientists. He walked a few steps and stopped among a collection of rounded boulders, many higher than their heads. When he donned latex gloves and bagged and marked a cigarette butt found on the dirt between rocks, Alexis understood. She leaned against a boulder and looked up at the top of the bluff. Tricky sniffed the area.

"Careful," Pat said. He bent to pick up a shell casing near her feet. She stood still. It was a long distance, but she thought she could pick out the place where they had been scrambling over the edge when Pat was shot. She turned to him. He nodded agreement with her unspoken question. From his expression, she did not envy the man who'd fired the rifle when Pat found him. He searched the area, taking several photographs of footprints in the dirt. He waved the others to join them. Not far from there, they arrived at a point where the stream split into several smaller flows and meandered among a protruding rocks and sandbars. Vegetation grew thick on the sand bars.

"We cross back here," Pat said.

"That place, where you stopped us, was a crime scene?" Leon asked.

"I was shot from here," Pat answered. He pointed to the top of the bluff. "Up there."

"When did that happen?"

"Three weeks ago." He jumped across to a sand bar. Professor Layne followed.

"Isn't it too late to collect evidence?" Mark asked Alexis.

"The canyon's been closed and guarded. It hasn't rained," she answered. A jury might disagree, but she would make that point, if she were prosecuting.

They followed Pat. On the beach, Alexis realized the dugout and campsite were invisible from here, and the river too shallow for boats. The group had chosen well, as had whoever built the dugout. Not far up the slope, she spotted the dugout door, but only because she knew what to look for. It was nearly as hard to see as it had been from the river. Not so, the makeshift kiln and campsite. As they approached, Alexis felt the familiar cloak of malaise settle over her, as it had on the day of her arrival in Central Oregon, and several times since. An eagle took off from its eyrie downstream and called out as it passed over. Its call chilled her as much as the place did. The eagles had paid her no attention before. Now, one could believe they, too, felt the evil in this place.

Tricky tugged at the end of his lengthened leash. She followed his lead. He bee-lined straight for the mounds they had decided covered waste ditches, sniffed one, then another and at the third, he began scratching the soil. Alexis frowned; her chill increased.

Pat watched, very still. "Professor Layne," he said after a few minutes, "the dugout is over here." He led the team toward it, and they trouped inside, out of view.

Tricky stopped digging. He stiffened and growled. Alexis followed his gaze. Dark Moon Kane stepped silently from a wide crack in the wall onto a pile of broken rock that appeared to have fallen from the crack. He crouched on the pile and pointed a rifle at her.

"Do not say a word," he said. She whistled a low note for Tricky and held him at her feet with the leash. He growled again. Hair stood upright from the back of his neck to between his shoulder blades. Pat stepped out of the dugout with a shovel.

"Pat! Watch out!" she cried. Kane seemed not to know which way to point the rifle for a few seconds. He stiffened when Pat stood upright, dropped the shovel and drew his gun. Alexis waited for him to fall with another bullet in his body.

Kane paled. His dark face took on a sickly hue and his jaw dropped.

"You are dead," he whispered. "You cannot be here." He dropped his rifle and fled, leaping from the rocks. Pat fired. Kane moved too fast. The bullet ricocheted off the wall. Pat ran after him, clambering over the pile of huge, rectangular stones. He grabbed Kane's rifle and tossed it behind him without looking back. Alexis picked it up and checked the magazine. The team from the university had heard the shot. They came out of the dugout, looking worried. Alexis dropped Tricky's leash and followed Pat.

"Stop! Police!" Pat shouted. He raised his gun and fired another shot. He ran, with Alexis following, but Kane had a head start and what he appeared to think was a ghost on his heels. He disappeared into the canyon, and his footsteps petered out on the grassy slope at the foot of the bluff. Alexis caught up with Pat when he stopped to locate them.

"He could be hidden anywhere here," she said. "You aren't ready for chasing criminals."

"I would, but he's good at hiding his tracks. I can't tell whether he went up, kept running, or hid. There are plenty of places for that here." He tried his radio, but no one responded.

"We're too close to the rocks," he said.

"Let's go back and see if our guests are frightened out of their wits, before he doubles back behind us," she said.

He nodded, frowning his reluctance to quit the chase. The scientists seemed relieved to see Alexis and Pat, but if they were terrified, no one was showing it. They had gathered their specimens and artifacts for study from the dugout and were using a tablet to catalogue what was there and what they were taking for further study. With the danger apparently past, they seemed excited by their find.

"Look!" Simon cried out. "Look what we found!" He opened a cloth bag he'd apparently brought with him and brought out a stone object. She closed the distance between them. The others looked equally excited.

"There is more," Simon added. He showed her a stone object with a representation of a fish carved on one end.

"It's a pipe," she said. "See? It's hollow all the way through."

With bulging eyes and wide, thick lips, the fish looked like other rare stone carvings she'd seen. He showed her a handful of chip-carved arrowheads, a stone knife, and a small bowl with a rounded instrument that was most likely used as mortar and pestle. Unlike the pottery in her father's office, these were real artifacts. If the gang had known it, these were worth far more than the pottery.

"I didn't see those last time we were here," Alexis answered. "Where were they?"

"There was an area beside one of the stones that was a different color. I think it's been dug up and reburied recently," Simon, looking over their shoulder, said.

Someone had tied Tricky to a bush. He whined, but Alexis ignored him. Pat released him, retrieved his shovel and approached the mound that had drawn Tricky's attention. He stood at the end of it examined it for a moment. Tricky began digging and scratching. Alexis left the scientists examining their finds and went to stand beside Pat.

"See anything different from the others?" he asked.

"It's wider."

"If you were digging a latrine, would you dig it two feet wide?"

"No."

Pat began digging. Alexis took the shovel from him and ordered him to sit down on a nearby stone. Surprisingly, he complied. He must be in pain. She dug for several minutes, starting at the end that was lower on the slope. If she didn't excavate the mound, he would. After digging a hole about a foot deep, she moved on. She had dug up half of a pit that was just under six feet long by 2 feet wide by a foot deep, when the scientists left the dugout, expressing curiosity.

"What is it? Professor Layne asked.

"We'll know when we finish," Pat answered. They offered to help, and the three took turns on the shovel, while Alexis turned her attention to Pat. A red spot had blossomed on the center of his back. She found some young sage leaves, mashed them between the palms of her hands, and lifted his shirt. While she worked, he tried to use his cell phone. She loosened the bandage on his back, examined the wound, and pressed mashed sage leaves over it, before replacing the bandage.

"It doesn't look serious," she said, "just seeping a little. Maybe only surface stitches are opened."

"Hurts," he answered. She placed her hands flat on his back, surrounding the wound, and closed her eyes, focusing all her thoughts and prayers. She chanted the Cherokee words her grandfather had taught her, not stopping when his shoulders visibly relaxed.

"Breathe," she reminded him. "Deeply." She felt the energy flow through her, through her hands.

"This looks like a grave," Mark said.

"Is that what this is?" The professor asked Pat.

Over his head, Alexis opened her eyes and nodded. The professor joined Mark in the hole and, using his hands and whatever else he could find, he helped. The other student used his tablet to take photographs of the entire area and the process.

"Oh, my God!" one of the boys cried. The scent of decomposition reached Alexis' nostrils.

"This is no ancient Indian grave," Layne said.

"No," Pat answered. "Let's throw some of the dirt back over it and get out where we can call backup. Be careful where you walk." Belatedly, they tried to avoid stepping on anything left at the scene, and any footprints. Leon used his tablet to photograph the bottoms of everyone's feet so police could tell which footprints were theirs. Without crossing the stream again, they walked back out of the canyon. Pat cautioned the guards to be extra careful about trespassers and told them Kane had been there. He was assured that Kane had not gone in past the guards. Pat radioed his office, requesting backup and a CSI team. The group waited.

"We'll do what we can to date these," Professor Lane told Pat while they waited. "And get them back to the tribes as soon as possible. Clearly, these will be greatly valued by your People."

"They will," Pat answered. "I'm glad Kane and his crew didn't know what they had."

"Maybe they found out, if they buried them and that guy you chased came back."

"I think if they did, they would have sold them."

"They're worth a lot of money in some markets. They are far more valuable as history. I can hardly wait to find out how old they are."

Half an hour later, the canyon was full of police personnel, one of whom appeared to have higher rank than Pat's, because he ordered him to return immediately to the residence of Chases Bear and get looked after. Pat agreed. "I will, sir, but Alexis took pretty good care of me."

"Get!" the cop ordered. "And take your scientists with you. They've contaminated the crime scene more than enough. The rest of you guys, we're not here to poke around the dugout. We're here to find out who died, why and when. Get at it."

"Sir?" Pat said.

"Yeah."

"I think it's a woman named Sarah McCaine, who disappeared about three years ago. She was reputedly Dark Moon Kane's girlfriend."

The cop let out a long breath. "Thanks, Collins. Go home." The police headed into the canyon.

The scientists were way ahead of Pat and Alexis. Good care or not, Pat was in pain. Alexis took his elbow and helped him back in the truck. She drove. They were with her grandfather at his home within the hour. Chases Bear gave him something for pain and Pat fell asleep within minutes.

Alexis sat at his bedside watching him for an unknown time, until she became aware her stomach was growling. When she left the bedroom, her grandfather was gone, called away, according to the note he left, for a child with a sore throat. For a moment, she was nervous at being left alone with their patient.

Granddad wouldn't be gone long, and if needed, he would be there. She made herself comfortable at Pat's bedside and dozed off.

Chases Bear woke her with an offer of food.

"That sounds good," Pat said.

Alexis grinned. "Hello, sleepyhead." She called home to say she was fine, and ask about her father. He said he was well, watching the news.

"Whose body did they find on the rez?" he asked.

"Wow! That got out fast. We think it may be a woman named Sarah McCaine," she said.

"That figures. She disappeared when she was ready to testify against her boyfriend."

"Dark Moon Kane."

"Yes."

"Damn. That bastard should have gone away for life."

"Maybe he will now."

"We can all hope, for everyone's safety."

Alexis bade him good-bye and hung up, as her grandfather called both Alexis and Pat to dinner. Alexis checked Pat, but he seemed able to manage getting up and dressing, albeit with a few cringes. She held a chair for him in the kitchen and placed her hands on his shoulders, focusing her thoughts. The now-familiar path of energy flowing through her body charged her with power and pleasure. When Granddad set plates on the table, she released Pat and sat with them.

They chatted over vegetable and chicken wraps, fresh and flavorful, with tall glasses of chilled whole milk. Pat seemed better. Alexis couldn't help wondering if his pain was truly eased, or if he wanted her to believe she helped him. His eyes shone, and he laughed easily with their chatter, leading her to conclude that the energy healing she was able to do was real and substantial.

At some point while they ate and talked, she set her food down on the plate and turned to Chases Bear.

"I had a dream," she said. "In my dream, a group of people were traveling south along the north coast. It snowed. They hid from warriors who were after them, by separating into small groups and building rough shelters from the snow in the forest, where they could see out over the beach. Enemy warriors found one of the small groups and stomped on them, trampling their shelter down on top of them. The People remained still, and not many were seriously injured. The warriors laughed and set

357

up camp, shouting that they would all be found in the morning. A white bear came to the water's edge, south of the warrior camp, just before dawn and caught many fish that he threw out onto the beach. Then he stood up and roared, waking all the People and the warriors. Several young warriors of the People slipped out of their shelters and circled behind the bear, beating sticks together, shouting and singing and moving toward the bear. He turned and ran toward the foreign warriors, who fled north, back the way they came, terrified of the Spirit Bear. Time passed and some of the People's young men returned, laughing at the warriors' fear. One was a very long time coming back."

Chases Bear gave a small smile and lowered his eyes, masking his thoughts. Pat looked confused, as if he understood the story but not its purpose. Alexis continued.

"The last young brave appeared as the women served cooked salmon to the entire group, using the fish the bear had thrown ashore for them. The braves gathered around the latecomer and asked what had kept him. He told them he had chased the bear and the terrified warriors all the way to the deep snows, and they would not be back. They would be lucky to survive the trek to their own homeland without supplies. The young braves of the tribe immediately dubbed the one warrior who had gone so far, "Chases Bear." They all ate and danced and slept and then continued south until they came to the confluence of two great rivers, too wide for crossing. There they stopped and built a village.

"Granddad, this all happened long ago and far from here. Why are you called Chases Bear?"

"I had that same dream when I was a boy, soon after my family came to Warm Springs. I told my father, and he named me "Chases Bear" after our spiritual Grandfather."

She was silent, looking at her food for a long time, before she spoke again.

"Teach me, Granddad. Teach me *everything*.

Chases Bear beamed with delight.

End

Made in the USA
Las Vegas, NV
09 March 2022

45297366R00203